The People of the Veil

By
Andrew M. Warren

AmErica House
Baltimore

ISBN: 1-59129-030-9
PUBLISHED BY AMERICA HOUSE BOOK PUBLISHERS
www.publishamerica.com
Baltimore

Printed in the United States of America

Dedication

This book is dedicated to all the men and women who faithfully and unselfishly serve the U.S. Government in our embassies abroad, they are true patriots in every sense of the word.

Acknowledgments

I'd like to thank a few people who helped me complete this novel. First and foremost I would like to thank my parents, Lewis and Viola, who taught me the value of hard work at an early age. Without their love and guidance this novel would not have been possible. I would also like to thank my siblings, Sandra, Lewis and Renee, for their unwavering support over the years.

I am also grateful to Todd Fritz for reading and commenting on each chapter. I am grateful to Todd for encouraging this project from the beginning. My thanks to Heather, who also helped me with revisions of this work. Also, I want to thank Mr. De La Touche for watching my back and being a good friend. Thanks for your support.

Many thanks to Professors William Alexander and Paul Clark for their early support and for sharing their knowledge with me.

I would also like to thank my many friends in Kuwait (especially A.I.), who gave me a better understanding of the culture, language and people of the Middle East.

I would like to thank El'va Anderson, who provided map illustrations, and Mel Wright, my photographer. And lastly, I am grateful to my agent Karen Carr of the Finesse Literary Agency.

This story is a work of fiction. Although it takes place against the backdrop of the Near East, the scenes, the characters and their interactions are purely imaginary. Any mistakes or misrepresentations are entirely the fault of the author.

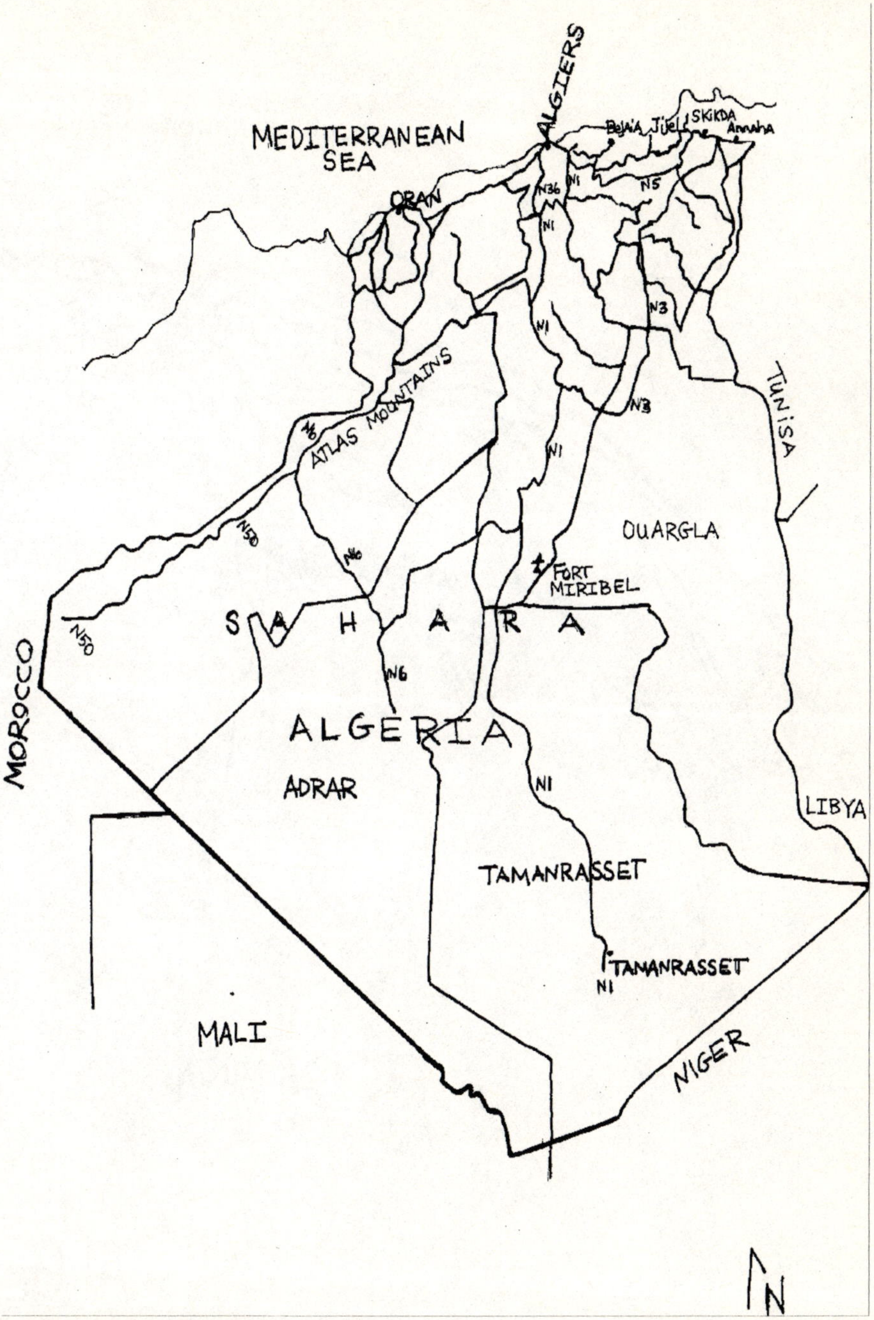

MEDITERRANEAN SEA
ALGIERS
Bejaia
Jijel
SKIKDA
Annaba
ORAN
N36
N1
N5
N3
ATLAS MOUNTAINS
N6
N50
TUNISA
OUARGLA
FORT MIRIBEL
SAHARA
ALGERIA
MOROCCO
ADRAR
LIBYA
TAMANRASSET
MALI
NIGER
N

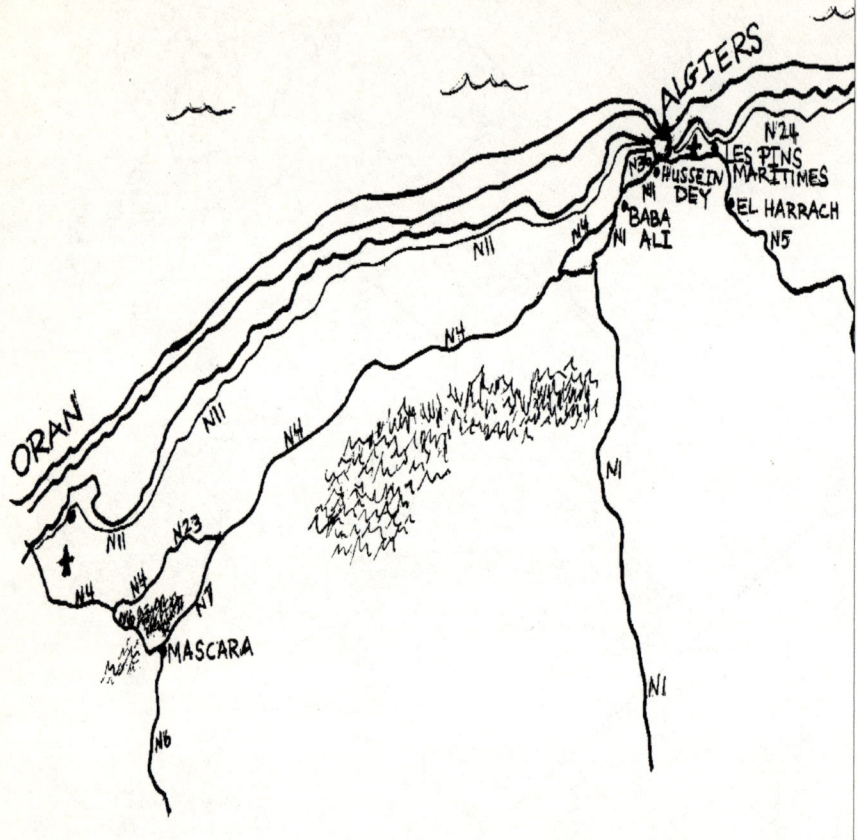

MEDITERRANEAN SEA

ALGIERS

N24
LES PINS
N35 MARITIMES
HUSSEIN
N1 DEY EL HARRACH
BABA N5
N1 ALI

N11

N4

ORAN

N11

N11 N23

N1

N4 N4

N6 N7

MASCARA

N1

N6

SAHARA

ALGE

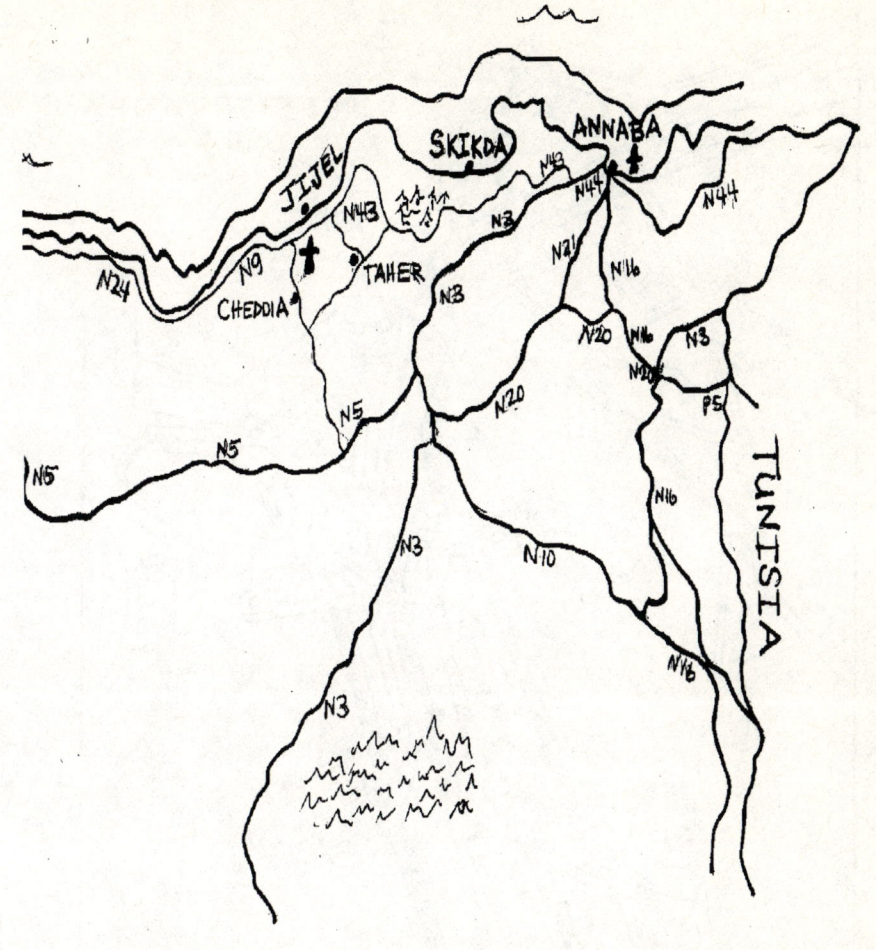

JIJEL
SKIKDA
ANNABA
N43
N9
N43
N44
N24
CHEDDIA
TAHER
N3
N44
N3
N21
N16
N5
N3
N20
N46
N3
N5
N20
N40
P5
N5
TUNISIA
N16
N3
N10
N16
N3

RIA

N

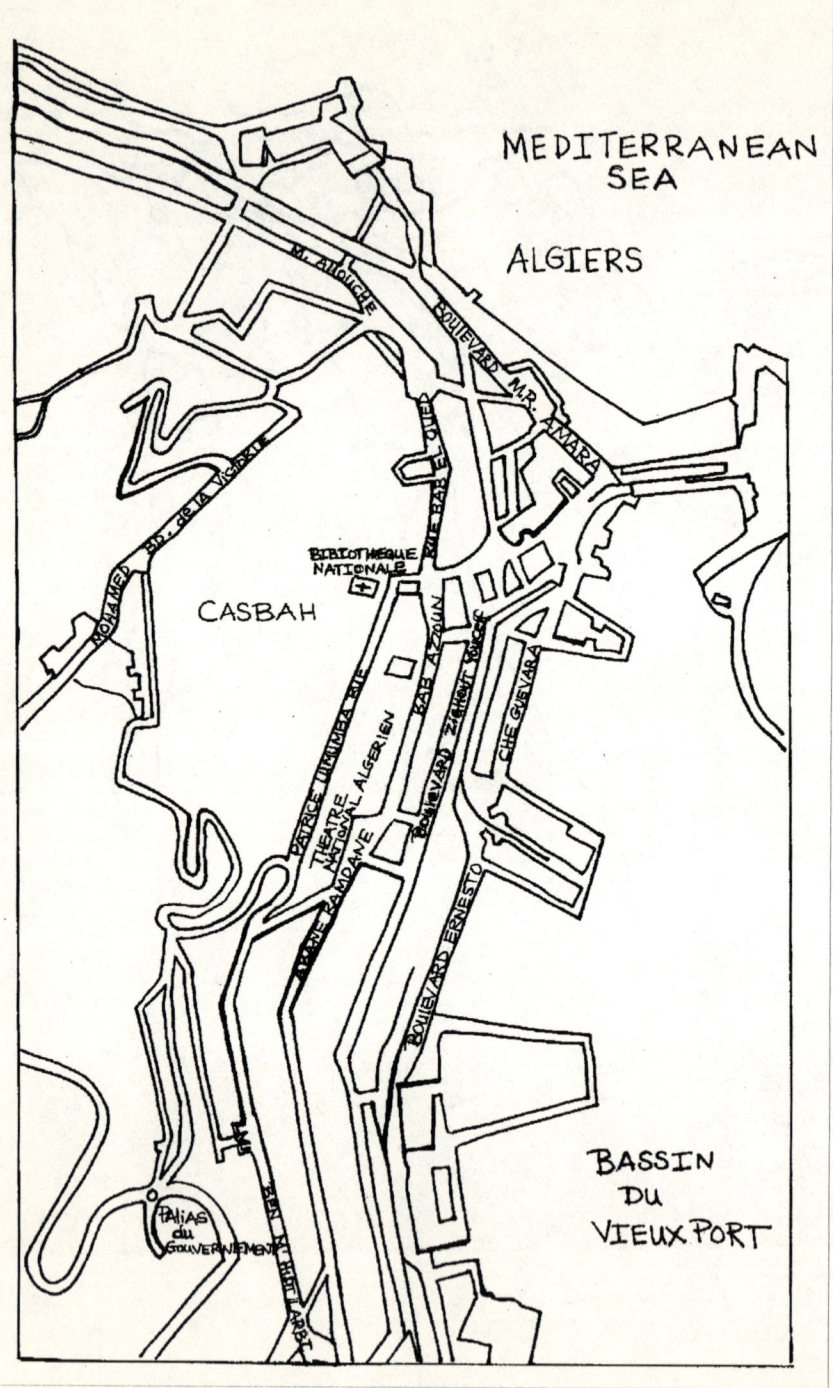

MEDITERRANEAN
SEA

ALGIERS

CASBAH

BIBLIOTHEQUE
NATIONALE

BASSIN
DU
VIEUX PORT

-One-

There is a means of polishing all things whereby rust may be removed.
That which polishes the heart is the invocation of Allah.

— Arab Proverb

Tuesday
11 December 2001

"Excuse me, I would like to apply for a business visa please," asked Abu Fahad.

"Yes sir, if you would fill out this application and provide two passport size photographs we could process it today," said the local guard.

After completing the application, Abu Fahad went to the entry of the chancery. "Please place any metal objects in the tray and step through the metal detector," commanded the Marine Security Guard. Abu Fahad took his keys and cell phone out slowly as he surveyed the first level of security at the embassy.

The three local guards in the booth had no weapons, but the Marine was armed with a pistol, noticed Abu Fahad. He stepped through the metal detector. He noticed the doors were the new magnalock doors that were probably centrally controlled from inside. Those types of doors were nearly impossible to open once they were sealed. Abu Fahad was given a ticket to collect his cell phone when he left. He noticed that the cell phone was placed in a box by the local guards; he decided to file this fact in his memory as significant.

Abu Fahad went through the outer security to the consular section. Because of the security situation in Algeria, only business visas were processed at the American Embassy in Algiers. People wanting to go to Disney World had to go to the American Embassy in Tunis to obtain a tourist visa.

Abu Fahad went into the consulate and took a number, and after twenty minutes, he heard his "name." "Muhammad Abdallouwi, window seven," boomed the loudspeaker.

"Why do you want to go to America?" asked the consul.

Abu Fahad noticed that his Arabic was formal. "I want to go over to do

a survey of companies that could provide us with computer spare parts," he replied, just as he had rehearsed several times before with his friends. "You see, I have a computer store in Algiers, and because of the volatility of the environment, few foreign companies operate in Algeria. Many of the stores can't service Apple or IBM computers here. I want to make an agreement with a few distributors in the U.S. so I can be the sole dealer here for parts and service."

The consul had a stern, authoritative look about him. He did not seem like the type to be easily fooled. Abu Fahad did not care about the visa; he wanted to see the security arrangements inside the embassy. "Let me see your company's documents and your bank statements," said the consul.

"Well, it's a start-up company, I have my bank statements and have made appointments with a few companies in the states via e-mail," explained Abu Fahad.

The consul examined the records. "It does not look like your business is very big from your bank records."

"That's why I need to expand," stated Abu Fahad.

The consul looked quickly though his passport. "I see that you have been to Iran, Bosnia, Egypt and Lebanon. What was the purpose of those trips?" inquired the consul.

"I traveled for business purposes," Abu Fahad answered.

"To obtain a business visa to the United States, I must see that you have solid business ties in Algeria, and thus far you have not proven that to me," said the consul. Abu Fahad could tell that this man was formidable.

"Well, if you do not give me the visa, then how will my business survive?"

"Sir, unfortunately that does not affect my decision; either you qualify for a visa or not. If you do not have any other information to show me, then I must refuse your request under U.S. Immigration Law, section 214b. If your situation changes, you can reapply after one year," stated the consul.

The consul stamped the passport and passed it through the slit at the bottom of the bulletproof glass. "Thank you, it has been a pleasure to meet you. May I have your good name sir?" asked Abu Fahad.

"Nick Phillips." He hated giving his name to visa applicants.

"I am sure we will meet again Mr. Phillips," said Abu Fahad.

Nick was weirded out a little. "I have another applicant, sir. If you don't mind, I must call the next person," Nick explained.

Abu Fahad left the consulate and knew that he would see Nick Phillips again, but it would be under completely different circumstances, under his terms. He made mental notes of all cameras, security gates, guard positions, cleaning force duties, and types of doors and windows as he went into the car that had been waiting in the parking lot.

"There were some weird applicants today. This last guy was a little strange," Nick told his visa clerk Arshad, one of the Foreign Service Nationals (FSN) who worked at the embassy. Because of the high financial cost of placing Americans in embassies abroad, the State Department hired local citizens to work in its missions. All of the foreign employees were required to pass local background checks and they did not have access to sensitive information. FSNs outnumbered Americans at every embassy and consulate. Arshad was his primary employee on the non-immigrant visa side of the consulate. He printed the visas after Nick had approved them. "Yes, madir (director), it almost seemed as if he did not want the visa," speculated Arshad.

Nick did his usual duties before closing up the consulate, such as making sure all the U.S. passports and visas were accounted for. As the consul, he was held personally responsible for those items.

"What's the good word, my friend?" Nick said to his employee.

"Mr. Nick, things are pretty bad now. Did you hear, last night Muslim rebels killed twenty soldiers and wounded ten others when they ambushed a military convoy," stated the employee.

"How did you hear that?" Nick asked.

"I read it in the French newspaper 'Al Watan' this morning."

"Can you read me the rest? My French is really rusty."

"Of course," replied Arshad. "The attack occurred near Tebessa about 630 km east of Algiers yesterday when a bomb exploded near a military convoy patrolling the area. Several newspapers confirmed that the Armed Islamic Group (GIA) was involved. The attack brought to at least 100 the number of people killed since Saturday. Over the past two months, the North African country has seen an upsurge in rebel attacks against civilians and soldiers, dealing a heavy blow to President Abdel Rahman Shayji's peace drive. The GIA has dismissed Shayji's peace plan as a sellout way to end more than eight years of violence. Hundreds of people, mostly civilians, have been killed since June when Shayji initiated his peace plan. The recent massacres in Algeria have sparked fears that diehard Islamic extremists have reorganized. Shayji's election in April 1999 sent a wave of hope across the country as he campaigned to make peace. Thus far, Shayji's campaign has been a dismal failure, his administration had been accused of rampant corruption and his decision to bring in young western advisors has only fueled the Islamist's cry that he is selling out the country. The new surge of attacks over the last six months have left more than 1,200 civilians shot dead or hacked to death making Algerians fearful of a return to the horrendous death tolls of 1993-1998, at the height of the civil war that broke out in 1992."

Arshad finished reading the article and shook his head. "That sounds serious," stated Nick, "I had speculated that the violence may be a prelude to something larger."

"Hey madir, if it sounds bad then it's probably worse."

Nick could not help but wonder if his worst fears were starting to be realized. He left the Consulate to go home.

-Two-

At home, Nick decided to call the Marine Security Guard Detachment Commander, Gunnery Sergeant Hank Johnson. "Let's work out, Gunny," said Nick.

"Roger that, I will meet you in the gym in 10 minutes. What do you feel like today, Nick?" asked Gunny. "I feel like doing some focus mitt drills and than some light sparring." Focus mitts are boxing tools that look like a large catcher's glove. Boxers and martial artist practice punching combinations with a partner using the mitts.

"Sounds good." After a few warm-up exercises, Nick began firing a flurry of potent jabs, crosses, hooks and elbows to the focus mitts.

"You always make me laugh when we start to train."

"Is that because I am supposed to be some pencil-neck paper pusher?" said Nick.

"Actually, I was thinking more along the lines of candy-ass pansy, but pencil-neck is fine by me," replied the Gunny.

Nick had never been a wimp by any means. At 6'2" and 200 pounds, he cut an imposing figure on the diplomatic circuit. Nick earned a black belt in Jeet Kune Do (JKD) kickboxing at 18. JKD was the style that Bruce Lee created out of western boxing, Thai boxing, Savate, Northern and Southern Gung Fu kicking, Sikaran, and modified Wing Chun. Nick discovered the style growing up in Virginia Beach, Virginia, where he had trained for 8 years under a master instructor. He was good, but knew he did not practice enough.

Nick sent in jabs, crosses, low hooks, uppercuts and elbows to the mitts. The Gunny had a hard time holding his arms up after Nick was finished. The Gunny was a traditional boxer but had learned some JKD from Nick. When it was the Gunny's turn, he fired powerful rights and lefts to the focus mitts. After ten two-minute rounds apiece, both Nick and Gunny were exhausted. "Still want to spar?" asked Gunny. Nick replied affirmatively.

Nick loved to spar; he equated it to a game of physical chess. It can be compared to a conversation between two individuals, in which an exchange of dialogue continues back and forth until it is ended somehow. Sparring is both rhythmic and unrhythmic; it includes pauses, interruptions, spurts of energy, feigning and subterfuge. When you are sparing you have to problem-solve. It requires instant analysis, decision-making, speed to carry out a strike in a fraction of a second, and the ability to react and adjust to the situation as it changes.

Nick faced his opponent in the basic Bai Joing stance while Gunny was in a typical boxer's stance. Gunny began by sending in a few punches that Nick easily slipped; he parried the next punch and sent a few of his own. He always started slowly and built up. The two participants traded punches, kicks and other techniques for about 10 minutes. The Gunny nailed Nick with a left jab and right hook. "Is that all you got, Devil dog?" taunted Nick.

"I was just being nice since you are my boss," replied the Gunny. "Are you ready for the heat?"

"Summer is a long way off," replied Nick.

The Gunny threw a strong front snap kick. As his foot was on the way, Nick angled his body to the left to parry the kick with a right block while simultaneously striking the Gunny in the face with a heel palm strike. The Gunny was stunned and Nick slid in under his guard and put him in a chokehold. The Gunny tapped Nick's arm, which meant he could have been incapacitated if Nick continued the pressure for a few more seconds. "Slick moves, I hate it when you use that martial arts shit. Real men just box."

"Yea, yea, and Marines always bitch."

The Gunny was joking, but he actually knew some marital arts and used it at times. He liked Nick; he felt that he could trust him, which in his opinion was a far cry from other State Department dolts in his opinion.

Gunny was a professional Marine who cared only about completing the assigned mission successfully and taking care of his men. Nick liked him. He was a no-nonsense grunt. Unlike other embassy officers, the Marines tended to be more realistic about their role in the embassy. Their job was to protect the embassy's property and its personnel. Gunny was an excellent commander and one of Nick's few friends at the embassy. Gunny had served in Operation Just Cause in Panama in 1989 and Grenada before that.

"Good workout, Nick."

"Thanks Gunny, I will see you tomorrow." Nick left the gym to go home, shower and get a good night's rest. In bed, Nick could not help but think about the news article and its ramifications.

-Three-

If you are a peg, endure the knocking; if you are a mallet, strike.
— Algerian proverb

Abu Fahad knew that now was the time. He was planning for his children's future and for the future of all Algerians. Abu Fahad was from the Taureg tribe, a nomadic tribe who lived in the North African desert for thousands of years. "Ya Shabab (oh men), tonight we will make the Kufar (infidels) pay for their misdeeds and take back Algeria for our children."

"Allahu Akbar!" the group yelled enthusiastically.

"I know Allah will smile upon us!" Abu Fahad exclaimed. Abu Fahad had drilled with his men for weeks on the best way to enter the villa and circumvent the security. All of his men were from the Taureg tribe, one of the fiercest tribes in North African history. Abu Fahad could not help but think about his seven-year-old son, Fahad. He could not let his son grow up in an Algeria and with such corrupt forces in power. In the election of the December 1991, the Islamic Salvation Front (FIS) won the majority of support and the military intervened in January 1992 to cancel the results. The National Liberation Front (FLN) took power in 1992 and tried to modernize Algeria by embracing the west. The nationalists wanted to remove from the constitution all references to the Islamic law (sharia). Sharia is the divinely mandated path that Muslims were to follow; it is God's law. Islamic law consists of four primary sources: the Qur'an which is the most authoritative source of Allah's revelation and law; the Sunna of the Prophet, which consists of the normative model behavior of Muhammad, that which he did and those actions which he permitted or allowed; the Hadith, or sayings and traditions of the Prophet; and Ijma, or consensus of the Muslim community. The FLN wanted to turn their back on their Islamic identity.

It was at that time the FIS and an extremist group supporting their cause, the Armed Islamic Group (GIA), had decided to take the battle to the streets. Abu Fahad was one of the first to join the GIA. Since the beginning of the violence in early 1992, approximately 100,000 people had been killed. Abu Fahad reflected how he was only a child at that time, 20 years old and not even married. He thought about how much his life has changed since 1992. He had married, fathered children and found a purpose in life. He had

17

achieved all of this because he had met the shaykh.

Abu Fahad thought about his three kids and felt that if western influence was not eradicated from the country and Islamic law implanted, they would have no real future. He knew that the FIS was the answer for Algeria; they would promote Islamic values within the families. Abu Fahad came out of his revelry, "I want you to remember the plan, we start at 11:00 p.m. Abu Musa provided us with the map of the grounds. We know that there are only six guards on duty at this time. I want the bombs to go off at 11:15 p.m. at the house down the street as a distraction. This will cause a panic among the security personnel who will send out a few men to investigate. We will swiftly intercept those going out and kill them. I will go over the east wall with four of you and I want Khalid to go over the west wall," Abu Fahad commanded.

Abu Fahad knew that he did not need to repeat the plan since the group had drilled for this mission many times, but he believed preparation was the key and he did not want to get overconfident. Abu Fahad reflected to himself, *did not the Prophet Muhammad say in the Hadith, 'Trust in Allah but tie up your camel'?* Abu Fahad knew that the group was being guided by Allah's hand, but that did not mean that the Almighty would do everything for them. "Once over the wall, Khalid's group will provide cover and take out any opposition while my group will find that infidel pig and do what Allah commands. Now to your positions," ordered Abu Fahad. All of the men had their faces covered and they wore blue robes.

He looked at his watch. It read 10:40 p.m. He hit the squelch button on the radio. He had told them not to break radio silence, but he would break squelch 20 minutes before they would go. At 10:55 p.m., he began a silent prayer, "bismallah al-rahman al-rahim (In the name of God the most merciful, the most compassionate)." He knew his other teams were at different locations around the city waiting to attack the other targets that they were planning to take out that night. Since this mission was the most important, he had decided to come on this one.

Muhammad Al-Zubaidi was sitting in the small shack outside of the villa when he heard the explosion. "Ahmad, I just heard an explosion," Muhammad yelled on his radio to his boss.

"Get up and check it out. I will send two guys from the house to go with you," Ahmad replied.

Muhammad had only taken this job because his uncle, the head of VIP protection in the Ministry of the Interior, had promised him that it would be easy and quiet. Muhamad remembered hearing his uncle say, "Hamudi, you can study at night and earn enough money to go abroad for college."

Muhamad was only 18, but was over 6 feet 4 inches tall, 260 pounds and very muscular. His uncle had explained to him that because of his size, any potential adversary would be too intimidated to attack.

Additionally, his uncle promised him that he would only work VIP residences at night, which was the quietest time to work. Muhammad got up and ran to the gate. "Allah, please protect me," Muhammad whispered to himself. He checked his Kalashnakov rifle to make sure it was loaded. He opened the gate and saw a car ablaze about 50 feet away. He was confused as to what to do next. Before he could decide, Muhammad heard a whistling sound through the air; he was hit in the neck with a crossbow arrow. The last thing that went through his mind was his uncle telling him that the job would be easy and quiet. The two other guards met the same fate.

Abu Fahad was already in the house with his tribesman. The villa was large, but he had the floor plan; the master bedroom suite was upstairs. His men took out the two security men downstairs with their short daggers. Abu Fahad found the rooms he was looking for, a man and a woman sleeping in the bed in one room and a younger man in another bedroom. His men had killed the younger man first because he was unimportant. "Allahu Abkar (God is great)!" yelled Abu Fahad. The man and woman awakened suddenly as Abu Fahad and his men unveiled their faces.

Abu Fahad started to speak, "Fight in the cause of Allah those who fight you; but do not transgress limits; for Allah loft not transgressors. And slay them, wherever ye catch them and turn them out from where they have turned you out; For tumult and oppression are worse than slaughter; but fight them not at the sacred Mosque, unless they fight you there; but if they fight you, slay them. Such is the reward of those who suppress the faith," declared Abu Fahad. Abu Fahad had memorized all of the Holy Qur'an at an early age, but especially liked this passage from Surah Al-Baqarah (The Cow, chapter 2, section 24, verse 189).

"Why are you here?" asked the frightened man.

"You are guilty of suppressing the faith," stated Abu Fahad flatly. "We are here to take back our country. Do not worry, for soon you shall see Allah." The couple's screams could be heard throughout the house as the men began hacking and slicing them to pieces with their daggers and knives. As they left, they recovered their faces.

-Four-

Wednesday
12 December 2001

"Nick, have you heard? The Prime Minister and his family were killed last night. I think the FIS and their goon squad, the GIA, have started to make their move," said Muhammad Al-Qadumi, the speaker of the house. "Other senior leaders of the National Liberation Front (NLF) are missing as well," said Muhammad.

Nick had feared this would happen. Over the last year, he had been writing reports stating that the so-called random violence was not so random; it was organized and escalating. All of his reports had been ignored in Washington. "Muhammad, are you in any danger?" asked Nick.

"I am moving from the house and taking my family with me. We will be moving around for the next few weeks until everything calms down," said Muhammad.

While Nick was concerned about his friend, he could not help but think about Mariam, his girlfriend, whose father was one of the leaders of the NLF and confidant of the President. He worried that she was in danger.

"Muhammad, do you think that the FIS will go after the rest of the senior officials?"

"I'm not sure but I think that the ministry of interior will be initiating another curfew," replied Muhammad.

"Mo, dier ballak (be careful) and call me once you have settled down. Let me know if there is anything I can do," Nick stated.

"Shokran, ya habibi (thank you my friend). I will call you in a week."

If only Nick had known that would be the last time that he would talk with Muhammad, he would have said more. Muhammad had been a mentor to him on Algerian politics and also a close friend. In the weeks to come, Nick would become sad and upset when he thought about their friendship and the memory of Muhammad being dragged through the streets. He remembered the crowd calling him an enemy of Islam, a kafir (an unbeliever), before stoning him to death.

After Nick got off the phone with Muhammad, he tried calling Mariam at her job at the ad agency, but her colleague told him that she had not come in.

21

Her co-worker wanted to know if he had heard the news and if he knew what was going on. It was all he could do to get off the phone by telling her he would call if he heard anything important about what happened last night. Nick thought to himself, *it seems that people are really scared this time.*

He next tried to call Mariam on her cell phone, which was not working. "Damn cell network, it never works when you want it to work." He needed to tell the ambassador, "the ass," but thought that he should make another phone call first.

"Allo Sami, Kaifak (how are you)?"

"Bakhair, ya ustad (fine, professor)," said Sami. Sami always called Nick professor as a sign of respect. Sami Bouteflica was the head of the American Embassy VIP protection detail. He was a detective with the ministry of interior (MOI) who had transferred over to this detail from its violent crimes investigations. He had confided in Nick that he did not like dealing with the families of the victims; it made him depressed to see the sadness he brought into people's lives. Unlike in America, the Algerian Ministry of Interior controlled the internal and external security services, including the police.

"You heard what happened last night, Nick?" asked Sami.

"Yea, what's going on, my friend?" inquired Nick.

"I am not sure, Nick, there were other outbreaks of violence and the MOI is on full alert. I was actually on my way to the embassy when you called. The only news I have is that we should be vigilant now, but word from the top is that it will fizzle out in a few days. Have you talked with al-hamar (the ass)?" Sami and Nick had this private joke between them; they both called the ambassador "al-hamar," and since the ambassador did not speak Arabic, he never got the insult. From day one, the ambassador treated Sami and his men with disdain and contempt, no better than "rent-a-cops." Sami's men were all educated – probably more educated than policemen in the states. They had to deal with diplomats on a daily basis and be respectful and courteous, and they also had to be good investigators to be ready for any contingency.

"No, I have not spoken with his Excellency today. I was hoping you would have some ideas about the situation," Nick stated.

"Wallahi (by god) I don't know. I think the top guys know more than they are telling us, but I am not sure. Look, I will be down in about one hour. I need to talk to you about something, but I have to make another stop first," said Sami.

"Thanks, Sami, see you soon." Nick decided to see the Ambassador. As he walked, Nick's thoughts dwelled on Mariam and if she was safe.

The Ambassador was a political appointee who had no idea what was going on in the country. As the senior diplomat in country, he was the president's personal representative and the person who liaises with the local heads of state, and reports on the current situations in the country and the official voice of the U.S. Government in that country. That was his official job, but this ambassador was a lazy SOB who did not want to leave the compound and delegated everything to Nick. Most political appointees have no concept of the job but like the title and the prestige of the position more than the daily work. Nick was sure the ambassador thought he would skate through this tour.

Nick went down to the ambassador's office. "Good morning, Sarah, is he in?" Sarah Garcia was the ambassador's secretary and had served at five U.S. embassies abroad. She was single, as most secretaries in the Foreign Service were. Nick and Sarah saw eye-to-eye when it came to the ambassador. He was a lightweight who should never have been appointed. Nick was a career foreign service officer (FSO) who had served in two other Middle Eastern posts. As far as political appointees went, Nick felt that Algiers got the dud of political appointees.

Sarah had worked for four other ambassadors and was thought to be one of the best secretaries working abroad. This was the reason the department decided to send her to help support this diplomat. "Nick, he is on the phone with his wife in Washington. He should be off in a few minutes." Nick decided to wait instead of barging in. He reflected on how he ended up in Algeria.

Algeria has been undergoing a civil war for the last eight years. This was not exactly Nick's first choice. Not many people put Algiers on their State Department bid list. So how did Nick get picked? He was told that it was because he spoke Arabic and specialized in the region. Well, Algeria is an Arab country, but Nick supposed that management forgot most educated people spoke French, while the majority of the populace spoke only Arabic. He was told that the department needed a young dynamic officer to go into Algiers (read naive and inexperienced into their statement) to make some changes. All the experienced officers had declined to accept this assignment, as Nick would find out later. He was told that he would run the visa and political sections as well as be the Deputy Chief of Mission (DCM), a great job for a relatively young officer.

Nick was 33 years old. He would have a staff of local hires or Foreign Service Nationals to help him run the sections. Nick thought how the Foreign Service loved political appointees in the department. This guy must have not given enough to the president's campaign to get Algiers as a reward.

Algeria underwent a political coup and the military government took over the government in 1992 and killed most of the old leaders. The coup initially went unchallenged, because the FIS leadership discouraged its followers from provoking clashes with the military. Relative calm prevailed and the military withdrew its tanks and troops in the following days. Some 300,000 demonstrators marched in Algeria protesting the Islamists and the main workers union, The General Union of Algerian Workers, in early January, and threatened to resist any Islamic government. The calm was deceptively brief. Within in a month, civil war erupted as Islamists struck back against the military crackdown.

The new government imposed a state of emergency, banned the FIS in March 1992, and dissolved the communal and municipal assemblies, most of which had been controlled by the FIS. The government also banned all political activity in and around mosques and arrested hundreds of Islamic activists on charges ranging from possession of a firearm to promotion of terrorism and conspiracy against the state. Military courts tried and sentenced the activists on charges brought against them. Civil liberties were dead; thousands were brought in, interrogated and tortured.

Most of the top FIS leadership was arrested and thousands of the rank and file members were forced underground. The press was reigned in and the omnipresent mukhabarat (secret police) became even more powerful. The repressive military actions against the Islamists were reminiscent of the military force used by the French colonial authorities against the nationalists during the war of independence. Thousands of troops were mobilized and assigned to cities and major urban areas. Curfews were imposed, removed, and reimposed from 1992 until 1999. Entire neighborhoods were sealed off for accused terrorists. The Islamists struck back by killing military personnel and government officials by the hundreds with axes and knives. Thousands were killed in the first year alone. The majority of Algerians were caught in the middle of both sides. Since 1992, about 100,000 people had been killed, including many westerners. Nick laughed to himself as to the obvious reasons Algiers was not on the A-list of assignments.

Nick heard the heavy door to the Ambassador's office open. "Nick, what's up? Sarah said you wanted to see me ASAP," bellowed Ambassador Curtis Alexander.

"Yea Curt, it's important." The Ambassador hated when he called him Curt. "Let's go in your office."

-Five-

Mariam Al-Qana'i could not believe her eyes. She had just come to her parents' house in the Al-Biar area, an upper class area where diplomats live outside of the city center. There were many police officers around her parents' house. She had spent the night in her apartment near the center of town and was supposed to meet her parents and her brother for breakfast that morning. Mariam and her seven-year old sister, Fatima, were having a girl's night at her apartment. Her sister loved sleepovers.

The police had the area blocked off. She stopped her car. "Stay in the car, Fatima."

"What's happening?" her sister asked.

"It's nothing, just stay in the car." She ran to the house. The police all knew her because of her father. "What happened, where are my parents?" she yelled. She tried to enter the house.

A older officer grabbed her. "You do not want to go in there."

"I want to know what is going on," demanded Mariam. She knew that something horrible had happened. For the first time she recognized Sami Bouteflica, Nick's friend who worked in the VIP protection at MOI.

"Come to my car," said Sami, "Calm down, I have to tell you something," Sami hated this part. He had heard the radio call this morning saying that Ahmad Al-Qana'i, his wife and his son had been butchered last night. He heard the call a few minutes before Nick called. He wanted to check it out before he told Nick. "Mariam, I am sorry that I am the one to tell you, but your parents and your brother were killed last night."

"What? You can't be serious. I just spoke to them last night." Tears began to stream down her face. "I just spoke to them last night, we were going to have breakfast today. I want to see them, to make sure."

"Several officers have already made the identification; it's messy inside there," Sami stated.

"Who did this, Sami? How could this happen?" she asked.

"We believe it was one of the terrorist's groups."

Mariam cried and cursed the men that did this act. Sami comforted her and tried to say some soothing words to her, but he could think of no words that could fill the void that had been torn open. Mariam asked, "Were they like the others we have heard about, you know...how bad was it in there?"

Sami sighed. He did not want to lie to her, but he knew she did not want to hear the whole truth of how they were killed. "No, Mariam, their bodies were not in bad shape."

This seemed to be what Mariam wanted to hear. She knew Sami was lying, but she could not think of them being horribly mutilated like the others killed by the terrorists. "Sami, can I see them to say goodbye?"

"Even though they were not in bad shape, it does you no good to see them this way. Remember them as they were."

Mariam had stopped weeping uncontrollably but tears continued to run down her face. Mariam came from an extremely close family, like most Arabs. She was having a hard time processing the whole thing. "I am cold, Sami." He turned on the heat in the car even though it was warm outside. Sami felt sorry for her. Sami knew that Nick cared for her and it caused him great pain to see his friend's girlfriend in anguish. "What about Fatima?" she asked. "What will happen to her?"

"Listen to me, Mariam. The Prime Minister was also killed last night and maybe a few others. We are still receiving reports."

"Can't the police protect me?" asked Mariam.

"I believe that the MOI does not want to cause a panic by giving protection to people, because that's like admitting the problem is out of hand. Also, the police are spread pretty thin right now. There is more you should know; I believe that more people will die before the killing is over. In all cases, the killers have gone after the whole family. You are in danger.

"The MOI asserts that these are isolated incidents. We do not know who's involved with these killings; it's chaotic right now. There were reports that some of the extremists have police uniforms; we do not know whether they were real police or just masquerading as police. There may be members of this extremist's group in the police. Do you understand?" Sami asked. He was not sure that she had understood everything he had said, maybe she was in shock. "You know where I live, I want you to take Fatima and go to my house. It's a security building and my maid will let you in. Other than Nick, do not tell anyone where you are. You have to take care of Fatima now." At the mention of her sister's name, she seemed to snap out of her trance.

"So we should go to your house and then what?" asked Mariam.

"Wait until you hear from Nick or me. You should be safe; police presence is very high today. One of us will call you in about an hour. I am on my way to the embassy now and I will talk to Nick," said Sami.

"OK, I will do what you say." Mariam exited out of Sami's car and went to her car. Sami could not help but notice how this normally very capable and self-assured girl walked as if her world had just collapsed. She composed herself as best she could so that Fatima would not know what happened.

"What's going on?" asked Fatima.

"Just some routine police exercises." Mariam decided that she would not tell Fatima at this time. She did not need a hysterical child on her hands. "We are not having breakfast with our parents today," said Mariam.

"Why not, what happened?" asked Fatima.

"Nothing. Just sit back and be quiet. We have to make another stop," Mariam snapped. She could not believe that her parents and brother were dead. She felt bad for snapping at her sister. "Look, how would you feel about another sister sleepover tonight?" asked Mariam.

Her sister perked up at the thought of another sleepover with Mariam. "That would be fun," she said.

Mariam had to be strong for Fatima. She started to well-up again as she thought about her parents and brother but kept it under control.

She thought of Nick. He was always strong. She thought about when she first met him. It was a diplomatic function at the Sheraton. Usually Americans did not come to such functions, especially American diplomats. There were only about ten non-diplomatic Americans in the country and only 20 percent of Algerians spoke English. Most U.S. officials had been too afraid to venture out at night, but Nick was not your typical American diplomat.

She was talking to her friends when she heard this strange Arabic accent coming from behind her. She was intrigued to find that it belonged to an American. Most Westerners do not speak Arabic but will usually speak French instead.

"Excuse me, I do not believe I know you," she said.

"Excuse me madam, allow me to introduce myself, my name is Nicholas Phillips, I am the Deputy Chief of Mission (DCM) at the American Embassy."

"Nice to meet you," she said. She noticed that he was quite tall by Algerian standards. He had dark features, dark hair and was handsome in a rugged way. "How did you come to speak Arabic?" she replied in perfect English.

"I studied it in graduate school in the States and in Jordan." She liked his accent. She had not met many Americans before. They talked for an hour about Algerian politics and what he thought about the country. They decided to get coffee at a cafe in the hotel after the event. Nick began calling on her at her office after the reception and they started to see each other socially after that.

At first, going out with an American was like a novelty, but after a few dates she discovered that he was a man of unique qualities. She had never liked dating Arab men because they were too controlling and tended to have affairs, and European men were too into themselves. She wanted someone to love and care about her because of who she was, not because she was attractive or came from a good tribe. Many guys had only met her once and then proceeded to ask her father to marry her. All that the prospective suitors wanted was a wife who came from a good family and who looked good on their arm. They did not want her, the real her.

She had decided a few years back that she would not be like her mother, but would marry for love. She had not dated much because all the men she met were either looking to have sex with no commitment or they wanted to marry her and keep her in the house like a prized trophy. She wanted passion, adventure and a person to share her life with. After dating Nick for almost eight months, she felt that he was the type of person she had been looking for. At 27, she had found love.

Nick cared for her, respected her and treated her as an equal. He never pressured her and he understood her culture. Because of Nick's expertise in the region, he was like a bridge between both cultures. He would know what to do; she could count on him. She drove to Sami's without going home to pick up any clothes. She arrived at Sami's apartment with Fatima and waited for Nick's call.

-Six-

"Curt, did you hear what happened last night with the Prime Minister and his family?" asked Nick.

"I heard. Is this why you wanted to see me so urgently?" the ambassador said impatiently. "More violence, that's all these people do is kill each other."

"No, this is different. I spoke with Muhammad Al-Qadumi this morning and he thinks it was the GIA and that maybe they are making their move," said Nick.

"Now, which group was the GIA?" interrupted the ambassador.

Nick sighed, "Sir, the GIA is the Armed Islamic Group or Jamat Islamiya Mousalaha, who began a series of violent attacks to create an Islamic state in Algeria about eight years ago," explained Nick.

"Yes, yes I remember," mumbled Curt.

"I have been writing for the last year that the upswing of violence was becoming more organized. Don't you remember those backgrounder pieces I wrote about the various groups a few months ago?"

The ambassador thought for a second. "Of course, it's my name that goes out on each cable as ambassador. But if I remember correctly, didn't Washington blow off your 'expert' assessment?" snapped Curt.

Nick knew that Curt was trying to needle him. Washington did blow off his assessment, one of the fatal flaws that the department committed, trusting its analysts in D.C. over the people in the field. Nick knew that Curt was delighted when Washington had responded that they thought the upsurge in violence was just seasonal without any real long-term threat connected with it. This was a clear slam against Nick's analysis.

Nick knew why the analysis was not well received. The Ambassador had sent an e-mail ahead to Washington to warn them that Nick's cables would be coming in and that he felt his assessment was inaccurate. Nick knew the only reason Curt released the cable was to make Nick look bad. If Nick wrote a cable that Washington disagreed with, it would hurt Nick's career – a career diplomat – and not the political appointee.

This was another problem with the ambassador; not only did he not know the issues and did not want to learn them, he did not let the professionals take the lead. Additionally, he took everything personally because he was insecure. He did not respect Nick's expertise but actually resented it because in his mind it made him look bad. At every turn, he tried to hurt Nick's career. In Nick's opinion, Curt was dangerous because he did not know his own incompetence and he had just enough power to cause an international incident, or, in this case, to prevent Nick from taking the correct safeguards to protect the lives of embassy personnel.

"It was not well received but I believe that the stakes have just been raised," explained Nick.

"Well, what do you propose?" replied the ambassador.

"First, I want us to write a cable stating the possibility that the situation could blow up so we can let Washington know the volatility of the situation," said Nick.

"Lay out your case for me, Nick." The ambassador almost seemed as if he had not already made up his mind.

"This is the first time a senior leader of the government has been killed since Boudiaf was killed in June 1992 by the Islamists. Boudiaf was one of the original founders of the FLN. After that time, the military cracked down so hard that while many civilians and government officials were killed, no senior leaders were killed because of the tight security procedures around them. Also, previously the MOI had arrested or killed most of the Islamist's leadership. Where did this attack come from and how could they organize it without the police sources finding out about it? Who carried out this attack? Is there another group we do not know about? This attack was well planned and was done for a specific reason, not as a random act. If you look at the last six months, more fake roadblocks, hostages being taken and violent crimes occurred than the previous twelve months. Just two weeks ago, nineteen people were killed at a fake roadblock near Larbaa just south of Algiers. This has never occurred so close to the city. The armed group was wearing military uniforms. Where did they get the military uniforms? There are too many hints that lead me to conclude that we are in the middle of something that Americans should not be in," stated Nick.

"Interesting analysis. I want to call the regional security officer (RSO) so he can hear your position.

John Machale, the RSO, was a close friend of the ambassador who sided with him on every issue. Nick knew that this was not proceeding as he had hoped. John was a 20-year veteran on diplomatic security, but had only served one tour abroad ten years ago in Canada. He was a weak officer who knew little about the Middle East. He volunteered to come to Algeria. As not many people wanted this posting, a volunteer is actually desired. Nick had heard through the grapevine that the only reason he took this job was because he was going through a divorce and he wanted to raise some quick cash. Algiers may be dangerous, but it's what you call a "moneymaker." Every State Department employee receives 10 % post allowance, plus a 15 % cost of living allowance, plus 50 % danger pay – and all of this is in addition to free housing. It's almost double your salary. The main drawback other than being dangerous is that the tour is unaccompanied, meaning no spouses. This is a tough selling point for many FSO's.

Diplomatic Security, or DS as they were called, are the security experts within the State Department. More often they were FBI wannabes who were incompetents with no grasp of the cultures they served in. Other federal agents actually called it "discount security" instead of Diplomatic Security.

Before Nick could say anything, Curt buzzed Sarah and asked for her to call John. "John will be down in a few moments," Sarah replied.

"Curt, Sami is on his way over. We can talk to him about what he thinks is going on," said Nick.

"He doesn't know shit," boomed John as he walked in through the door. "Sami's a fucking washout from the detective squad. What's up Curtis?" said John.

"Nick's been giving me his take on what he believes is occurring in Algeria. Could you please tell John what you told me, Nick?" Nick quickly went through his case.

"That's horse shit. Your so-called expert on Middle East affairs is seeing conspiracies where there are none. It's random violence; these people have been killing each other for eight years. Don't get me wrong, Curtis, it is disconcerting that the Prime Minister was killed, but the MOI has it under control," John said.

While the Ambassador was a lightweight, he was not stupid. "John, Nick does have a point – this is the first time a senior government official have been killed," interjected the Ambassador.

"Trust me, Curtis. My MOI contacts assured me that everything will be under control in a few days, a week at the outside."

"What are they going to say, John? 'Oh, our country is going in the crapper and you Americans should leave.' Of course they will reassure you. That's part of Arab culture, since we are their guests. If we listen to them, we will not be in a position to leave," Nick replied forcefully.

Sarah stuck her head in the doorway, "Sir, Sami is here to see Nick."

"Send him in."

Sami walked up and greeted the ambassador with the usual warmness that all Arabs use to greet men of rank. Next, Sami went to Nick, and after shaking his hand, he placed his right hand over his heart, which was a sign of respect and friendship to Arabs. No one else in the room understood the gesture other than Nick. "Sir, thank you for seeing me." Sami said hello to John last. John could not even muster enough manners to be nice to Sami. In an Arab's eyes, this was not only disrespectful but also challenging.

"What can you tell me about what's happening in the country?" asked the ambassador.

Sami began, "Sir, I just came over to give you and Nick a situation report. As of this morning, we have not caught the people who killed the Prime Minister. We are confident that we will apprehend the perpetrators. In the meantime, as a precautionary measure, we have decided to increase the security around the embassy's parameters."

"Is there any evidence that this is the start of something countrywide?" asked John.

"My ministry's position is that it's isolated," replied Sami.

"That's my assessment too, that it is isolated," said John.

"Sami, I know that you have to give the official view of the MOI, but what's your personal opinion as an Algerian citizen? You live here and work here," said Nick.

Sami was clearly hesitant. He probably thought that John would call his superiors if he said something different than his ministry. He began, "Personally, and remember that this is not the view of the ministry, I believe that the situation is very precarious. Extreme caution should be taken at this time. Our PM has been killed, people are scared and who knows what the fear can spark."

"Do you think that a full blown civil war will break out?" asked John. John knew that Sami and Nick were friends. If Sami answered the question affirmatively, he would have grounds to have Sami removed and possibly have one of his local friends put in his position. The Algerian Ministry of Interior did not look kindly on its officers stating their own opinions. The ministry wanted its officers to state the party line; any deviation was grounds for immediate dismissal. Sami looked at Nick. Nick shook his head.

"It is our ministry's position that the assassination of the PM was an isolated incident."

"Sir, I think that's what I said earlier," said John.

"Sami, do you have anything else?" asked the ambassador.

"No, sir."

"Thanks for coming in, Sami," said Nick.

Sami stood up to leave. "Because of the situation, I will be at MOI's security office on the compound for the rest of the day. I need to talk you, Nick, after you finish here," said Sami. He left the room.

"See, it's all speculation, sir. We do not want to alarm Washington," John said.

"Nick, draft a cable telling Washington want happened to the Prime Minister and the official MOI position, that's all. Let me take the rest under advisement. Clear your cable through John."

"Yes sir."

"We will meet back here in two hours."

Nick was clearly disappointed; he hoped that they would not regret their decision. John left elated; he thought to himself that he'd put Nick in his place. Unfortunately, he was so concerned about putting Nick in his place that he did not think about the merits of Nick's case. Nick walked back to his office. Because he was so dejected, he forgot to call Sami.

The ambassador sat in his chair and thought about the meeting. He felt unsettled about what Nick and Sami had said. He pondered the situation. He hated Nick and the way he disrespected him. He was the ambassador and he should receive a certain amount of respect from his employees, regardless of whether or not he was a political appointee. He had been able to basically stick it to Nick during the last year. He thought about his last year at post. Nick always treated him as if he knew nothing about this field. Curtis ran a successful multi-national company for years. This was no different than that, wasn't it? But deep down he knew what Nick and Sami said about the recent upscale in violence in the country had made sense. When he was running his corporation, what would he have done? This job was supposed to be a reward for his efforts in the election campaign. Since the first days, it had been a headache, Curtis opined. "The staff does not respect me, Nick has been on my ass, waiting for me to screw up." He felt really tired and thought that he needed a break.

Curtis came up with a solution. He would go to Washington for consultations this evening to explain the state of affairs. This would accomplish a few things. If there were really a threat, he would be safely back in D.C. with his wife. Nick wanted the helm so badly, he could have it for a few weeks. If the situation did settle in a few weeks, he would return to the country and tell Nick how he over-reacted once again. He could probably use it against Nick over the next year. He would tell Nick that he is going back to fight his cause and be back soon.

"Sarah, tell Nick and John that I want to see them ASAP," said the ambassador.

"Yes, sir."

"Also, book me on a flight to Washington. The connection does not matter as long as it's the earliest."

Nick and John came to the ambassador's office. Nick passed the ambassador the cable. The ambassador skimmed the cable. "Looks good Nick, send it out. Now, this is what I decided to do. I am going back to Washington to discuss the matter with them. I think Nick's analysis has merit, but if he sent it out now they would not understand it or support it. I will leave this evening and be back in probably a week. Once I talk with senior Near East Affairs Bureau management, I will let you know what I want you to do. In the interim, per procedure, Nick will be Charge D'Affaires until I return. I will send an e-mail out to the rest of the embassy staff. Any questions?" asked the ambassador.

"You can't leave in the middle of a crisis," Nick said incredulously. This was unreal. Any career ambassador would stay because it would be a chance to be at the forefront of the crisis. This was a time when careers are made; it was unthinkable that an ambassador would leave.

"There is no crisis at this point. That is what John said earlier and that is what your cable says. This is not a debate. I just wanted to inform you of my decision. Now if you will excuse me, I have to pack, because I have asked to leave on the earliest flight," stated the Ambassador.

Nick and John both left the ambassador's office in shock. "Because of this new development, I will stop down at your office in the afternoon to discuss the embassy's security arrangements," Nick said to John. As Nick left he could not help but think, *so the rats are abandoning the ship.*

-Seven-

Your dwellings are before you, and your life is after your death.
               – 9th century Muslim Ascetic

"Haya Al-Salat Ayuha muslimim, Ashaduaallah la illa ila allah wa muhammadu rasul Allah, (come to prayer Muslims, I witness that there is no god but Allah and Muhammad is the prophet of God)." Abu Fahad listened to the soothing sound of the idhan, or call to prayer, as he performed the wadhu (ritual ablutions) or purification before prayer. He washed his hands, wrists, arms, head, feet and ankles, as his father had taught him so many years ago. After the ablutions, he walked into the mosque after taking off his shoes. With his fellow Muslims he walked to the line on the floor that indicated the direction of Mecca, the direction all Muslims should face when praying. The imam said, "Qad qammatis salah (the prayer has begun)." He raised his hands to his ears and said "Allahu Akbar" in unison with the other worshippers. He bowed at the waist and began the prayer before standing up straight again. He prostrated himself on the floor and let his head touch the carpet as the Prophet did 1400 years ago. At the end of the prayer, after doing several iterations of the same movements, he turned his head to the right and to the left, and said in the direction of each neighbor, "Asaslamu alaikum ahmatuallah (peace be upon you and Allah's blessings)."

He sat on the floor after the prayer and contemplated what it meant to him. Unlike other religions, Islam is a very structured religion. All Muslims have prayed the same way for each of the five daily prayers for over fourteen hundred years; it was what made him feel connected with all his Muslim brothers and sisters. It was truly an "umma," or community, as the Prophet Muhammad had envisioned so many years ago. In his and the shaykh's opinion, The Prophet of God did not plan for the community to become so fractionalized and ungrateful. Everything in this world was dependent on Allah, His mercy and magnificence. How could people become so arrogant as to forget Him? Allah should be praised, worshipped and feared. If the people did not voluntarily come into the fold then it was his and every true Muslim's duty to bring the people back.

It was as if he had been asleep for all those years before he met the shaykh and he had opened his eyes. He remembered the meeting as if it was yesterday. He was only 20 when his father and uncle were killed in the first wave of retaliatory strikes after the military took over in 1992. His father and uncle were attending a peaceful rally to protest the military canceling the election when the army came in and without warning begin shooting into the crowd. His father and uncle, along with 100 other people, were killed. The government claimed that the crowd became unruly and they had no choice, but the people who escaped told the story of the massacre, which sparked the Islamists to take up arms.

He had gone to the Badar Mosque, named for the Prophet's decisive military victory over the infidels in Arabia in 623, to perform a funeral prayer for them after the event. The mosque was located down a winding street in middle-class quarter of Algiers. It was a large building with one tall minaret where the muezzin summoned the faithful to the five daily prayers. The style of the mosque was Moorish with painted tiles and turquoise glazed bricks on the outside.

It is obligatory for Muslims to pray to Allah for a deceased love one. After the prayer was done, he was sitting there when an old man walked up to him. "Who were you praying for, my brother?" said the old man.

"My father and uncle, who were killed yesterday at the square," replied Abu Fahad.

"There were many that were killed yesterday. It's the fault of the Kufar (infidels) ruling this country," he said.

"Kufar, why do you call them that?" Abu Fahad, like many of his friends, did not really follow politics. "I blame the army who killed my family members, not the government," said Abu Fahad.

"It's not the army that we should be upset with, but the leaders who ordered the army to commit that crime. The army is jahil (ignorant), like the people before the appearance of Islam. They were ignorant, too, that is why that time is called the jahiliya in the Qur'an, the time of ignorance. The Quraysh tribe fought against our Prophet in sixth century because they were afraid and did not understand. They were ordered by the influential merchant families to stop the man who was disturbing their way of life." Abu Fahad became enthralled with this old man's story.

"The tribes did not understand the message that our Prophet was giving them. They convinced the people that he was a soothsayer, a madman, in order to rally support against him. The ruling families of sixth century Arabia wanted to protect their wealth; they wanted to continue living a hedonistic lifestyle. They did not want to be responsible for their actions or take care of the poor. They said that this man and his followers were backward and dangerous to the society as a whole. This is what the government is saying about the true Muslims today. The military government says that we are backward, dangerous and threaten the progress of the country. The Muslims won the election in December 1991 with popular support. Who canceled the elections, who outlawed the Islamic party, who is trying to protect their way of life, a life without morals or directions for our children? We have prostitution in our Algiers; why do women sell themselves? If we lived in a true 'Umma' (Islamic community), the women would be taken care of, not taken advantage of."

The man's words and ideas moved Abu Fahad. He had never met someone so eloquent. The old man spoke in classical Arabic, which was the sign that he was an educated man. He used phases from the Qur'an in his speech. He had a presence about him that demanded respect. This old man dressed as a peasant but spoke like a shaykh of a large tribe.

"The leaders have lost their way, and the ignorant people help them. They are not Muslims. They will send our children to hell by their example."

"What do you mean?"

"How many mosques have you seen built in the last year?" asked the old man.

"I don't know, maybe one or two," replied Abu Fahad.

"How many hotels, bars and discos?"

"I am not sure," said Abu Fahad.

"About thirty new places where alcohol is served have been built in a year. In addition to that, those are the type of places where the French and other westerners come to meet and eventually defile our women. The leaders are not setting the example and Muslims like you and me are suffering the consequences. In the Qur'an (al-nisa, chapter 4, verse 76) it says that our duty as Muslims is 'to fight in the cause of Allah and those who reject faith, fight in the cause of evil: so fight against ye friends of Satan.' The Qur'an also states, 'those who strive in our cause, we will certainly guide them to our paths for verily Allah is with those who do right (Al-'Ankabut, chapter 29, verse 69).' You should also remember the reward of the evil ones, 'Ye such for the wrongdoers will be an evil place of final return. Hell – they will burn therein – an evil bed, indeed to lie on! Yea such – then they shall taste it – a boiling fluid and other penalties of a similar kind and truly they will burn in the fire (Al-Sad, chapter 38, verses 55-59.)' Does this make sense to you?" asked the shaykh.

"Sort of, but I am not sure I understand," said Abu Fahad.

"What I am trying to explain to you is that you are responsible, as well as all other Muslims, if you allow the leaders to continue perverting Islam. You have a religious duty to make a change." The shaykh went on to explain the concept of Jihad to him. He called it the sixth pillar of Islam:

The duty of every Muslim to strive for the Islamic Umma. This is an order ordained by Allah and his Islamic law (sharia). All laws that are currently in effect in all so-called Muslim countries are not in accordance with Allah's will. The true Muslims must declare war (jihad) against their leaders who are trained in the West by the Christians, communists and Zionists. Muslim leaders who reject the laws of Islam must be considered apostates. There is no sin higher than apostasy. Cooperation with an infidel ruler who claims to be a Muslim is a sin. The punishment for such a leader is death. Perpetual jihad against an infidel state is the highest obligation and the only solution is for Muslims to destroy that society and revive Islam. Armed struggle is the only acceptable form of Jihad. Jihad through peace is not Jihad. First fight the internal infidel, then the external infidel (the non-Muslim world). Jihad should be taught by every Muslim and can be learned by anyone. Leadership in the new Islamic country must be granted to the strongest of the believers.

All of the shyakh's language was said in such a way, using Qur'anic illustrations that all Muslims know, that Abu Fahad could not help but to respond positively to it. "How can I make a change? I am only one," said Abu Fahad.

"So was Khalid Ibn Walid, our most famous Muslim general who took Al-Andalus (Spain) in 711," stated the shaykh. "I am offering you a chance to achieve paradise by working with some friends of mine. You will help bring about this change. Are you married?"

"No," replied Abu Fahad.

"Come over to my house today. My niece will be there. I want you to meet her."

Abu Fahad had gone to the shaykh's house that day in 1992. His niece was beautiful, conservative and looking to get married. She wore the traditional headscarf, or hijab. Abu Fahad had married her at the end of the year, and she gave him a son the following year. Because of the shaykh, he had a life, a complete life. His father and uncle were killed by the Algerian military, which would be enough motivation to fight against the government; but he had found a spiritual guide, a mentor, a substitute father in the shaykh. He was an integral part of a larger family, the shaykh's family. Being married to his niece made him a relative.

As the Arabic saying goes, "me and brother against my cousin, but me and my cousin against the world." As to all Arabs, family was important to him. Arab society was built around family loyalty. Relatives are expected to help each other. Family affiliation provided security. It assures that one will never be without resources, emotional or material. Family was the ultimate refuge. He was not going to let his new family down. The shaykh needed him to be the sword of Allah, and he would die fulfilling that duty if necessary. Another old Arab proverb summed it up for Abu Fahad: "Support your brother, whether he is the tyrant or the tyrannized." Abu Fahad went on to memorize the shaykh's concept of Jihad and teach it to others.

For the first two years, they had trained him in the desert in hand-to-hand combat, explosives, and other insurgency tactics. In the evenings, he would sit in the shaykh's tent for hours learning about the Islamic glory years between 700 and 1258 AD. He memorized the Qur'an and learned about Islamic law, as well as the sayings and traditions of the Prophet. The shaykh had told him that he had never seen a better student. This type of praise only made Abu Fahad push himself harder to learn in order to fulfill his duty.

At the end of his training, he went to Bosnia to hone his skills against the infidel Serbs for 24 months. In 1997, he returned to Algeria to work with the shaykh's group performing small hit-and-run operations against soft targets and civilians who broke Allah's laws. He had risen in the ranks over the years to become the shaykh's best and most reliable Mujahid (holy warrior) fighter. The shaykh had given him more responsibility and he was now one of the shaykh's most trusted advisors. He owed the shaykh much; he had a purpose and an assured place in paradise for his efforts.

He was brought out of his thoughts as an individual approached.

"So, it's done."

"Yes, oh shaykh, and I took pleasure in seeing the blood drain from their faces," stated Abu Fahad.

"We must talk, my son, about our next step. Come to the back room so we can talk."

In the room, Abu Fahad started, "Ya sayyidi, (Oh, my lord), I have a plan that will shake the infidels to their core and it will be an excellent follow-up to our action last night." The shaykh urged him to continue. "I have a plan that will allow me to infiltrate the American Embassy and kill all the Americans there. This will let the country know that we are powerful, serious and a major player in the Arab world. This one act will unite all the religious groups to our cause in the country and send a clear message to the world that our time is now. We must drive all the foreign embassies out of the country. If the Americans go, then the rest will follow. May I proceed?" said Abu Fahad.

"You have my permission and blessings," said the old man.

*

Curtis called Sarah. "When is the flight leaving?"

"It leaves in two hours from the International Airport. I made you a reservation on Olympic Air."

"Olympic Air, I heard that airline is horrible. Why didn't you book me on a better airline?"

"Well, you said you wanted the earliest flight out of the country, and that was it."

"Well, if that's the only flight, I hope you booked me in first class, at least."

"Under State Department regulations you are only authorized for economy class, so that's what I booked you in. I will be happy to change it, but you will have to pay the difference."

"Just make the change. Have the driver pick me up at my quarters in 30 minutes."

Sarah laughed to herself. There were other flights leaving but she specifically put him on this airline because it was so bad.

Nick stopped by Sarah's desk. "Can you believe that he's leaving?"

"No, I can't. I have worked for several other ambassadors and none would have done this, but I think that it shows how awful this guy is at his job. Even with career ambassadors, there are good ones and bad ones, but that has to do with how they manage people, not how to do the basic job of diplomacy. Everyone I have worked with previously would have given anything to work in a crisis situation, because it puts them in the spotlight. Every ambassador wants to be in the limelight, hoping that the crisis will either put him in Congress, give him a better posting in the future, or put him on the cover of *Newsweek*."

"I knew that he didn't like being here but to leave like this is inexcusable. I think it lends credibility to what I have been saying for the last year – he should never been appointed in the first place. Sarah, please send an administrative notice around telling everyone that the ambassador left for consultations and that my name should appear on all outgoing cables. If anyone asks why he is leaving, down-play it. I don't want anybody to think that his leaving has anything to do with the current situation."

Curtis went to his house and packed only what he needed. He was glad he was going to leave. He waited outside for the driver to come. He would go back and talk with his friends in the President's administration; maybe he could get them to transfer him to a better place like in Europe. When he was offered the post, he was told it was the country where the Casbah was located. They described it as glamorous and exciting. They made it seem like Morocco or Tunisia. No one had told him that a civil war was going on. He had readily accepted the post without question. He believed he would be lying by the Mediterranean Sea soaking up the sun. As it was, he couldn't even go out of the embassy without security. He would enjoy leaving this place. His driver put his bags in the car.

"Where to sir?"

"The airport." He didn't even look back as he left the embassy.

-Eight-

Nick decided to take a walk after leaving Sarah's office. As he crossed the compound, he was always taken aback by the size and beauty of the embassy compound. From the outside, the embassy was a fortress with several layers of security checks. From the inside, the compound was beautifully designed with luscious date palms lining the yard, a large fountain sitting in the middle of the chancery, flowers adorning the paths, and a running path encircling the inner perimeter. There was a cafeteria, a gym, two pools, four tennis courts, and a bar all for eleven Americans residing inside the walls of the compound.

Of the eleven, five were Marine embassy security guards (MSG), there were two regional security officers, one communications person, one admin officer, the ambassador, his secretary, and Nick, as both political counselor and consul. Nick had two jobs because Algiers did not process too many visas and the U.S. did not have much of a political interest in the country.

Nick thought about why he was here. He wanted to make a difference, to be at the tip of the foreign policy spear. He was out here on the frontier doing what he wanted. He had earned a master's degree in Middle East history and Arabic and went overseas while most of his friends were trying to figure out what life was about or were still in school. He guessed he owed his determination and focus to his parents. His father was in the Navy for twenty years before starting a successful real estate business. He learned from him the concept of duty and honor, especially that one should give back to society and serve one's country. From his mother he learned patience in achieving one's goals. She had sacrificed for the family until her children were adults; at that time, she went back to school to obtain a degree in fine arts. She had always wanted to be an artist and never had the opportunity. At 55 years old, she began painting, and four years later she had a small gallery featuring her work. Nick thought that she was an amazing woman. He knew they often worried about him, especially with all the bad news coming from Algiers every week.

Nick knew that Algiers was what you called a typical hardship post. The Americans could not leave the post unless they had an escort with local guards or a regional security officer. Some of the Americans said it was like living in a prison. Because the Americans had to stay on post most of the time, the Department decided to at least make the post aesthetically pleasing.

The Americans did go out into town but could only go out in groups. Nick thought the concept of going out in packs was somewhat backwards, since it made you look like a more attractive target. Why try and kill one American when you can kill eleven Americans in one fell swoop? Like most precautions coming from diplomatic security, it was utter lunacy, he mused. Sometimes their security suggestions just did not pass the logic test. In the same vein, Nick thought that having all the Americans living on one compound was irrational and irresponsible. Didn't they learn anything from the attacks on the marine barracks in Lebanon or Khobar towers bombing in Saudi Arabia? Nick decided to go back to his office so he could begin reviewing the things he had change in order to make this place safe.

Sami was standing outside the door leading to the Classified Access Area (CAA) when Nick walked back into the embassy. No foreigners could cross the "hard line" without a cleared American escort. "Mr. Nick, I have to talk to you," said Sami.

"Sure, follow me." Nick punched in the number to the cipher lock leading into the CAA. Nick had forgotten that Sami wanted to speak to him.

In Nick's office, Sami seemed in a strange mood. "Azaig, ya habibi (how are you, my friend)?" asked Nick.

"Not good, Mr. Nick. I heard a report at work this morning before I talked with you. It had said that Ahmad Al-Qan'ai and his family were killed last night. Before you think the worst, Mariam is safe. She is at my house."

"Are you sure she is all right?" asked Nick.

"Yes," replied Sami.

"What happened?" asked Nick. Once he knew that Mariam was safe, he could breath a little easier. He was still upset over her family. Her father had been so alive and full of energy. He remembered the hours of conversation he had with him. Her mother had been a gracious host who always knew how to engage everyone in conversation at their dinner parties. While Nick was sad, he could not imagine what Mariam was going through. Sami took the next ten minutes to explain what had happened.

"Sami, I do not know how I can thank you. You are my brother."

"La shokran alla wajab (no thanks is necessary because it was a duty)," replied Sami.

"Do you believe she is in danger?" asked Nick.

"Yes, Nick. She should maintain a low profile for a few weeks. The group wanted to kill the whole family. They know that Mariam and Fatima escaped. She must be careful."

Sami was plugged into the local scene and knew what was going on. "What have you heard about the new round of killings? Are they just targeting all the people from the ruling party?" asked Nick.

"I am not sure, because we have very little information on who is responsible for these crimes. All I can say for sure is that our informants say that not only do they appear to have grudges against the ruling party, but foreigners, too. Mariam is safe for now, but I believe you have a larger problem at hand. I believe that these unknown extremists may target the American Embassy," stated Sami.

Nick had enough to worry about with the ambassador's absence, the current security situation, Mariam, and now a possible threat. He had to meet with the RSO and the Marines ASAP to go over the security posture of the embassy.

"Do you have any concrete evidence about this threat, Sami?"

"No, my friend, but I have asked several of my informants to keep their eyes open. The moment I hear something, I will inform you."

Nick pondered. If Sami believed that a threat existed, then he took his warning seriously.

"Well, as long as there may be a threat here, do you mind if Mariam stays at your house?"

"Not at all," replied Sami.

"I need to talk with my guys here to go over security, but I will call Mariam right now. Let's meet in two hours, at 2:00 p.m." After Sami left the office, Nick immediately picked up the phone to call Mariam.

-Nine-

Abu Fahad left the mosque to go to his second home in Fort de Lou, one of the areas known to be sympathetic to extremists outside of the Algiers. His group had rented an entire apartment building in the area. Algerian security officers rarely ventured into the area for fear of bloody reprisals by the extremists. Abu Fahad had several such houses or apartment buildings around Algeria. They preferred areas that were sympathetic to their cause, such as Bentaha, Miftah, Benaki and Harash.

Algeria had become increasingly more like two separate countries. One was the heavily populated northern part, where Islamic extremists fighting the government since 1992 have been lashing out against the population.

The army had continued to rely on force and repression to crush the Islamists in the conflict. In this part of Algeria, factories did not work, and many people were unemployed or underemployed. The leaders had placed all their hopes for economic well-being on economic reforms guided by the International Monetary Fund and the World Bank. Both the organizations had repeatedly stated that stability was essential to attracting the foreign investment needed to reform the huge and inefficient state sector which dominates the economy.

Foreign investment was the last thing Abu Fahad and the shaykh wanted. Abu Fahad was upset because the leaders were giving away the country. The current regime had already given away the southern half of the country. They called it a success; they allowed British Petroleum and the Atlantic Richfield company into the south to develop the oil- and gas-rich regions. Abu Fahad thought that there was enough expertise in the Arab world to get fellow Muslims to come to Algeria to develop the oil fields. Many of the areas developed by these foreigners were in the desert south, the historical lands of Abu Fahad's people, the Tuaregs.

The Algerian government thought they had the problem of the Islamists under control. They had assassinated many of the leaders and jailed the rest. They decimated the villages where they lived. The government made deals with Western companies to exploit and develop the southern desert region for gas oil. They took away the land that belonged to Tuareg tribes, known as the legendary "blue men" of the desert because of their indigo-dyed cotton robes, and as "people of the veil" because the men, not the women, wore veils. The

Taureg have inhabited the Sahara from the southwest of Libya to Mali. In Southern Algeria, they were concentrated in the highlands of Tassili-n-Ajjer and Ahaggar. They were organized into tribes into a three-tiered class of nobles, vassals and slaves. As Abu Fahad's father was a noble, so was he.

In a supreme irony, just as the situation in Algeria improved enough to bring in more foreign investment, the initiative to push the Tuareg off their ancestral land gave the dying Islamic movement a new ally. Historically, the Tuareg, a Berber subgroup, and the Algerian Arabs never fully became integrated. The Tuareg were a fierce nomadic group, while the Arabs were more of an urban population. The Tuareg spoke Berber and Arabic while the Arabs, descendants of the Arab invaders, spoke Arabic. The urban Arabs were more apt to identify with the Algerian nation, whereas the Tuareg had more tribal loyalties. Both groups were Muslim and had intermarried over the years, but they had different political agendas.

As the Arabic proverb states, "the enemy of my enemy is my friend." When the Algerian government started taking the land from the Tuareg in the mid 1990's, it was Abu Fahad, since he had already been working with the Islamists, who had brokered introductions and brought the two groups together. Who would have thought that nomadic desert fighters would be working alongside the Islamists? Thanks to the greed of the government, a new tribal Islamic movement was born.

Abu Fahad knew that as a noble he could get the tribes to join in the fight to take the country from the corrupt leaders. He brought the shaykh to meet the head of the tribe, he spoke native Berber and translated for the shaykh. He helped come up with an agreement of cooperation between the two groups. He now had a place of distinction with both the Islamists and his tribe. The government was not prepared to go against a tough tribal fighting force who was determined and committed to their cause. It has been one year since the two groups had agreed to work together. Now was the time to make their mark. *Allah Yajib (Allah will provide),* Abu Fahad thought. Allah had guided his tribe into the fight. He knew he was truly blessed.

Abu Fahad was the first to arrive at the apartment. He was expecting his Shura (high council) within the hour to start planning their biggest attack.

-Ten-

Lock your door rather accuse your neighbor.

— Lebanese proverb

"Mariam, are you all right?"

"Yes, Nick, but my family, did you hear...?" Mariam started crying and Nick could hear the pain in her voice.

"I am so sorry for what happened. How is Fatima?" he asked.

"She is fine. I have not told her yet, I can't just yet. When can I see you?" Mariam asked.

"I want to see you, but I just found out from Sami that there may be a threat against the embassy. If that's the case, I could be bringing trouble to you. Right now no one knows where you are. You and Fatima are safe. If I come to you, maybe I will be followed. Also, I would have to bring the whole security detail with me, which will only bring more attention to you. I thought about bringing you here, but now with the threat, it does not make sense.

"I am truly sorry, your parents and brother did not deserve to die; they were good people. I think our biggest concern now is to protect you and Fatima. I am hoping that everything will settle down in a week. Sami told me that the Ministry of Interior will have the situation under control soon." Nick lied, but felt she needed some reassurance since her world had just imploded.

Nick spoke with Mariam for another 20 minutes, not only to comfort her, but to reassure himself as well. *I almost lost her,* he thought. She seemed to be doing amazingly well for someone who had lost her parents but he knew that she was just being strong. "I will call you every few hours; you can page me at any time if you want to talk or need anything. I love you, Mariam. Everything will be all right. Nothing's going to happen to you and Fatima. Get some rest and we will talk in a few hours to figure out the best course of action, okay?"

"Okay, Nick. I love you."

Nick hung up the phone and thought how everything had just changed. He loved Mariam. They had been talking about taking a vacation together just a few weeks ago. He knew that she wanted to get married, but he was not sure if he was ready. He had dated many women in his life but he never truly

met the one that had connected with him like Mariam. He had thought that he would have another twelve months of his tour to date and would get to know her before he had to make a decision whether he would marry her or not. Was he ready to take her to the States with him if he had to leave the country now? He was not sure. He would protect her and do everything in his power to make sure that she and Fatima were safe, but was he ready for marriage? For now, he had to table that thought because he had an embassy to run; other people depended on him.

Nick asked Carmen, his secretary, to alert all American staff of a meeting at 1600 hours in the conference room for an Emergency Action Committee (EAC). The EAC was the committee that was called when information was learned that threatened the American community. The EAC was in charge of maintaining the Emergency Action Plan (EAP). The EAP provided for procedures in a crisis situation with each foreseeable contingencies. Successful planning involved periodic exercises to provide a backdrop for a real emergency. It was the ambassador's responsibility to establish the EAC and appoint members on the committee, but since he didn't much concern himself with the more mundane affairs of the embassy, Nick was left to choose members, to organize and to chair the meetings.

Carmen had worked for the embassy for eight years. She was divorced and quite striking. "Carmen, you have lived here all your life. What do you think will happen?"

"Mr. Nick, I am scared because I think that we have yet to see the worst of the violence." Carmen always called him Mr. Nick instead of just Nick. Carmen had worked for him for almost one year and she always had good instincts – even better than the so-called security expert in the RSO's office. There were some State Department officers who believed that FSNs were all working for the local security services and that they knew better than them because they were officers. Nick believed that one must respect the FSNs for their experience.

He was not naive enough to think that none of the FSNs worked for the Algerian State Security or reported on what was happening inside the embassy. But there were good FSNs who deserved respect, like Carmen. Nick could not blame many of the FSNs for reporting on the activities within the embassy to the local security service or a foreign security service. Almost all FSNs were treated with contempt by the American officers. It always happens, an officer arrives in country and immediately starts changing all procedures and proceeds to the put the local hire in his or her place. The arrogance of most FSOs was incredible. It was actually rare when American Foreign Service Officers actually treated the locals with respect.

Nick decided to call the Gunny. "Gunny, are you in your office? I want to talk to you."

"Yes sir, I will be here all afternoon," he replied. Nick rung off and left his office to see the Gunny.

"Gunny, how's it going?" Nick asked.

"Fucked up!" he replied. "I am not getting any info from John about what's really going on in the country. That motherfucker has been holding out on me, and I will not compromise when it comes to the lives of my Marines."

"You know how John is. It's not that he's holding out; he doesn't know shit, but he is too incompetent to say he doesn't know shit," Nick said to the Gunny.

"Nick, what's going on here?"

"Gunny, here's the deal. I think the situation is deteriorating but I don't know how bad it is yet. Sami told me that there is a possible threat against the embassy. You know Sami, if he says something, believe it. I have not heard from all of my contacts in the Ministry of Foreign Affairs. One of my friends was killed in the attacks last night. So I think prudence should be our best approach. I want you to organize a react drill ASAP. I want to be ready in case the situation gets worse. I am not sure if we will be evacuated or not," Nick replied as honestly as he could. Nick explained that he was sending a report to Washington but would probably not hear anything until the next day.

"Well, at least I can count on you for straight answers, Nick. I will plan the react drill for 2000 tonight. I think you should know there is a good chance that many of our local guard force soldiers may decide not to show up for work if the problems in the country continue," stated the Gunny.

"I think you should have a meeting with the local guards and tell them that all of them will receive a one step increase in pay for maintaining their regular shifts. I will clear it with the department. Second, see if your contacts within the Ministry of Interior can give you a situation report."

"Roger that, sir," replied Gunny.

"Hank, stay on your toes and expect anything," said Nick. "I want an update every two hours even if you have to say no update."

The Gunny grunted affirmatively.

"I have to talk with John now." Nick was not looking forward to that conversation as he returned to his office.

Nick picked up the phone to call John, the RSO. "John, can you come to my office?" asked Nick.

"Sure," replied John. He came to Nick's office, and Nick could tell that he was not happy about reporting to Nick.

"John, first thing I want to say is that I know you don't like me, but we don't have to like each other to work together. The only thing that you need to remember is that I am in charge now, and all security decisions must be approved by me. I know that Curt gave you carte blanche to run security as you saw fit, but as long as he is gone, all decisions go through me first. Do you understand?"

"It seems clear to me," John replied sarcastically.

"Now that I have said what I wanted to say, let's get to business. Sami told me that he learned from his informants that the embassy may be in danger."

"Sami don't know shit, and if he keeps speaking out of school about things he doesn't know anything about, he will probably find himself out of a job," replied John. Although John was an idiot, he did have contacts at the Ministry of Interior.

"The ministry is not giving us any answers. Until I hear differently, I am taking this seriously and I think you should, too."

"Now you are telling me how to do my job," interjected John.

"No, John. By law all threats must be taken seriously, and that's what I intend to do."

"Suit yourself." Nick thought that he had to play John carefully if he wanted any sort of cooperation.

"John, although the final decision is mine, you are the expert. I want your help. What if there is some truth to this threat, what then? I need your help."

"Okay, I will help; but you said it, I am the expert." Just as Nick thought, playing to his ego was probably be the best way to go.

"I asked Gunny to plan a react drill for tonight just to make sure his guys are sharp."

"That is my responsibly to call those drills."

"I know you would have called it, but I bumped into Gunny and just mentioned it. The Gunny thought it was a good idea." John looked at Nick suspiciously. Although Nick had told John that he was the expert, John thought that Nick was still trying to encroach into his area of expertise. "I also told Carmen to call an EAC meeting for 4:00 p.m. I will lead the meeting and give my suggestions and recommendations. I want to get ahead of this in case it does turn out to be something."

"Fine, what else do you want done?" John had already seemed to forget they had a truce.

"Gunny told me that he expected some of the guards to call in sick. He said he would speak to them to keep them motivated." Nick did not want to tell him about the one step increase in pay; John would make an issue of it. "Can you prepare me a brief on the contingency plans for different types of attacks, such as an armed group storming the embassy, a truck bomb, a stand off rocket attack and so on? I would like to have that on my desk by 5:00 p.m. today, at least the bare bones on how we would weather an attack. Also pull out the NEO (non-combatant evacuation operation) orders. Who knows, we may have to evacuate." Nick wanted to keep John on his toes and keep him busy. He believed that the NEO orders would not be necessary.

"That's quite a list. I will get on it and brief Michael on what you want." John was clearly brooding. He did not like to have his domain intruded upon, but Nick did not care; he wanted to be ready for anything. Michael Stefini was the assistant regional security officer and this was his first post. Michael seemed like a good guy, but it was hard for Nick to tell, since John kept him away from anyone who could say that John was an ass. John was Michael's immediate supervisor and he made sure that Michael did not forget it. Nick believed that Michael could be counted on in a pinch. "I have to give Washington an update. I will see you at 1600 hours, John." As John left, Nick could clearly see that he was not happy. Nick could not dwell on that, he had to draft a cable to the Department.

Nick started to write:

> *Immediate for SecState Wash DC*
> *From Embassy Algiers*
> *Classified by Charge Nick Phillips*

> *During the night of 11 Dec 2001, the Algerian Prime Minister and his wife were brutally murdered. They were found hacked to pieces in their house by local security forces. Ahmad Al-Qan'ai, one of the senior FLN leaders and a confidant of the president, was assassinated during the night. The Ministry of Interior believes that the crime was done by Islamic extremists, but thus far have no suspects in custody. Although these crimes were spectacular, the Ministry of Interior has claimed that they were isolated incidents. The general sense among the population is fear. Some senior FLN leaders believe that the Islamists are making their move to topple the military government. The Ministry of Interior has not reinstated the curfew as of yet. Many locals believe that the violence will likely worsen before this round of killings is over. (Comment: There have been some rumors that these unknown extremists may be considering the American Embassy as a target, but this rumor has not been substantiated. American Embassy*

Algiers is taking these rumors seriously and have begun to make the necessary security precautions, to include holding an EAC. End Comment.)

Nick pushed the send button and the cable was gone. He had hoped he was not being an alarmist, but he wanted to let Washington know what was going on.

Nick's phone rang. "Yes," said Nick. "Hello, Sami, come on up."

Sami came into Nick's office a few moments later. "Usted, how are you?" asked Sami.

"I am fine but everything seems to be in an upheaval. Have you heard anything else from your side?"

"Yes, the Ministry of Interior has instituted a curfew. Anyone who is not on official business after 8 p.m. at night will be arrested."

"W'allahi (really)? They have not had a curfew in almost three years. It seems as if the situation is getting more tense by the moment. What do you think is happening?"

Sami looked at Nick and thought about how to phrase what he was going to say. "Nick, you mean more to me than my own brother. I do not want anything to happen to you. The ministry's new official statement is that they are only initiating a curfew as a precautionary measure. They stand by their assessment that the new wave of violence will be over in a few days. In my opinion, we are facing the greatest crisis since the violence started in 1992."

Nick was floored. "Are you telling me that the extremists may take over the country?" Sami nodded slowly. "It's hard for me to understand all this. What about the army, can't they just crush the extremists with their sheer size?" asked Nick.

"It's not that simple, Nick. The government cannot go into neighborhoods and indiscriminately arrest people. The fighting has been going on for eight years, and the people are tired. Remember, the citizens elected the Islamists into power and the military took over. There is a powerful sentiment in the country that maybe the Islamists should have their way. That's one reason; secondly, these attacks were carried out by a new, stronger group. We have crushed most of the old guard. Who are these new people? Maybe the Islamists are receiving support from a new segment in Algeria. If the Islamists get a foothold in the country, there may be a general uprising and parts of the army and police may go with them. It will be anarchy on a widespread scale, and it will take a long time before it settles down. All I know is that you, as an American, should not be here if the government goes."

All of a sudden Nick's chair felt much larger. "I can't believe I am hearing this. You mean that there is a real possibility that we may have to evacuate the embassy?" Nick asked.

"Yes. I hate to be the one telling you this, but if things radically change and the Islamisits decide to take over the embassy, there will be no hostages like in Iran. They will kill every living person within the walls of this compound."

-Eleven-

Abu Fahad was meditating on the floor when members of his tribe started entering the apartment. The apartment had been set up as a meeting place for the group or as a hide out in case the police were after one of the tribe. One by one the group begin sitting on the floor in a circle. For centuries, the Tuareg tribe had sat like this to discuss matters of importance.

"You should all know that the shaykh was pleased with all of your deeds last night. He sends his regards and thanks." Abu Fahad was the only person in the group who met with the shaykh regularly. For security reasons, no others were allowed to attend their meetings. Of course, all of the members of the tribe had met the old man but only Abu Fahad knew how to contact him. The shaykh had convinced Abu Fahad's group that living life under the current situation was not only intolerable, but also un-Islamic. He had shown them the light as he had shown Abu Fahad so many years ago. Abu Fahad had brought the GIA and his tribe together. Although he was seen as first among equals in his tribe, he felt he rightly deserved a seat beside the old man. He was the most capable and he had the trust of the old man. He knew that he and the shaykh would put the country back on track.

"The shaykh told me to tell you that each act 'fi sabil Allah (in the duty of God)' gets you one step closer to paradise." To a Muslim who came from the desert like the Tuareg, paradise was highly sought. All of one's dreams would be realized in the afterlife. Paradise for the Muslim male was described in detail in the Qur'an; rivers and lush gardens will be in abundance, man will have every adornment that he wants, he will never tire, virgins with big, beautiful, and luscious eyes would tend to his every need and he would be surrounded by his family. Hell, on the other hand, was described in equally vivid detail. The shaykh knew how to evoke the right images in his follower's minds. Abu Fahad had realized this fact from the first moment he met the shaykh.

"We are not done yet, my brothers. We are about to embark on the most dangerous mission." He looked into the eyes of each of his tribesmen. There were eight people around the circle; each controlled a group of twenty men. Abu Fahad knew that each would be leaders in the new Islamic republic of Algeria in the future. Those 160 men made of the core of the Tuareg fighters in the tribe. Each one would give their lives for the other and the cause. Abu Fahad did not want to meet the members of each group unless it was necessary for the mission. He had learned this philosophy from the Bosnians.

They called it the hydra principle, though he did not even know what a hydra was before that. They told him that he should have a core group who also had followers; if someone was killed or captured then the whole group would not be compromised because only the leader knew everything. They also told him that if one head was cut off, another would grow in its place. He thought that was a strange example at first, but now he understood.

Abu Fahad would plan the attack with his core eight leaders and then decide which group would participate in the attack. Only the eight people in the room would know the complete plan. He could count on them and he needed their feedback. Only the core eight knew how to contact Abu Fahad. If any of the group members were captured and tortured, then they could only say that he existed, but could not lead them to where he was. He would instruct each leader not tell their followers the details of the plan until they needed to know.

"We will attack the American Embassy," stated Abu Fahad. There were murmurs around the group. He could see that they thought it was an ambitious task. "I know you think the Americans are invincible, but we will attack them and succeed, and then the world will see that they are only a paper tiger. Do you want to reach salvation? Are you ready to make the infidels pay for ruining our country?"

"Allahu Akbar," the group yelled.

"You will each choose one person from your groups to help us succeed. We will only need eight to mount the primary attack and the rest will support us by conducting other attacks."

"How will we get though their security checks?" asked Khalid.

"I have figured out how to do that but our biggest concern will not be the Americans, but Algerian State Security. Once we begin our attack on the embassy, they will surely call for help. That is why we need our tribal brothers to launch some diversionary attacks in town about 20-30 minutes before the attack and during the attack. I want five car bombs to go off in town near the most popular tourist spots; target the major hotels and discos. These are places that destroy the Islamic identity. This will create a panic and keep the security services so busy that they will not be able to come to the aid of the Americans. These attacks will flood the switchboards of the police and make it even harder for the Americans to call for help. We do not need much time; I anticipate being able to enter in the embassy and do what we have to do very quickly. I will have a secondary group waiting away for back-up

58

nearby. Our other groups will be conducting attacks west of Algiers tonight and tomorrow morning."

"How will we breach their security in the first place?" asked Ahmad.

"That's the easy part," replied Abu Fahad. "They will let us in."

-Twelve-

Nick sat in his office thinking about what Sami had told him. He had wanted John to prepare for any contingency, but he never thought that the government would actually go or that they would need to evacuate the embassy. Nick was glad that Sami was so candid. Nick had ten Americans to protect. He would make sure that the embassy would be ready if an attack took place.

"Sami, I understand. If the situation in the country does start to rupture, I want to know ASAP. I would rather evacuate the compound than try and weather the storm."

"I will let you know immediately if it becomes too dangerous, because the problem is that if the Islamists do take over the country, it will happen without much warning, so you should be prepared if that does happen," said Sami.

"Thanks. I knew I could count on you. I know John's contacts will probably only give him the ministry's standard line of 'everything will be under control soon.'"

"You have to understand, Nick, that nobody wants to admit that the situation could possibly get out of control. We have been fighting the Islamists for eight years, and since 1998, the government has been saying that we have been winning this 'non-war' – I say non-war because we have dedicated more resources to combating the terrorism in eight years than our whole defense budget for the previous ten years. But, now if the government says that all of a sudden there is a real threat from these people, it would give a real surge to their movement. You have to remember the government invalidated the election results of 1991. Part of their reasoning was that it wasn't a fair election and that the military came in and restored the peace. The government has been telling its citizens that the attacks were not organized and that their movement does not represent the main stream. In fact, the Islamists won that election fairly and more people than they care to admit support their agenda. Now, this is not the whole government that has been turning a blind eye to the Islamists. There have been some that have been calling for new, fair elections but the military will never go for that."

Nick thought that made sense, especially since the government had done everything in its power to kill off any leaders within the Islamist's movement.

"I have a favor to ask of you, Sami. Do you mind if Mariam stays at your house for the time being? I am worried about her and do not think it's safe it she goes back to her house."

"No problem, anything I can do for you or her just let me know."

"Shokran, habibi (thanks, my friend). I will talk to her about leaving the country until everything calms down."

"That would be best if she did leave," said Sami.

"I need to prepare for the EAC meeting. Page me as soon as you hear something. If nothing changes, let's get together later this afternoon."

"I will be here until 6 or 7," said Sami.

Nick sat in his office before going to the conference room. Everyone was already there when he walked in. Everyone stood up as he walked in, as was the policy when either the ambassador or the charge d'affaires, when the ambassador was outside the country, walked in. "Would everybody please sit."

Nick began, "I am glad to see everyone today. I wanted to meet with everyone and to let you know what's happening in the country. Please let your sections know what I am about to tell you. We do not know a lot at this time. Several senior FLN leaders have been killed, including the Prime Minister. You read the e-mail; the ambassador left a few hours ago for consultations. The situation is very volatile at this time and anything could happen, including the Islamists taking over. That's the worse case scenario but I want us to keep it in mind. If that happens, I will order an NEO, because I feel that the security situation will be such that it would be too dangerous for Americans to stay. Additionally, I have learned that a possible threat exists against the embassy. I want Sarah to pull out the Emergency Action Handbook. She will go through the checklist and be the official log keeper." Nick wanted to make sure all his actions were on record. He had heard of more than one officer's career being ruined because of how different people described the course of events after it had happened. He knew that if there was an official record, it would be harder for anyone to misrepresent the facts.

"I want the Marines and the RSO section to review the defense plan of the embassy and 'use of force' regulations. I also want you to test communications and identify likely staging points, assembly areas and embarkation points. Also, I want every member of the embassy personnel to know what to do in an attack and where his or her safe haven is." The safe haven was important because in case of an attack, everyone would meet there. The FSNs would be in one side of embassy and the American staff on the other in the CAA.

"I want public affairs to develop a plan to deal with the press, because you know whenever a crisis happens, everyone wants to know what the Americans will do. I want the Ministry of the Interior notified that we believe that there is a threat. I don't care it they don't believe it or won't tell us; we will put them on notice that we assess that there is a crisis. I want John to check the safe haven for barriers, supplies and communication equipment. John should also brief the security personnel inside the embassy compound of the threat as well as the char force, mailroom personnel and telephone operators. I want admin to contact the airlines to see if they are still maintaining their flights. Now, I know this is a lot to do right now, but this is our priority. Everything else is secondary."

Nick looked at his senior staff: the Gunny; John; Thomas Burton, the admin officer; Sarah; and Rick Williams, the communications officer. All seemed receptive but John, who was clearly pissed that he was not consulted before Nick started mentioning an NEO, security recommendations or the threat. Nick was becoming aware that John would be a problem for him if things got dicey.

"An NEO, aren't you sort of jumping the gun by even considering an NEO?" asked John.

"I think we should keep all our options open and be ready for any contingency. I also want to let everyone know that all operations will still function as before. We will maintain the same hours and still conduct visa and American citizen service hours. I want the consular section to contact all Americans to let them know that we are monitoring the situation. All other duties take a backseat to help locating the Americans. I want all admin and political FSNs to help consular in this regard. There are only about ten Americans in country, but I want to know where these people are in case we have to evacuate. All leave is canceled at this point. If there is anything that any of you need to discuss with me, call Carmen if it deals with unclassified issues, since she is an FSN, or Sarah if it deals with classified things. I hope we can ride this out. I need your help. If you have suggestions let me know. We are all family and I want to make sure that if this situation does change quickly we can make the necessary adjustments. Are there any questions?" asked Nick.

Sarah asked the first question, "Do you really think the situation could change that much that we would need to have an NEO?" An NEO was carried out by an aircraft carrier and it involved a lot of logistics. Several helicopters would take off from a carrier and evacuate the embassy employees. In the past eleven years, 144 diplomatic missions had been evacuated, disrupting personal lives and embassy operations. In addition, eleven separate attacks were made against Americans and U.S. interests in 1998 alone. The embassy in Mogadishu was one the most famous ones. Unpredictability was one of the key aspects about living oversees. Who could have anticipated the accidental bombing of the Chinese Embassy in Belgrade that led to a major civil disturbance and siege of the American Embassy in Beijing by demonstrators? It was impossible to know that huge forest fires in Sumatra and Kalimantan, Indonesia, would cause the embassy in Kuala Lumpur to be evacuated for health reasons. And lastly, who would have thought a failed pyramid scheme in Albania would lead to civil war and the evacuation of the U.S. Embassy?

"I think that is a distinct possibility. The one fact that keeps going through my mind is what Sami said: If the Islamists take over and decide they want to attack the embassy, they will probably kill all of us." Sarah was visibly shaken when Nick explained this part. "For this reason, I will request an evacuation if the civil unrest becomes unmanageable." Nick knew that while all Foreign Service employees joined the organization because of adventure and excitement, it was everyone's worse fear that an uprising would occur. After the Iran hostage crisis, the State Department had incorporated crisis management exercises in its training program. Nick thought about how that was usually the day when people called in sick. No one took that part of the training seriously and Nick hoped that they would not regret it.

It was John's turn to ask a question, "If the situation does deteriorate, I hope you know that as RSO I will have to take command of situation."

He was clearly challenging Nick in front of the group. "Well, depending on what happens, we would have to discuss it at that time, but hopefully it will not come to that. In the meantime, hopefully you will have those security contingency plans for me soon," replied Nick.

"I will have it on your desk at 1700 hours," replied John.

"If there are no other questions, then we will meet again tomorrow at the same time. Thanks for coming. Gunny, can I have a word with you?" The Gunny stayed behind.

"What's up, Nick?"

Nick briefed Gunny on the killing of Mariam's family and told him that she was at Sami's house. Gunny had met her on several occasions. "I agree that she is safest there. Let me know if you need me to do anything." Gunny liked Mariam and felt that Nick had met the perfect woman.

"Thanks, Hank. I want you to tighten physical security controls and inspect all barriers this evening."

"Roger that." The Gunny exited the room.
Nick left the room thinking that John would be an obstacle.

-Thirteen-

Abu Fahad began explaining his idea to the men. "The Americans will let us inside the walls of the embassy. When I was there last week, I saw several of their cleaning crews pushing large dumpsters outside of the embassy compound to a group of larger trash dumpsters outside of the security barricade. Every day, twice a day, four of their local workers push these dumpsters, one at a time, to the trash pick-up area. What we will do is be in the large dumpster outside of the security perimeter when they arrive. Once there, we will get into the smaller dumpster and they will push us through the jersey barricades, past the security check, and into the compound itself. We will put two to three men in each dumpster, fully loaded with Kalashnakovs, grenades and pistols."

He could tell by the looks on their faces that they liked the plan. Abu Fahad continued, "We will be inside the barricade before they know what has happened. They do not have that much security inside and the local guards do not have weapons; they will surely run when we start our show. As for the Marines, they will be our biggest problem. We will take them by surprise and then open the gates for our secondary group to enter. No one will use the radio until we start the attack. I will let the second group know when to approach the embassy.

"Inside, our group will split up into two groups of four people and each will go to the opposite ends of the embassy and force the doors open. We will take over their central control room and we will open the gates for the other twenty tribe members. We do not want to alert them of our presence until we have control of their control room. Once we have control, we will kill everyone and regroup back at this apartment later that night. If something bad happens, go to the apartments in either Bentaha or Miftah," continued Abu Fahad.

"How will we get the four workers who work for the embassy to help us?" asked Ahmad.

"Mahmud, tell the brothers what you have been doing for the last week," commanded Abu Fahad. Mahmud was Abu Fahad's brother and most trusted Mujahidin fighter. At 20, Mahmud was eight years younger than Abu Fahad but was totally devoted to his brother. After Abu Fahad's father was killed, Abu Fahad became like a substitute father to his brother because he was the oldest male. Although he trained in the desert with the GIA and in Bosnia, he taught Mahmud everything he had learned. He taught him about the Qur'an and what a person needed to do to reach Jinna (Paradise). In many ways, his brother was more extreme in his thoughts and actions than Abu Fahad. He showed no mercy for his victims. Not only did he kill them with his dagger up close but he killed them slowly so they felt the pain as the life drained out of them. Abu Fahad swelled with pride when he thought of his brother.

"I have the names and addresses of the four people who clean the embassy," said Mahmud.

"But how do we know that they will help us?" Ahmad persisted.

"They are Muslims, surely they will help us. Also we will break into their homes the night before and hold their families hostage while we carry out our mission. This is to ensure that they do their religious duty in Islam." Abu Fahad knew in Arab society that family obligations take precedence over the demands of any job.

"We will explain to them that as Muslims they must help their Muslim brothers in order to expiate their sins. They have served Shaitan (Satan) long enough. We will give them a choice, 'Help us or we will flay the skin off your family members in front of you before we slowly kill you.' They are beneath contempt, they have served the Kufar (infidels) and therefore must do penitence. This will be their penance."

The group all nodded in agreement to Abu Fahad's plan.

-Fourteen-

"Gunny, can we go over security from your standpoint?" asked Nick over the phone.

"Roger that. Come to my office," said Gunny. He wasn't a talker. He believed in economy of words. Nick saw him as a serious man who just did not believe in a lot of wasted motion. Nick and Gunny had worked out together since Nick arrived a year earlier and had smoked dozens of Romeo y Julieta Cuban cigars together. Nick and the Gunny had no problem obtaining Cuban cigars, because Algeria did not have a ban on Cuban products. Many times when they got together to smoke cigars under the stars, they would not say a word to each other but not feel uncomfortable. They both enjoyed good company and a great cigar.

Gunny's office was inside Post One. Nick had seen Post One everyday since he had been in Algeria, but he was now seeing it as if it was for the first time. When Nick arrived at Post One, he was let in by Gunny.

"Where do you want to start?" asked Gunny.

"Let's start from the basics. I am looking at this from a different perspective now." It almost looked like a glass-enclosed cage. A Marine was always on duty inside Post One. Almost every embassy in the world had a Post One with a Marine that answered the phone 24 hours a day. Nick thought it was one of the uniform things about embassies: "American Embassy, Marine Guard, how can I help you?" The standard greeting used by every Marine.

"OK," began the Gunny. "This is Post One, the security nerve center of the embassy. This is the best protected area in the embassy. The glass that surrounds Post One is bullet proof and impact resistant. It will repel any force and repulse it back where it was fired. Everything is controlled from these panels. The doors on the outer perimeter are magnalock so that if anything happens, not even the FSN guard will be able to enter the main area of the embassy."

"What are magnalock doors?" asked Nick.

"Magnalock doors are super heavy magnetic doors that can not even be opened by a rocket-propelled grenade. If an attack happens, each of my Marines are instructed to lift up all the jersey barriers, seal the magnalock doors, then call me and the rest of the Marines to the main building."

"Now, Gunny, what is this thing that John was talking about if something breaks out that he would be in charge?" asked Nick.

"Technically he is in charge of the security of the embassy, but you are in charge of the mission. In case an attack does happen, he should be in Post One coordinating the defense. Some ambassadors or chiefs of missions would probably choose to let the RSO control the situation. But make no mistake: you are the highest ranking person on post; therefore, you are in charge."

"If an external attack occurred, what would happen after those first steps are taken?" asked Nick.

"Hopefully, my Marine would see it on the cameras before it happened. We have cameras at each entrance of the embassy. Once he saw it, he would secure all entrances and then hit the alarm button to alert everyone of an attack. Everyone should go to the safe haven but we would announce it as well. Next, he would alert the local guard force and the Ministry of the Interior that an attack has occurred. He would move all staff and visitors to the safe haven area and secure elevators to upper floors and disable them. At the same time, the air conditioning unit would be cut off to prevent the spread of gas if it's a chemical attack. We would defend the building according to our defense strategy, withdrawing as necessary after laying down suppressing fire and securing barriers."

Nick's confidence was up after hearing the Gunny go through the procedures for attack. He had known Gunny would have everything in order but this proved it. If something did happen, Nick would be glad that Gunny was on his side.

"Can you see in all directions from Post One and spot everything that is coming?" asked Nick.

"Not quite. There are some blind spots but that is where the local guards help us by providing us with some warning. We asked the State Department for the money for security upgrades but we are still waiting. You would think after the embassy attacks in Dar Essalam and Nairobi in 1998, they would get off their ass and take this shit seriously," stated Gunny. Gunny may not talk a lot but he never had a problem telling it as he saw it. "We have a weapons locker that has a shotgun inside. Each of my Marines wear a nine millimeter as a sidearm," continued the Gunny.

"You don't keep an M-16 or other heavy type of weapons around here?" asked Nick.

"No, Sir. We are not supposed to engage an enemy unless they are coming over the wall. We are only supposed to use our weapons defensively. That is why we do not have any sniper weapons here. We have a few M-16s in the

RSO's office in the weapons safe, but I do not think anyone in the RSO'S office is qualified to use them."

Nick laughed, "Are you serious?"

"Yes."

"But you are Marines. You guys fire more rounds through M-16s then any other branch of the military, " said Nick.

"Yes, but that is how John has laid out the security procedures and he is my so-called supervisor."

"If you had access to those weapons, what would you do?" asked Nick.

"I would keep them in our weapons locker at Post One. If a hostile event happened, I would send two of my Marines on the roof to take up sniper positions until we were either evacuated or the threat was neutralized."

"OK, Gunny, you got it. I will smooth it over with John, you will have those weapons." Gunny gave Nick a wry smile because he knew that John would not take it well. "You know what the problem with that guy is, he's got little dick complex. You know guys with little dicks want to compensate for their inadequacies by giving people shit all the time."

"If you need me you know where I am," stated Gunny.

"Need you? You can't be serious," replied Nick.

"Not to help you, but to perform first aid on him after you finish hurting John."

Nick laughed as he walked away.

Nick returned to his office at 1630 to a message that Sami wanted to see him. Nick thought that it could not be good information.

Sami came to Nick's office and was clearly unsettled. "Nick, I just received a call from my ministry; all personnel have been put on alert. The army, police and all other security forces have been told to come on duty. I have to leave but I will try and come back later this evening."

"What does that mean, Sami?" asked Nick.

"It means that things are out of control. We have reports that there have been skirmishes in various enclaves around Algeria. It hasn't been all from the Islamists. Our reports say that various tribal sections of the society have begun to rise up. I feel that the ministry is scared. I still do not have any word from them as to the long-term viability of the government."

"This sounds as if a general uprising may be in the cards, like you mentioned earlier." Nick sat there and thought that he would need to send another cable to the department about the deteriorating situation.

"I have to check in at the ministries' complex and then I will be back. My bosses are obviously looking to stabilize the situation inside the country before worrying about the safety of any foreigners, or they would not have asked me to come in. This is another indication that the problem is serious. I hate to leave but I am also hoping that I can learn more from my friends when I see them. All of my friends who work within the security services will be coming in to the ministry. They will be able to tell me what's going on around the country. I will have more information when I return."

"Thanks, Sami. I appreciate anything you can do." Sami got up to leave and was stopped by John in the hall. "I see that your country is finally going to shit," said John.

"Unlike your country, we did not get independence until 1962. We are still trying to find our way. I believe you fought a bloody civil war 100 years after you gained your independence. History is like that," said Sami.

"Whatever. All I know is that this is a fucked up country," said John as he walked away.

Sami left the building thinking that it was unfortunate that Nick had to work with such a person. *May Allah protect you, my friend,* thought Sami.

John barged in Nick's office. "I just talked with one of Gunny's Marines. He said that they were going to be issued M-16s. How are you going to do that, since those weapons are in our weapons locker?"

Nick did not want the conversation to start out this way. "John, I don't want to step on your feet, but I talked with Gunny and we believe that since the Marines are better trained on those weapons, they should have access to them. I want you to take those M-16s over to the Post One after this conversation."

"I am in charge of security," exploded John. "You can't do this. I dictate what happens on this post when it comes to security."

"John, I am in charge of the mission. That means everything. That is the chain of command at this post for all matters of security: me, then you and then Gunny. That is laid out in the Emergency Action Handbook. I can order you but I want your cooperation on this. I will expect those weapons to be over at Post One within the hour. The Gunny will sign and be accountable for them." John was upset again. Nick thought that this would be getting more difficult at each meeting with John. "So show me what you have in terms of contingency plans."

"Each possible attack will have a different type of response. For an armed group attacking, that's the easiest. We are fortified and it would be useless to attack head-on. If an attack did happen, the Marines would defend the embassy and depending on the level of the attack, we would probably order an evacuation using from military transport," said John. "For a stand-off attack, we should get a warning from the FSNs or the cameras. If that's the case, we could probably withstand the attack."

"If we have to evacuate, what is the plan?" asked Nick.

"We will order the evacuation from the aircraft carrier that is in the Mediterranean."

"Which ship would do the evacuation and how long would it take for them to get here?" Nick queried.

"I am not sure which ship is out there. Maybe it would take one hour."

"Can you find out which ship would evacuate us and how long it would take exactly?" asked Nick.

"I will let you know." John went on for a few more minutes.

Nick thought that he had never heard a worse debrief in his life. He did not want to press John on security matters since now he knew that John was totally incompetent. Nick knew that he could rely on Gunny and his Marines if thing got really out of hand. If an attack did occur, Nick would take charge, because John would only get in the way.

"I just want to update you. I have heard that not only will there be a curfew initiated but all of the security forces have just gone on alert. There have been reports that fighting has broken out between some tribes and the security forces. I am going to let Washington know that the situation is deteriorating. Let's meet in the evening," stated Nick. "Have you heard anything more from your contacts, John?"

"Not yet, but as I said earlier, if the situation worsens they will call me." John hated having to report to this guy. He thought he knew everything about the region. He wished Curtis was here; he knew how to neutralize Nick. He would talk to the ambassador when he returned. He would let Nick have his day now but would make sure that he made note of everything so as to inform the ambassador. John got along well with the ambassador. They were both from small towns in Indiana and they both thought Nick was an arrogant prick. The ambassador had watched John's back ever since he had arrived in the country. John would just have to wait until he returned.

"John, don't you think it's strange that your contacts have refused to tell you anything about what's going on in the country?"

"Well, they aren't alarmist like some we know." John got up and went out. He would not have security dictated to him by a fucking amateur.

Nick watched John leave and thought that if an emergency situation did happen, he would look to Gunny to provide him with advice. John thought to himself how DS could let some of these guys go overseas. Some guys like John weren't qualified to protect something as important as an embassy.

Gunny went back to Post One and asked his Marines to initiate a radio check of the embassy system. He did not want any problems with the communications system if a crisis occurred. He pulled out his hand-held radio and checked to make sure the front gate and back gate could hear him. He walked through Post One area by area, he checked the barricades and the gates that protected the embassy. All seemed well, but as a career Marine, he knew that things could change quickly. He decided to check on the security near the inner perimeter.

-Fifteen-

The doctor must heal his own bald head.

— Persian proverb

Nick had been running around all day worrying about the embassy, but he was distracted because of his concern for Mariam. He called her.

"How are you?" asked Nick.

"I got some sleep but I can't help but keep thinking of what those people did to my family. Nick I am scared and I don't know what's going on here." Nick updated Mariam on what had happened in the last few hours.

"I have a bad feeling about this, Nick. I need to do something, talk to my other relatives or my father's friends. I feel so cut off from everyone. Fatima still doesn't know anything yet, but I can't keep it from her for long."

"I think you need to be careful about who you talk to. Whatever you do, do not tell anyone where you are." said Nick. "We still do not know what is going on so let's play it very cautious, okay?"

"I understand, Nick. I trust you. When can I see you?"

"I don't know. I miss you, Mariam. I want to be with you, but the situation is too volatile. I think the best place for you right now is where you are. I don't want anything to happen to you. I think you and Fatima should plan on leaving the country tomorrow until everything calms down."

"Nick, I can't just leave my home, never knowing when I can come back. I hate the fact that they are trying to run us out of the country. Also, I must bury my parents in the prescribed Islamic way." All Muslims must be washed and purified after they die. After the ritual purification, the dead are then wrapped in strips of white cloth before they enter the ground. All Muslims must be buried within three days. The three days prior to the burial, members of the family will sit up and read portions of the Qur'an. It was very important to all Muslims that they be buried in the right manner.

"I believe that it's too dangerous for you to be in public. You should talk to your uncles or cousins to see if they can assist in the burial. Mariam, I love you. I don't want to sound callous or hard, but you must take care of yourself and Fatima now. Your parents would understand," Nick stated.

Mariam sighed, but knew that Nick was right. "I know, but I feel so helpless." Mariam was not the type of woman to sit by and wait for things to happen around her. She was a doer. Although she was a graphic artist, she was also active in Algerian politics. She led a drive to get women out to vote. She was an important person in the women's political movement. She supported the Algerian modernist's movement, and the Islamists knew this fact. This is another reason Sami and Nick wanted her to maintain a low profile. Even aside from being her father's daughter, she was a valid target in their eyes.

"I will call some of my relatives and have them make the arrangements. I will also try to find out from senior FLN leadership what is going on in the country. I want answers," declared Mariam.

"Are they in any danger from these people?" asked Nick.

"I asked Sami that and he said that they were only killing the immediate family members." Nick could tell that Mariam was now recovering somewhat from the shock. She was becoming her old self in Nick's eyes; she was starting to take her life back.

"I will call you as soon as I hear something on the situation. If you hear anything call me," stated Nick.

"Okay, be safe, Nick."

Nick decided to start on a new cable when his phone rang. It was Rick, the communications officer. "Nick, we just got an immediate cable from Washington. I will bring it up to you."

"What is it, Rick?"

"A response to your earlier message."

Rick left the cable and returned to his office. Nick read the cable:

> *Immediate for Embassy Algiers*
> *From SecState Wash DC*
> *Classified by Secretary of State*
>
> *We read your cable with concern and agree that the situation may become volatile at any moment. If post feels that the threat reaches a critical level, post is authorized to evacuate the embassy. There is currently no news coming out of Algeria. Continue to keep us updated. The USS John F. Kennedy is in the Mediterranean and ready to assist if the need arises. Please review your security posture and NEO procedures.*
>
> *Powell*

Nick finished reading the cable and thought that at least there was some adult supervision at the Department. When Nick had sent his last cable he was not sure how it would be received, but he hoped they would be supportive, and it looked as if they backed his assessment. He knew that sometimes in Washington, the managers backed the analyst in the building over the people in the field. It may seem irrational to anyone looking from the outside in, but he knew that many of the analysts did not want to take the risk of being wrong. Consequently, they played it safe and never made concrete predictions. The same flaw existed in management also. They worked with these analysts on a daily basis, so they tended to support the people in their offices. Because of this trend, everyone was afraid of being wrong. It made you look like a bad analyst or bad diplomat if you could not even predict what would happen in your country of responsibility.

-Sixteen-

Nick decided to take a few minutes to assess the situation. It was already 7:30 p.m. and the Gunny was going to start the reaction drill at 8:00 p.m. He would try to get Mariam out of the country tomorrow night. So much had happened in one day that he forgot that it was Wednesday. He would try to appeal to her that it would only be temporary. She was a smart and savvy woman, but under these circumstances he had a hard time imagining what she would do. Nick decided to have all the Americans rounded up and brought to the embassy on Friday evening. Luckily, there were only about ten Americans in the country. He would have Arshad send drivers for them Friday afternoon. He knew that some Americans would probably want to stay, but he would give them the option to leave.

On Friday, the Muslim holy day, the violence would probably settle down. If things were still shaky, he would plan for the evacuation on Friday with a possible departure on Saturday morning, considering the country did not crumple the next day.

Nick's phone rang. It was Gunny. "Nick, I will start the react drill in about 10 minutes. You want to come down?"

"I will be at Post One in a few minutes."

Nick arrived to see Gunny with another marine inside Post One. Gunny began by setting up the drill, "We just received a call from the local guard force that a suspicious truck has pulled up to the embassy. What do you do corporal?" asked the Gunny.

"I hit the delta barriers to keep the truck from entering the compound," replied Corporal Jeff Swafford.

"Now the drill begins. Several unfriendlies have just killed the local guards and are moving to the compound. Go," ordered the Gunny.

Jeff immediately locked the magnalock doors which sealed the outer doors. He hit the alarm and called the RSO. "Sir, we have a situation. Several intruders have entered the compound. I sealed the outer door and have hit the alarm. I am waiting for Gunny."

Gunny whispered to Nick, "We will do this drill as if I am not here. I want to see how they react on their own."

One minute later, three other Marines burst into Post One in full riot gear. Sergeant Peter Clark, the assistant detachment commander, asked what had happened. At the same time, one Marine went to the weapons locker and pulled out the two M-16s, while Jeff pulled the shotgun off the wall. Jeff explained what had happened. Peter ordered Jim Coleman, a lance corporal, to go to the roof to set up as a sniper and told Jeff to make an announcement telling all employees to go to the safe haven.

The safe haven was an area inside an embassy deemed to be most secure. It was away from windows to avoid fragment damage from glass. It usually contained gas masks and enough food and water to hold out for a week in case of a gas or chemical attack. Nick had always thought that they did not do enough training with the embassy staff in case an emergency broke out. Nick had asked the ambassador several times to have emergency drills, but he refused every time because he said it would interfere too much with the daily operations of the embassy. Nick had even written a cable saying that the embassy needed to conduct more drills, but the ambassador refused to send the cable.

Gunny barked, "They have just entered the embassy compound."

Peter commanded, "Swafford, you stay here and let us know what happens. We will be on channel-1 of the network." They called it net-1 for short, the internal communications system used by the Marines. They carried small hand-held radios that had multiple channels.

"Mike, you come with me." Mike was another sergeant but had just joined the MSG program. Although he did not have a lot of experience in embassies, he was in the infantry and had a lot of combat experience.

They went through the embassy expertly, Nick and Gunny following at a discreet distance. Gunny had set up cardboard cutouts of bad guys in various hallways before the drill. The two Marines had no idea if they would find anything. They saw the first three targets, and they rolled CS gas down the hall, donned gas masks and entered the corridor once the gas grenades "exploded." They "fired" several shots into their enemies. Gunny had given Nick a gas mask as they left Post One; Nick did not know why. All of the bullets and gas were fake, but Gunny wanted Nick to practice putting the gas mask on.

The group moved down the hall and cleared every room. Room clearing was a technique where the Marines would check it for any bad guys. If the threat was eliminated then the room was declared "clear from danger."

They proceeded to check every room of the embassy. Once the threat was over, they sounded the all-clear alarm. Afterwards in Post One, the Gunny had a "hot wash," a review of how the drill went.

Gunny began, "That was a good exercise, guys, but I want your coordination to be better. If you are all together, I want everybody to already have his duties designated. You should only call out positions if the group is separated or the situation demands it. For example, Coleman always goes to the roof so you should not have to order him to do that. He should know and just say that he going there. Overall not bad. I want everyone here to review the NEO procedures."

Gunny continued, "Everybody is on duty tonight. I want sweeps made of the perimeter every two hours with the local guards. You guys rotate one person out to sleep. I leave it up to you to work it out. I don't want to hear that the local guards are sleeping on the job. It's your job to keep those guys sharp. I want no fuck-ups. We are in a serious situation. I will rip your heart out if I catch anyone clowning around. The chargé has told me and I believe that there is a real threat against the embassy. This is what we are trained for. Woe be it to any motherfucker who goes up against a U.S. Marine." Gunny emitted a loud bark. The four other Marines barked in unison.

"Sir, do you have any thing to add?" asked Gunny of Nick.

"I echo Gunny's words: stay sharp. Your chain of command is Gunny first, then me. Do not call John unless you can't find either of us. I will be taking control of any emergency situation in conjuction with Gunny. Do you understand?" stated Nick.

Yes, sir," roared the Marines.

Nick looked at his watch. It was already 10:00 p.m.

"Sir, we have a visitor at the back gate, "said Jeff.

Both Nick and Gunny looked at the camera and noticed it was Sami. Gunny said, "Let him through."

"Gunny please come to my office. I want you to hear this, "stated Nick. They left to go to Nick's office.

Sami walked into Nick's office with a weary look on his face. Nick felt bad for him since he had to watch his own county fall apart. Sami was fiercely loyal to Algeria. He was Berber from the Kabyle tribe, by far the largest of the Berber-speaking groups. He could trace his ancestors back 1000 years and he was proud to be from a tribe that called Algeria home for so long. But Nick had noticed that the day's events had put a unique strain on him. He had always treated Nick as an honored guest in his country. Nick and Sami had become more than friends, almost like bothers. Sami had taken Nick to visit his relatives in the desert near the Chelif River. Many of his relatives remained unassimilated to Arab culture and retained their own language and some of the cultural differences. If it was one thing the Kabyle knew, it was loyalty. Historically, the Kabyle were very unsociable people. It was said that if one of their tribe took you as a true friend, that friendship was separated only by death.

Nick knew Sami saw him as a true friend. Nick, for his part, felt the same about Sami. When Nick arrived in the country, not many of the Ministry of Interior officers had much contact with embassy personnel, let alone were friends with the embassy staff. Nick, as he knew both the Arabic language and the region, immediately invited the ministry contingent that protected the embassy to his house. While most of the officers were still standoffish, Nick had struck up a friendship with Sami. Sami loved American books but could not find any in the country. Nick discovered that Sami and he had similar tastes in literature. He let Sami borrow books from his library and they would discuss them afterward. During the past year, Sami had let Nick get a glimpse of an Algeria that very few foreigners had seen, especially Americans.

Sami began by greeting both Nick and Gunny warmly, as was his custom. "I talked with many of my friends who work in various parts of the country. It is bad news. There appear to be spurts of violence breaking out around the country. The GIA is definitely behind it, but there is one curious dynamic: many of the reports say that some of the tribes are participating in the violence, especially the Tuaregs."

"Who are these Tuaregs?" asked Gunny.

"They are a fierce desert tribe who are an offshoot of the Berbers. We have had problems with them in the south because of the government's decision to relocate some of them. But we have heard nothing from them this far north," Sami explained. "The Ministry of Interior's resources are being taxed to the fullest. We still believe that we can contain the threat, but it may take some time. We expected violence in areas such as Oran and Arzew, areas to the east of Algiers. But we are seeing violence in places like Ghardaia and Hassi Messaoud in the west; we have never seen violence in those areas. Groups have been ambushing people on the streets and bodies have been found headless and chopped to pieces. Various mosques have been broadcasting a demand from the FIS stating that the violence will increase unless the government steps down and the military surrenders. This is why we believe the tribes are helping. They want an end to all the violence and the current government. The FIS is demanding a total transfer of power; they will not stop until the election results of 1991 are reinstated.

"Also, you have to keep in mind that for the last eight years these extremists have felt threatened by Westernization. For an Arab who cherishes traditions and feels that his identity is jeopardized, Islamic extremism is an ideology he can cling to. This is another reason why many of the tribes are now joining the terrorists groups."

Nick and Gunny looked at each other. "What is your assessment, Sami?" asked Nick.

"At this point I can't say. The government's resources have never been stretched this far before and we are seeing violence from disparate segments of society as well. I talked with my friends in the army and police. Some believe that the government will prevail and others believe that the government only has about a week. Some of my friends have been talking about leaving Algeria. As you know, these Islamic terrorists have made it one of their priorities to kill anyone working for the Ministry of Defense or Interior. Some prefer to watch it unfold from outside the country. I will stay and fight. This is my country. I am Kabyle. I will not leave, at least not at this time. I will help you in any way I can. For the record, the ministry has decided to cut the local guard force at all foreign embassies by one third. As of tomorrow, your guard force will be cut by 15 people," said Sami.

Nick and Gunny both had spoke at once, "What!"

"This will leave us even more vulnerable to an attack," Nick stated.

"The government feels that the primary threat is to them, not you. I know it doesn't make any sense but it's their men. By the way, I was ordered to report to another department tomorrow to augment the violent crime department. It appears they want me back there," stated Sami.

Gunny spoke up, "First they cut our guard force and now they recall the most experienced officer from here. That's fucking great."

Nick was thoughtful for a moment before he spoke. "So I guess that you have no choice. Will you continue to let us know what's going on?"

"I am not going anywhere. I will be here tomorrow. I told them that the situation is too precarious to take away both the guards and me. They ordered me to report tomorrow. I told them either I stay here or I quit. I think at first they were probably going to take my resignation, but I reminded them that many of my tribesmen were in the police and army, and that if they let me quit, they would quit, too. They know we Kabyle always stick together. Regardless of what John thinks, I am not without a little influence. I think because of the threat to internal security they had no choice but to give in to me. I am sure that I will have some problems once all of this blows over. My bosses are not ones to forget incidents such as this. Unfortunately, I could not do anything about the 15 guards. I am sorry."

"There is nothing to be sorry for. On the contrary, mushkur (you act is appreciated). You have done more than was expected. We will forever be in your debt," Nick stated. The Gunny expressed his thanks for Sami's loyalty.

"Sami, what's your plan now?" asked Nick.

"I will return home and make sure Mariam is fine. I plan to be back here by 7:00 a.m."

"I want to thank you for that as well. Tisbah alla Khair wa salamat, ya akhi (good night and be safe my brother)."

"Inta kaman (you too)," replied Sami.

Sami left Nick office. "That's some friend you got there. I would take one of him for fifty like John," said Gunny.

"You and me both. I will see you later. I will probably not sleep much, so I will be around. Where will you be Gunny?"

"I will be mostly in my office, but if I am not, I will be checking the perimeter and making rounds. I will be on net-1. Take this so we will never be out of communication contact." Gunny handed Nick a radio.

"Good idea. Thanks, Gunny."

Gunny decided to return to his office to check on what was going on there. In his office he decided to call the assistant regional security officer, Michael. While John was an ass, Michael was new and gung-ho. "Michael, I wanted to let you know what was going on here. I talked with Sami. The situation is getting worse and we don't know what might happen as a result of it." Gunny told Michael what he heard from Sami. "Now, I have been checking on the various security procedures at Post One but I wanted you to know the situation in case any thing happened."

"Thanks, Gunny. I know you and John don't get along, but I appreciate you keeping me in the loop." Gunny hung up the phone and decided to check the embassy's perimeter.

Nick sat back in his chair, exhausted. He still had to write a cable and call Mariam. It was almost 11:00 p.m. He begin to draft the cable:

> *Immediate for SecState Wash DC*
> *From Embassy Algiers*
> *Classified by Chargé Nick Phillips*
>
> *As of 2300 hours, the situation on the streets has deteriorated. A general curfew has been initiated and all security forces have been put on alert. Anyone on the streets not on official government business after 2000 hours will be arrested. Reports from the Ministry of the Interior (MOI) indicate that tribal forces have joined the Islamists in the violent attacks. The Islamists have demanded a reinstatement of the 1991 election results or warn that the violence will increase exponentially. Although the violence has spread, the MOI is still claiming that they can subdue the forces shortly.*
>
> *The MOI believes that the Algerian government has more to fear from the Islamists than the foreigners residing in Algeria. Thus, in an*

unprecedented step, they have cut security from foreign embassies by a third. These local guards have been reassigned to other department to combat the violence. (Comment: This move suggests that the MOI is worried that they will not have enough strength to crush the uprising. Embassy Algiers remains alert and believes that an evacuation may be necessary if this violent trend continues. Please alert the USS John F. Kennedy to stand by. Will advise. End Comment).

Nick sent the cable and decided to lay back in his chair and rest for a few minutes.

-Seventeen-

"Mariam, how are you?"

"I am well," replied Mariam.

"Sami should be there in about 30 minutes. So were you able to contact anyone?" asked Nick.

"Yes, first I talked with my uncle Yusif, who had thought I was killed as well. He had already started organizing the burial proceedings. He was so happy that I was alive, he actually started crying on the phone. He called my aunt and cousins to the phone. It made me sad all over again. I asked them if they thought I should leave, and they said yes. I told them that I was concerned about them being here and they told me not to worry. They said that many of my relatives have been worried about me. Also, they told me that people had called asking about me. My uncle thought that they were friends who wanted to express their condolences about me but they would not leave their names. They asked whether he had heard from me. He thought it was strange, especially since they believed I was dead. I think you are right Nick, there may be some people after me."

That thought chilled Nick. He had thought it was a possibility that she was still in danger but had hoped he was wrong. "Mariam, make sure that you are careful. Don't go out or tell anyone where you are. I think that you have to consider whether these people are still after you."

"I will, Nick. It's not just me that I have to worry about. I have Fatima to think about."

"How is she today?"

"She is fine. We have been playing some games. She loves having sleepovers with her big sister. I wanted to tell you that Yusif got me in contact with Sulaiman Al-Barum, the FNL party chairman and a close friend of my father. Sulaiman also thought they had killed me. He explained that the FLN is in hiding now but they are not leaving the country. The leadership has vowed to fight back. As you know, the FLN and the military have had a close alliance since 1992. He told me that they are looking for suitable replacements to take the place of the Prime Minister and senior parliament leaders who were killed in the first wave of attacks. He was adamant that the FLN was not leaving and that they would not let the Islamists take the country. Sulaiman is planning a meeting with the FLN central committee in a few days. He wants me to be there to stand in for my father. He thinks that my presence will motivate a lot of people, and he says if I am staying then it will sway others to stay."

"You can't seriously be considering going?" asked Nick.

"I don't know, Nick. My father spent in whole life in service to Algeria. It is hard to think that along with his death, his legacy is dead as well. I am trying to find my way, Nick. I know I have to protect Fatima because she is probably in trouble, too. But they killed my family and now they want to push us out of the country. If I go, what will come of all my father's sacrifices?"

"Mariam, I think it's too dangerous for you to stay. I am not saying that you can't ever come back, but just at this time, when everything is crazy. Sami also agrees that you should leave, and he knows the situation better than either of us."

"Nick, I love you and trust you, but they didn't kill your family. My uncle told me that their bodies were so mutilated that it was hard to identify them. He barely recognized his own brother, my father. Do you know how that makes me feel?"

"I can't imagine. All I know is that I love you and don't want anything to happen to you or Fatima."

"I know, Nick. I am just confused right now. I promise I will not do anything unless I talk to you and Sami first." Nick and Mariam talked for a few more minutes before ringing off.

Nick stayed in his office and decided to rest on the couch instead of heading home.

Mariam sat looking at the phone. She had hoped that she did not sound too hard-hearted to Nick. She respected his opinions and judgement; his assessment had never been wrong. While she was handling the deaths of her family better, she was still having trouble with her emotions. Earlier she had snapped at Fatima and now she was short with Nick. She loved Nick, and while it was hard to forget about her situation, she knew Nick was under pressure, too. He had told her that the ambassador had left the country and that there was a possible threat against the embassy. She was worried about him. She remembered the first time he came over to her house about five months ago when all of her relatives were there. Nick had spent all day with them answering questions about himself and America. He did not even see her the whole day; her uncles, aunts and cousins practically interrogated him during his time at her house.

She had to laugh at the situation when she thought back to it. Here was this American diplomat invited to her family's house for dinner, and she didn't even think that he had a chance to enjoy the food. He was gracious and patient with all of her relatives. He didn't even understand most of them since they spoke the Algerian dialect, which was very different then the modern standard Arabic that Nick knew. She knew that she loved him at that point. Someone who could put up with so much just because of her was truly special.

Because her father was very well known, Mariam had only dated a few Algerian men. She did not want to embarrass her family or ruin the family's name. Family honor was important to Arab families and she did not want anyone saying that her father raised a "shamuta" (girl with no morals). The maintenance of family honor is one of the highest values in Arab society. Since misbehavior by women did more damage to family honor than misbehavior by men, clearly defined patterns of behavior and social rules had been developed to protect women and help them avoid situations which could give rise to false impressions or unfound gossip. Mariam was always keenly aware of how to conduct herself in public and in private.

Although she did not have much experience with men, she also did not have the same baggage as so many of her friends who had bad love affairs. She saw Nick as someone who could not only read her thoughts, but look into her soul. Nick had been a teacher, a friend, a confident and a lover to her. She did not want to push him away now when she needed him the most. She was brought out of her thoughts when she heard a key in the door.

Sami entered the house and yelled out for Mariam. He did not want to walk in on her if she was not dressed. Mariam came out and asked him to lower his voice because Fatima was asleep in the guest bedroom. Sami apologized for shouting and again offered his condolences for her parents and brother. Mariam asked, "How bad is it Sami?" Sami gave her a brief rundown of the day's events. "I am worried about Nick."

"He is fine, Mariam. Although his main responsibility is the embassy, I know he is greatly concerned about you. He wants you and Fatima to leave tomorrow."

"I can't just yet Sami." Mariam told him about her call with Sulaiman and Nick's reaction.

"Nick's right, you should leave now. It doesn't mean you can't return."

"I know, but I haven't made my mind up yet. I am so confused, Sami."

"You are like a sister to me, Mariam, and I am worried about you, too. I also knew your father well, and I know he would have wanted me to watch over you. I can't force you to do anything but it's just becoming too dangerous for you to be here." Mariam thanked Sami for his concern. "You should get some sleep, I hope the maid has provided you with everything."

"Thanks, Sami, she has." Mariam thought about Sami. She was happy that Nick had a friend like him. She knew they were extremely close and met almost daily. She knew that Nick cared a lot for him and that Sami felt the same way. She felt so much better knowing that Sami was there with her that night and that he would be with Nick at the embassy in the morning.

"I will not see you tomorrow morning because I have to leave early. If you have any problems, call either Nick's pager or mine."

"I understand. Good night, Sami."

"Good night." Sami left the room to go to his bedroom. He had hoped that Mariam would leave the country soon. She had already been through so much pain. No good could come of Mariam staying in the country. Although Mariam and her sister were in his house for such a sad reason, he was glad that he could open his house to them.

He had divorced nine months earlier and his wife had left the house at that time. The divorce had been hard on him but Nick had been there for him. As an Arab man, you were taught not to share your feelings with other Arab men. That was considered a sign of weakness. The Arab concept of Maruwa, or manliness, was still a trait that Arabs followed. It was similar to Latin machismo. Nick had given him an outlet to talk where his other friends could not. He hoped that Nick and Mariam's relationship would survive. Sami dozed off within a few minutes after his head hit the pillow.

-Eighteen-

A book of verses underneath the Bough, A jug of wine, a loaf of bread -
and thou beside me singing in the wilderness-, Oh, wilderness were Paradise
(Jinna) enow.

           – Umar Khayyam, Rubiayat.

Thursday
13 December 2001

Abu Fahad sat up in the apartment going over the plan. He had just woken up for the early morning prayers. His watch read 4:00 a.m. His group would be at the houses of the four embassy employees today and then they would attack the embassy tomorrow, on Friday. No one would expect an attack to occur on the Muslim holy day. The Jews observed the Sabbath on Saturday and the Christians observed it on Sunday. Those two groups were bound by their beliefs to rest on those days and to not take part of any labor or employment. He was sure that the Americans would not be expecting an attack on the Muslim Sabbath. Fortunately, the Muslims were emancipated from such stringent restrictions as explained in chapter 16 (Al-Nahl), verse 124 of the holy Qur'an.

Abu Fahad felt the next week would decide the fate of Algeria. The war that he and the shaykh fought was for the heart of the country; he specifically saw it as a war to find the Algerian personality. The year 1962 saw an end to 133 years of French colonial rule. Since that time, the almost 30 year rule of a one-party totalitarian system existed in the country. In 1991, the Islamists were finally able to prevail. The years of bombs, ambushes and slitting of throats came down to the next seven days. Abu Fahad wanted to free the country from its legacy of colonial domination, which he viewed as ongoing through the influence of a political and military elite that even now remained bound to French business and political interests. Abu Fahad knew this elite class. They had been protected by the security forces that seized power in 1992 and they viewed the Islamists movement as a manifestation of the negative effects of past failures.

Abu Fahad had coordinated with various tribal groups around Algeria over the last six months. Once his group began the assassinations, the tribal groups would begin their random attacks on civilians. The GIA would launch attacks on the military and police targets, which were better trained. After the Americans were dealt with, they would send notices to the rest of the western embassies in the country stating that they had 48 hours to leave the country before a similar fate met them.

His supporters were in every segment of the Algerian population, including the Ministry of Interior and the army. The shaykh's goal was to create enough anarchy and discontent to spark a general uprising like the one in Iran. He would receive reports from his network throughout the day about the police and army's reactions and movements. He would use that information to coordinate his other followers' actions.

All of his core followers knew the plan and had their instructions. Two of his tribesmen would go to each house of the four embassy employees this evening and hold them hostage until they agreed to help them enter the embassy. His brother Mahmud would accompany each group. No Arab would dare not cooperate for fear of losing the one thing more precious than their own life: their family's lives. Abu Fahad went over the plans again. He was going to stay at the apartment all day and use it as a control center. He was too important to the movement to be on the streets today. He would not venture out until he led the raid on the embassy tomorrow.

Abu Fahad was not afraid to die; in fact he was prepared to die. He and all of his men had already received their Islamic last rites and saw themselves as already dead. If they did die in battle, they would be immediately accepted into heaven by the Prophet as shahids (martyrs). While he did not view dying as something to be afraid of, he did not want to push Allah's will too much. He was willing to die for what he believed in to make a better Algeria for his children. If Allah smiled upon him and he came out of this battle unharmed, he and the shaykh would be the first two people who sat on the Islamic Shura (high council). The high council would be made up of holy men and mujahidin (holy warriors) like him; the council would make all of the country's decisions. Every province or city would have a local council that would be hand-picked by the high council. This was to ensure that all decisions would be done in accordance with Allah's law.

Any person who broke Allah's law would be punished based on what Islamic law prescribed. As the Americans would pay tomorrow, the Algerian Muslims who had turned their backs on their religion would also be required to pay their debts. The price for both would be the same: a river of blood and a pound of flesh.

-Nineteen-

Sami quietly left the house to go into the ministry. He wanted to check on what had happened during the night before he went to the American Embassy. Sami could not help but think of the significance of everything that had happened. It seemed impossible that it was being played out this way. During the war of independence, Islamists, tribalists and nationalists all fought together for one Algeria. How could it go so wrong in less than forty years? Sami thought that the return of the Arab Afghans between 1988 and 1992 helped to fuel the crisis. During those years, approximately one thousand Algerians returned home from Afghanistan looking to inject energy into the Algerian Islamist political scene. He felt that those individuals, in addition to the ones who came from Bosnia, created another deadly wave of terrorists inside the country.

Sami understood that the collision the between the fundamentalists and the FLN was building at the same time that the Arab Afghans were returning. Since independence, Algeria's population had nearly tripled to 24 million, sixty percent of whom were under the age of twenty-five. Through careless management, the government had acquired a huge foreign debt. In the middle 1980's, when the gas and oil market collapsed, the income on which the FLN relied on to provide social services dropped severely. In the face of an economic crisis, the government had no disposable income and the first wave of discontent began. From there, massive riots occurred. Sami always thought that the rioters began protesting for purely economic reasons, without ideological content. He had concluded that the Islamic leaders quickly seized command of the streets, providing direction for thousands of young men who were looking to improve their situation by any means necessary.

Sami drove to the ministry complex building. He loved the drive outside of the city because it was so beautiful. The narrow streets that wound near the Mediterranean Sea were lined with the tall, elegant townhouses with their intricate iron railings. Even during the bright morning sun, the splendor of the city was evident. The city swept dramatically through the bay where palm trees lined the streets. This was the Algiers of old, remnants of the city before the war started. As he entered the city center, the roads twisted and turned and were lined with burnt-out cars. This was the Algiers of today. He passed buildings draped with barbed wire and surrounded by concrete blocks to prevent car bombers from parking their vehicles in places to do the utmost damage. He parked his car in its usual space.

Spirals of razor wire were slung over the Ministry of Interior building. The entry ways were patrolled by security men with masked faces. No one wanted the Islamists to know who they were since all were targets of the terrorists. He saw that the men were more on edge than usual. They had their fingers on the triggers of their Kalashikovs and carefully checked each visitor.

Sami walked to his office and started going through that night's reports on the computer.

"Sami, come here," said Husayn Al-Shami. Husayn was Sami's supervisor. "How's everything? You know why I wanted you reassigned to another detail; it's because I think we have more to worry about the internal security than the Americans, but I understand why you want to stay. So what's the news at the embassy?"

"Well, the ambassador left yesterday and Nick is running the embassy. They are all very worried about the situation in the country. Have you heard anything that is not in the reports?"

"No, but if I hear something, I will call you. By the way, keep me informed as to what happens at the embassy. If any trouble occurs, call me first and I will send some of my men to assist. I would hate anything to happen to our American friends."

"Thanks, Husayn." Sami went back to reading the reports. One report from the duty officer grabbed his attention. It read:

At 0500 hours, a group of armed men seized the international airport in Algiers. The group immediately blew up several of the runways and airplanes on the tarmac. The Army responded to the crisis and began to battle with the perpetrators. Several Islamists were killed, as were 5 soldiers. The fighting was still going on as of 0800 hours.

Sami put the report down. He thought that if the Islamists had taken the airport, they wanted to be able to control who entered and departed the country. This was a critical development, Sami thought. Other reports stated that various attacks had occurred around the city during the night. The reports actually made it seem like everything was under control. Sami knew better than that. It was a smoke screen. His superiors were trying to maintain the calm. He called a few friends who could give him some more information about the situation. After several conversations, he decided to head to the embassy. He reached into his drawer and took out his back-up pistol, a Sig Sauer P230. Even though it was only a 380 caliber that held seven rounds, he liked the little gun because it was easy to conceal, and at 23 ounces, it was extremely light.

His primary weapon was the Glock 17 nine millimeter which held nineteen rounds with its extended magazine. He pulled out a few extra magazines just in case. He practiced with both of these guns several times a month. He shot expertly according to his ministry's standards. He carried a boot knife on his left ankle. He would make himself a hard target if the Islamists came after him. He left the office on the way to the American Embassy.

-Twenty-

A stone from the hand of a friend is an apple.
— North African proverb

Nick woke up and looked at his watch. It was 6:30 a.m. He decided to spend 30 minutes meditating and practicing martial arts before starting his day. He went through a shorter routine since he wanted to get back to the embassy. He began with simple relaxation techniques, such as stationary exercises. He sat down and concentrated on removing tension. Nick needed to re-focus himself to reinvigorate his chi, or life energy. His instructor had told him twenty years ago that relaxation was a fundamental aspect of all martial arts. He stressed to Nick that relaxation at key points in each technique could facilitate the speed and flexibility essential for true power. Nick had followed his advice since that day.

After completing his routine, Nick went to the locker room for a shower. Inside, he saw John, who had just finished his workout. Nick stripped down to take a shower, as did John. "Good morning John."

"Morning, Nick."

"Can you stop by my office at 11:00 a.m. so we can update each other?" asked Nick.

"Sure, no problem."

During the exchange, Nick noticed that Gunny was right: John had reason to suffer from little dick complex. Nick left the locker room laughing to himself.

He went to the cafeteria to grab something to eat before returning to his office at 7:30 a.m. After checking his e-mail, he began to think about the situation. Nick was in a position of authority and in the middle of a volatile and dangerous situation. He knew that he would have to make decisions over the next few days that he wouldn't have thought he'd have to make this early in his career. This was only his third tour. He had served tours in Amman and Damascus before being transferred to Algiers. Normally, FSOs were not offered positions such as DCM until after their fourth tour. Nick was fortunate because no one else wanted the position, so the Department had agreed to his request to be posted there. He didn't want to make any mistakes, but he knew that he was bound to make some because he did not have the experience. A lot depended on him. He would rather err on the side of caution instead of putting people's lives in danger.

Nick remembered a quote from Theodore Roosevelt that his father had told him when he was about to go to college:

"Far better it is to dare mighty things, to win glorious triumphs, even though checkered by failure, than to take rank with those poor spirits who neither enjoy much nor suffer much, because they live in the gray twilight that knows not victory nor defeat."

Those words always inspired Nick. He would not let his staff or Mariam down.

Sami called Nick from the front gate. Nick told Post One to escort him upstairs to the CAA. Nick called Sarah to let her know that Sami was coming up. "Do you think he has any news?" Sarah asked.

"I think so. After he leaves, come in and I will give you the update."

"Thanks Nick." Nick thought that the Foreign Service ran efficiently because of people like Sarah.

Sami entered in a hurry. Nick and Sami exchanged greetings. "So my friend, is the state still run by the nationalists?"

"Barely. This is what I know: there is currently a battle going on at the international airport in Algiers between security forces and the Islamists. They have blown up several planes and damaged parts of the runway. For all intents and purposes, the airport is closed at this time. If we can get control of it, then the government will obviously reopen the undamaged runways at that time. More fighting has taken place during the night. It seems that an organized effort is underway by the Islamists to create revolutionary conditions in the country. Many segments of the society have responded and the government have been receiving calls for the removal of the FLN."

"What's the bottom line?"

"We are losing, Nick. The government still has a viable army and police force, but we are slowly losing ground to the Islamists. The government is being overwhelmed."

"Do you know how much time the country has before the government collapses?"

Sami looked tired for it to be so early in the morning. "Maybe a week. The government may be able to prevail, but odds are they will not be able to withstand the challenges from so many different elements within the society. My friends are telling me that people are tired of living in fear of the Islamists. They are questioning whether an Islamic state would be so bad. Considering how many people have died, who can blame them for starting to support the Islamists?"

Nick sat there looking at Sami. "Do you remember that time you took me to Tizi-Ouzou, the capital of the Kabyle region?"

"Naam (yes)," replied Sami, "I recall the drive there from Algiers, the road was lined with eucalyptus trees. You told me that you had never seen such a beautiful, remarkably untouched region in the world before."

"It's sad to think that the progress this country has made in the last forty years is about to come to an end," stated Nick. Nick was lost in thought for a few moments. "Sami, thanks again. Did you learn anything else?"

"No, that's all I know at this time."

"Sami, can I ask you a question?"

"Ta'ban (of course)," replied Sami.

"What will you do if the Islamists take the country? Will you stay or leave?"

He looked down for a second before he answered. "I have been asking myself that same question. I think I will stay and fight. I will not make a mad exodus if the government crumbles. I am Kabyle. My people have lived near the Atlas Mountains for over one thousand years. When the Arab invaders came in the early seventh century, we were here and did not leave. Most people think Islam was spread by the sword. It was not. The Muslims of that era gave the tribes an option either to convert to Islam or pay the tax of superiority. No one was slaughtered or killed because they refused to convert. Actually, the Muslims preferred that the indigenous people did not convert because they were paid more money. By Islamic law you could not extort money from your fellow Muslims. I will not leave my land because some group who incorrectly interprets the Qur'an says that I am a kafir (infidel) and must go. I have a duty to fight against these madmen. They are not Algeria. We are Algeria and I and my relatives will fight to keep this country as it is. You know why I joined the security forces?"

"No, why?"

"I was too young to fight in the war of independence. I heard the heroic stories from my father about how the country came together and fought the great western nation of France and won. A small colony was able to beat a much larger imperial power. We won because we were right in our ideals, and Allah supported us because we helped ourselves. After hearing those stories, I decided that I wanted to enter a career that would contribute to maintaining the balance of what is right. I know people say that the police and army are brutal in this country, but I have never let brutality or unfairness fester when I was around. I have taken every opportunity to set things straight. That is why I worked in the violent crimes department for so long. I wanted to make it right for those who were killed. It got to me after a while, but I know I made a difference and will continue to."

Nick was surprised by the force of Sami's conviction. These events had obviously affected Sami in a very profound way. "I understand what you mean. My father taught me at an early age that service to one's country is the highest aim a person can achieve. Will you be on compound all day?"

"Yes," replied Sami.

"I will stop by later today." Sami nodded and left Nick's office.

Sarah called Nick and asked if she could come in. "Sure, Sarah. How are you today?"

"Well, actually I am fine, but just a little worried."

"I know everyone is concerned about the civil unrest. I have decided that I will order an NEO for tomorrow evening. I think the situation is too volatile to risk people's lives." Sarah seemed relieved. Nick explained what Sami had told him. "Please arrange an EAC for 1:00 p.m. after lunch so I can tell the section heads what the plans are. Also, schedule a general embassy staff meeting so I can talk to everyone at 4:00 p.m."

"Sure, Nick. For what it's worth, I have served at many posts, and I think you are doing the right thing. It's better to be prudent than foolhardy." Sarah knew that many diplomats in Nick's place would not have the courage to call an evacuation. It was never seen as a career-enhancing thing to call an evacuation if nothing happened, but if something did happen then you were heralded as a hero. She knew that most people would not want to take the chance, especially when the RSO did not agree with it. This was why she liked working with Nick, and it was what made him stand out as an exceptional person. Sarah started to go.

"Thanks for the support, Sarah. You must have read my mind. I wasn't sure that I was doing the right thing." As he left the office, Nick's pager went off. It was Mariam calling from Sami's House.

-Twenty-One-

"Mariam, how are you?"

"I am well, Nick, and you?"

"It's hectic. It looks like the international airport in Algiers is closed. Sami thinks that the situation will change drastically by the end of the week. He believes the Islamists will win this time. What have you heard from your friends?"

"I talked with Sulaiman and the other FLN leaders and they still want me to get together with them. I called some of my women activist friends who are also thinking of staying. I need time to think about that one. Before we get into that, I wanted to apologize for how I acted yesterday. I know I sounded short with you yesterday. I am still upset and confused over my parents' and brother's deaths."

"Mariam, you don't have to apologize to me. I understand. I think you are handling this extremely well. You have always been so strong. I need to tell you something. Because of the deteriorating situation and Sami's suggestion, I am ordering an evacuation tomorrow evening at the close of business. I don't want to take the risk that the country is overrun and my people are endangered. It's not my first choice to leave you here, but since it's a military transport, they will only evacuate U.S. citizens or embassy personnel. I want you to meet me in Tunis. You can take a flight out of the airport at Oran or Annaba the same day or the next. I can have Sami arrange it for you. What do you think?"

"Nick, I didn't think that you would be leaving so soon. I would feel very alone if you left too. I will talk to some of my father's friends and relatives to get their thoughts. I think I will go. You will meet me in Tunis?"

"Yes, sweetheart. After I am evacuated, I will take a transport to Tunis to monitor the situation from there. I am so happy to hear you say that you will leave. I will give you a call in a few hours. I love you."

"I love you very much, Nick."

Nick clicked off the line. He loved Mariam. Like everyone's, his life had been a long series of interwoven relationships, both good and bad. With Mariam, he had known more happy moments than with any other woman. He entered into the relationship with her without expectations. He was looking for someone to have fun with, but also to help him better understand Algerian culture and traditions. He realized through their long walks together and their late night conversations that they shared the same dreams and aspirations.

Nick now understood that he had to give love a chance, because there was nothing greater in life than loving another and being loved in return, for loving is the ultimate of experiences. He had been waiting for some artificial time period that would tell him that he was ready to make a serious commitment. One could not judge the profundity of love by a calendar. He would meet her in Tunis and ask her to marry him there.

Nick sat back at his desk and composed his thoughts to write the cable:

Immediate for SecState Wash DC
From Embassy Algiers
Classified by Chargé Nick Phillips

As of 0800 hours, fighting continues to take place between the government forces and the rebels. The rebel forces are composed of the both Islamists and various tribal groups. The Islamists have taken the international airport in Algiers and destroyed many of the airplanes and the runways. There have been reports that a general uprising may occur. Sources within the Ministry of the Interior (MOI) believe that the Islamists are gaining ground and that the government may fold within one week. Multiple segments of the Algerian population have called for the FLN government to step down in favor of the FIS. (Comment: We believe that the situation has deteriorated enough to warrant an evacuation. If an Islamic government takes over, all Americans living in Algeria will be in extreme danger. End Comment.) Embassy Algiers will alert the American population of the threat and ask those who desire evacuation to enter the embassy compound by 1400 on 14 December. Request a Non Combatant Evacuation for all Americans to take place at 1800 hours local time on 14 December 2001. We will conduct business hours on that day until 1630 hours to get ready for the evacuation. Please alert the USS John F. Kennedy that approximately 20 individuals will need transport. Will advise if that number changes significantly.

Nick sent the cable hoping that he was not overreacting to the situation.

-Twenty-Two-

John sat in his office with Michael, his assistant RSO. John had been trying to get some news from his contacts, but many were not returning his phone calls, or when they did reply, they told him that everything was under control.

"Do you think that we will have to evacuate?" asked Michael.

"No, I don't think so, because my contacts have assured me that the situation should calm down soon."

Michael was young and looking for action, but did not relish being in a firefight with Islamic extremists who chopped up their victims. "I was talking to Gunny and he told me that Sami believes we are in the middle of a power keg," said Michael.

"Don't believe anything that dirtbag has to say," replied John.

"I think we should take some precautions though," stated Michael.

"Oh, now I get it, you think because you get a little information about what's going on that you are an expert on the security situation here in Algeria and you don't trust my assessment. You listen, youngster, I have worked in DS for twenty years. Unless your name is on that door as Regional Security Officer, I'd advise you to shut the fuck up. Don't forget who writes your evaluation, kid."

Michael tried to be calm. He hated having this guy for a boss because he never listened to anyone. "I am not saying that I don't trust your assessment, but the level of violence has been rising for the last few months. I am just getting my info from the newspapers. What have your contacts been saying?" John had purposely not allowed Michael to cultivate any contacts within the Ministry of Interior. He told Michael that all communication had to be done through him. Michael was upset, but he couldn't do anything because John was his supervisor. John had been running the section as a tribal fiefdom: all decisions no matter how trivial had to be approved by him.

"I have not been able to get in touch with many of them, but they would have called if it becomes really bad. I will try again."

John called the head of the Criminal Investigative Department, Muhammad Al-Shamlan. "Mo, how's it going?"

"Not good. You have heard all the problems that we are having."

"Yes, I have heard, but I am calling to ask if we are in any danger."

"My ministry has taken calls from various embassies today. We believe the threat level is the same for foreigners as it was before these attacks."

"So what you are saying is that nothing has changed for us?"

"Yes."

"Thanks Mo, that's what I wanted to hear." John sat back and thought, *No threat, just as I said. Nick is just trying to get everyone spun up for nothing.* "He just told me that everything is fine and that we don't have anything to worry about."

"And you believe him?" asked Michael.

"Why would they lie to me? They like us being here."

Michael thought that since John did not have many overseas tours, he took what the security service told him as the truth. If a situation did occur, would he be able to handle the crisis if his contacts were wrong? Michael may not have had much overseas experience, but he knew from talking to Gunny and reading the newspapers that something serious was going on. Michael trusted Gunny and his instincts, and therefore trusted Nick. If they felt that the embassy was in danger, he believed it.

John decided that he had enough of this first tour kid. "I am going to see Nick."

Nick left his office to go to the Consulate. He still had duties down there that had to be attended to.

"Arshad, Shlonik (what's up)?"

"I am fine, madir."

"Have you contacted all of the Americans in country?"

"Yes, sir. Of the ten Americans we had listed as being here, only five are still in country. The rest were businessman who have left. I have contacted them to inform them that we are monitoring the situation."

"Thanks, my friend. I want to send out another notice today." Fortunately for Nick, all the citizens were on-line and had access to e-mail. One of the first things he did when he came to Algeria was to allow American citizens to register with the embassy, as well as ask questions by e-mail instead of having to come into the embassy.

Nick sat at the stand-alone computer to compose the e-mail message. He wrote:

From: Nick Phillips
Charge D'Affaires
American Embassy Algiers

To: The American Community
13 December 2001

As you know, Algeria has been experiencing major fighting over the last two days. Because we feel that the threat by the Islamists is escalating, it is dangerous for any American living in Algeria. I have ordered a Non Combatant Evacuation for 1800 on 14 December 2001. All Americans are entitled to be evacuated. To facilitate departure as efficiently as possible, please adhere to the following conditions:

1) Bring a passport for yourself, and passports or birth certificates for any underage children.

2) You are allowed one small carry on bag. This bag should be no larger than 24'' by 24''. Anything larger will not be allowed.

3) No pets will be allowed on the helicopter.

4) You must be at the American Embassy compound no later than 1400 hours on 14 December to be evacuated.

If these conditions are not followed to the letter, you will not be allowed to board the aircraft. Please keep in mind that we will be evacuated by a military helicopter to an aircraft carrier and these rules have been enacted by the military. There are no exceptions.

If you want to remain, it is your right to do so, but please inform us of that decision. Please do not call the embassy to ask about bringing anything not on the above list. We understand that this is probably a very difficult time for you and your family.

Sincerely,
Nick Philips

Nick sent the e-mail and printed a copy for Arshad. Nick hated writing such a harsh message, but if he did not, people would be coming with suitcases and pets of all kinds. Nick remembered in Mogadishu that the Marines on the helicopters just threw suitcases on the ground and pets were either shot or let free while their owners sat there wide-eyed. Nick want to avoid that scenario in Algiers.

"Are you serious? You are leaving?" asked Arshad. He was definitely upset by the news, as if the departure of the Americans meant the definite take over of the country by the Islamists.

"I think it's best for the Americans. If the country does fall into the hands of the extremists, they will kill us," said Nick. "I can't take the chance, so I am ordering the evacuation now."

"But what about us? If the extremists find out that we locals have been working at the embassy, we are in danger, too." Nick knew that he was right. "They will kill us," said Arshad. Nick thought about Carmen and his other friends.

"Arshad, by law, we can only evacuate Americans if it's under dire circumstances. I will check the regulations though. The Marines who will come on those helicopters will not allow non-Americans to come aboard." Arshad was clearly hurt. Nick felt bad and sympathized with Arshad and the rest of the FSNs. He knew by evacuating he was leaving these people to horrible fates. He thought back to when the Americans left Saigon in 1975 and the stories of all the FSNs who were left behind. Nick had read about how many of the FSNs were sent to re-education camps. He remembered some of them saying in subsequent years how they were tortured by the communists.

"Madir, maybe in some countries it's prestigious to work at the American Embassy, but not for us in Algeria, from the Islamists standpoint. For the last eight years, many of us have lived in fear that the Islamists will accuse us of being Kufar (infidels) and that we will be killed. We have earned a good salary here but it has caused our families much grief. You know this region and these people. You know what will happen once you leave. We will be on the run until they catch us, and only Allah knows what they will do to us."

Nick knew that they would not be tortured like in Vietnam. They would be killed and so would their families. Nick could not have that on his conscience. The U.S. should not let their friends down like that.

"Arshad, you are my friend, and you have given the embassy many years of service. There is nothing I can do about the evacuation. That's the military's decision, and by law they can not evacuate non-Americans. But I will not let you down. I will probably be convicted for visa fraud, but I will issue you, your family and all the FSNs valid U.S. visas. I can't take you with me, but this will allow you to leave from one of the airports if it gets bad for you here." Nick would not get prosecuted, but he would probably get in some trouble for deciding to issue visas to all the FSNs.

Arshad was about to cry because he knew that Nick was putting his career on the line. Since Arshad had been at the embassy, FSNs were not issued tourist's visas in Algiers because of the guidelines coming out of Washington. All FSNs had to go abroad to apply for the tourist visa like any other applicant. Arshad hugged Nick and thanked him profusely.

"Now, you know on the B-1/B-2 visa that you are only allowed up to a six month stay, unless you petition the Immigration and Naturalization Service for a longer period. Don't make me have to come after you as an overstay violator."

Arshad laughed and thanked Nick again. "You are in charge of letting the FSNs know. Tell everyone to bring their families' passports tomorrow. I will only issue for immediate family members. You process them and I will approve it. Also, make sure all the Americans understand the restrictions. No dogs or cats, okay?"

"Sure thing, madir." Arshad left in a good mood. The one thing that always made his job enjoyable was that he knew that Mr. Nick always did the right thing. He backed him up when other section heads gave him problems for no reason, like the RSO. Arshad hoped that they would not be gone long. He liked Mr. Nick.

Nick thought that he would have some explaining to do in Washington, but he would rather explain to them than to God about why he did not try to help these people. Nick went back to his office.

-Twenty-Three-

You can't pick up two melons with one hand.
                                             — Persian proverb

Nick went back to his office to find Gunny there. "Five of the local guards called in 'sick' today. We had fifty locals working on the guard staff, now because of the situation, fifteen were reassigned. That leaves us with only thirty local guards," Gunny said.

"Do we have enough security to adequately protect the embassy?" asked Nick.

"Just barely, those ungrateful motherfuckers. I even gave them the one step increase you mentioned."

Gunny always made Nick laugh. "Gunny, they are more scared of the Islamists than they are of you. At least you won't hack them in pieces."

"Says who?" replied Gunny. Nick laughed again.

"Any problems last night, Gunny?"

"None, except I caught some of the local guards sleeping. I swear they aren't worth a shit."

"You can't blame these guys. They have the worst duty possible and receive the least amount of pay. You know how hot it gets in the daytime, and they have no AC or even access to water. It's a wonder nobody has dehydrated out there," said Nick. "Don't forget Gunny, every time an embassy has been hit, it's one of those poor bastards who gets killed." Nick was reminded of those local guards who were killed in Dar and Nairobi in 1998. They were not allowed to have any weapons, which made them extremely vulnerable.

Gunny had to admit that Nick was right. "I know, but they are such a sorry group. Nick, I came for a couple of reasons. Take this." Gunny opened up a satchel and took out a pistol. "Because our security is becoming thinner every day, I want you to carry this. I know you are Mr. Kung Fu, but Confucius say, 'Even-tough-man-can-get-bullet-in-ass.'" Gunny said the last words in the worst Asian accent Nick had ever heard.

"Don't give up your day job. What do we have here?" asked Nick.

"This is a nine millimeter Beretta, which holds fifteen rounds in the magazine. You fired this one before, remember our outing six months ago?"

"I remember."

"Now, I just want to go over a few things again. It's double action, which means that you do not have to cock the hammer to fire. Just pull the trigger and it will fire. Also, there is a safety, but I want you to keep the safety off because if shit happens you will not remember to disengage it before trying to shoot. You will get your ass shot up and probably blame me. So keep the safety off. Don't worry, it will not go off accidentally. It needs about thirteen pounds of pressure on the trigger to fire a round off. This is the magazine and this is how you work the slide to put a round in the chamber." Gunny expertly handled the pistol as if he was born with it in his hands. "I brought you a leather Galco Hip holster. You can wear it under your jacket without drawing attention to yourself. I want to you to chamber a round now."

Gunny handed Nick the gun butt first. Nick chambered a round, put the pistol in the holster and then attached it to his belt.

"Good. Now go forth my son and kill some motherfuckers." Although Gunny was Nick's friend, at times he thought his sense of humor was a bit morbid.

"Thanks, Gunny. I do feel better knowing that I have a gun nearby."

John entered Nick's office without knocking. Sarah came in after him. "Nick, he just came in. I could not stop him."

"It's all right. Have a seat, John. I was just about to explain the new situation and what I have decided to do," stated Nick.

John was somewhat startled to see Gunny. He knew Gunny didn't like him and that he would not allow him to disrespect Nick while he was there. Nick had thought that Gunny would probably hurt John before this tour was up.

"Gunny, how are you?" John asked.

"Fine."

"John, I heard from Sami this morning and he gave me an update. What have you heard from your contacts?" Nick asked.

John began to squirm in his seat. "Well, my contacts have been busy with the problems, but those I have heard from have assured me that the terrorist threat should be over soon. They mostly say that the biggest threat is to them, not us. I believe that if something did happen that would affect us, they would tell us."

Nick briefed the two on what Sami had told him. "I have decided to order an NEO for tomorrow at 1800. I feel this is the most prudent thing to do."

How can you make this decision without consulting me? I am the RSO. I should be the one making recommendations to you for this type of situation, but you know that I don't think there is a threat. My contacts are there; they know what's going on. Why wasn't I informed when you made this decision?" John thought he should have been consulted about this. This was a security decision, not something Nick should decide. Since John wasn't a part of this decision, he would surely look bad in the eyes of Diplomatic Security back home.

"I was about to call you when you came in," replied Nick. "I think it's best for the community. I have already sent an e-mail to the Americans living in Algeria. I have set the deadline for 1400 hours for all Americans to be here."

John was upset again because he wasn't brought in on the process, and Nick knew that he would never say anything in front of Gunny.

"There is supposed to be a segment on CNN at 10:00 a.m. on the Algerian civil war," said Nick. He turned on the TV to see what CNN had on the fighting:

"Today is December 13th and we had heard several conflicting reports coming out of Algiers. Two days ago, several senior government leaders were assassinated, including the Prime Minister. Since that time rebel forces have been on the move within the North African State. One report has stated that the Islamists have taken over every major airport and have captured many cities. Another report has said that the violence is under control and that fighting is sporadic. What we do know is that there is no official news coming out of the country. We here at CNN have tried to arrange entry into the country only to be refused. We have received the following fax from the Armed Islamic Group: 'The journalists who fight against Islamism through the pen will perish by the sword. Everyone who does not support the creation of an Islamic state in Algeria is a legitimate target.' We are currently reporting from Tunis, Tunisia and we hope to have more news for you later on this afternoon."

The report continued for another fifteen minutes, but only covered the background of the conflict and did not have any live information from the country.

"Even CNN's smart enough not to come to this fucking country. No story is worth getting your head chopped off for," stated Gunny. Nick thought he had a point.

"John, Arshad will process the Americans tomorrow staring at 0800. I only expect five. I want you to supervise an organized shredding of all documents inside this embassy. I want everything shredded by 1200 hours tomorrow. I don't want this to be another Tehran where all of our cables were taped back together and published in books. Every piece of classified material, I want destroyed. This is serious. I also want all employee records shredded by tomorrow." Nick called Sarah into the office.

"Sarah, I want you to instruct the admin staff to start copying all relevant employee records and send them in e-mails to our desk officer at the department in Washington. I just told John that I want him to supervise an embassy-wide destruction of all paper records by 1200 hours tomorrow. I especially want all personnel records shredded. I don't want any of those files getting in the hands of the Islamists and them using the information against our employees.

"John, do you understand what I expect?"

"Yes, you want all paper destroyed by 1200 hours tomorrow," replied John.

"Sarah, I want you to work with John so that we will have a copy of the personnel records when we eventually come back into the country. I want an update of this by COB today." John left in a huff and Sarah departed with him. Gunny waited until everyone left to speak.

"Nick, I just wanted to tell you that if something does happen before we leave this place, I don't trust John. Watch your back. You know you can count on me and my Marines."

"Thanks Gunny. I knew that, but it's good to hear."

Gunny went back to Post One.

-Twenty-Four-

Sherif, Mahmud and Ibrahim walked up the stairs to the building. Mahmud was leading each group that would take the family hostage. The first name on the list was Jamil Al-Hawi. Jamil had worked for the embassy for six years. He would pay for working for the Americans. Abu Fahad wanted to make sure that each operation was done right, so he entrusted his brother to lead the groups. Also, Mahmud spoke English, which was another reason Abu Fahad wanted him there.

Mahmud thought everything would go as Abu Fahad had planned. He knocked on the door. "Naam (yes)," a voice called out.

"Madam, I am from the American Embassy. Your husband has been an accident. We need to talk to you."

The door opened up and Jamil's wife was immediately taken aback when she saw the three men. They did not seem like the regular embassy employees.

"What happened to him? Is he all right?"

"It's not serious, but he wants to see you," replied Mahmud.

"Please come in. I am Nariman, Jamil's wife. It will take me a few minutes to get ready and I must call my cousin to come and look after the kids," said Nariman.

Mahmud slapped her across the face. "Shamuta (woman with no morals). You bed down with a kafir, therefore you shall be treated as an infidel. Sherif, Ibrahim, get the kids," ordered Mahmud.

Nariman lay on the floor bleeding from the mouth and nose. She was shocked. What was this man talking about? He had called her a shamuta. The two other men brought her three kids into the room.

"Sit down and shut up," ordered one man to her kids. "Your husband is guilty of destroying the Islamic Identity. He has worked for the Americans far too long; he has to pay for his arrogance. We should kill him, but we will give him a choice. He can help us or he can watch you and his children die before we kill him. When will he be home?" asked Mahmud.

"Around 5:00," replied Nariman. She was scared because she had heard the stories of these extremists doing heinous acts to people they deemed to be infidels. She prayed that her husband would not be late today.

113

"Sherif and Ibrahim will stay until Jamil returns. You will not see me again. When your husband arrives, they will tell him what is required of him."

As Mahmud was leaving, he slapped her again hard across the face. "You are lucky. If we did not need you, I would slice the skin off your body in front of your kids." He spat on her as he left.

Nariman began saying a silent prayer to herself as he walked out.

Mahmud went downstairs and got into the waiting car. They had timed it so he would be picked after exactly 10 minutes after he entered into the apartment.

Mahmud greeted his tribesmen and directed them to the next address. He knew the name from memory, Kamal Abdal Aziz.

They parked their car and walked toward a small villa in Hydra. This house had a gate with a speaker system. He pressed the ringer. "Oui."

"Hello, madam. I am from the American Embassy. Kamal has had an accident."

Mahmud and his group were buzzed into the villa. He laughed to himself and thought how easy it would be. They repeated the same routine and Mahmud was back in the next car in 10 minutes.

Mahmud thought the operation was proceeding smoothly. He had finished with two of the targets and only had two more to go. Abu Fahad had told the men to free the hostages after their husbands had helped them. Mahmud thought that they should all be executed after he was finished with them. He would respect Abu Fahad's wishes because he was the older brother and knew best.

The next target was named Hamza Zeidan, and he lived across the city. Mahmud arrived at his apartment in 20 minutes. At the door, Mahmud told Hamza's wife that he was from the American Embassy and that he needed to talk to her about Hamza.

"Hold on for a minute," she said. Mahmud was surprised because the others had gone so easily. The door opened and standing in front him was Hamza. "You are from the embassy. I don't recognize you," said Hamza.

"Shut up, pig," said Mahmud. He hit Hamza across the face, which made him lose his balance. His two other tribesmen stepped through the door and grabbed the wife. She screamed and a melee broke out. After a few moments, Mahmud's men had the wife subdued. Mahmud hit Hamza in the stomach and pulled out his knife. "You make a sound, I will cut off one of your wife's fingers."

"Please don't. What do you want?"

"Yusif, hit the wife," ordered Mahmud. Yusif hit the women with an open-handed strike.

"That was a warning. Do not speak unless I ask you a question. Why are you not at work today?"

Hamza was upset and trying to get a handle on the situation. *What do these men want?* he thought. "I was sick, so I called them and told them I would be in tomorrow."

"You are fortunate you still work there. What I want is your help. You are filth; you have served the Americans for too many years. It's people like you who have ruined this country. You probably don't even pray. You are no better than the infidels, because you were born a Muslim and you have turned your back on your religion. There may be a chance to redeem your soul. You will help us. If you do, your family will live. If you do not, we will rape your wife and daughter then peel the skin off them like a grape before we kill them in front of you. Now, do you want to help your fellow Muslim brothers?"

Hamza was in a state of shock, he could not believe what he was happening.

"Yusif!"

"Okay, I will help you. Just please do not hurt my family. What is it you want me to do?"

"Just your job. At what time do you take the trash dumpster outside of the compound?"

"At 1:00 p.m."

"Tomorrow, you will go to work as usual and my men will stay here. If you tell anyone or anything strange happens here, they will kill your wife and family. They are prepared to die for their cause. Is your family?"

"I will do whatever you say. Please do not hurt my wife and children."

"When you, Kamal, Jamil and Bassam start pushing the trash dumpsters to the outside, just pretend that everything is normal. After you dump the trash in the larger container, you will see my men and me in that dumpster. Act natural and we will climb into the smaller dumpsters. You and your friends will push us through the parking lot and inside the embassy. Once inside, do nothing until you hear the action start. Just slip out of the embassy while everyone is running around. If all goes well, my friends will release your family in the evening. If it goes poorly then you will be attending the funeral of your loved ones on Sunday. Do you understand everything that I have told you?"

"Yes. I do. Do you promise not to hurt my family if I help you?"

"Yusif!"

Yusif slapped Hamza's wife again.

"I told you that you do not ask questions."

Hamza was racked with fear. "I'm sorry. Please do not hit her again."

"One last thing. Kamal, Jamil and Bassam are in the same situation as you. Do not talk about this with them. Just do your duty. They will be instructed as I have instructed you. You will see me again in the dumpster. We will be in contact with our men at all the houses. If you do not carry out the act, we will order the men to kill your families at that time. It will not be quick or neat. Fahimpt (do you understand)?"

"Yes."

"Draw me a map of the compound and indicate where everything is located. If you are deceptive or draw it inaccurately, my brothers will severely punish your family."

Hamza took out a pen and paper and begin drawing a schematic of the embassy's grounds. He drew the layout of Post One and the main embassy building.

"Where are the dumpsters located?" Hamza added the dumpsters to the drawing. "We will see how good an artist you are tomorrow."

Mahmud left the building; he looked at his watch knowing he was off schedule. He exited the building and looked for his tribesmen. They had probably circled around the block. He began walking down the sidewalk when a car pulled up. He jumped inside.

"What happened, Mahmud? We were worried," asked Tareq.

"A little surprise. The kafir was there. He had called in sick. It was fortunate because he drew us a map of the grounds. Also, I am glad that I had a chance to persuade him to help us." Mahmud laughed. "Yalla (let's go) to Bassam's house."

The last target went as planned. Mahmud was out of the apartment within 10 minutes and went back to the apartment where his brother was staying.

"How did it go?" asked Abu Fahad.

"It went as planned. By tomorrow at this time, the grounds of the American Embassy would be flowing with blood.

-Twenty-Five-

Nick sat in his office thinking about the evacuation. If all went well, by 2000 hours tomorrow they would all be aboard the USS John F. Kennedy. Nick thought he was doing the right thing. No diplomat wanted to leave the embassy under these circumstances. The ambassador had left before seeing whether the situation got really bad. He did not want to be seen as a coward or someone who would run at the slightest hint of problems. The State Department had left the Sudan in 1992 under similar circumstances. A civil war was going on in the Sudan when the ambassador had ordered an involuntary evacuation. The Department had two types of evacuations: involuntary and voluntary. Involuntary departures from post only occurred under extreme conditions.

Before joining the State Department, Nick had envisioned himself as an ambassador. He did not know how this whole experience would affect his future assignments. His ambassador hated him and had undermined him since he arrived a year ago. Any career ambassador would relish the fact that Nick was a Middle East expert. If Nick's analysis had not been sabotaged by his ambassador, Washington would be hailing him as the person who predicted this event. As it was now, he would probably be the fall guy, since he was the career diplomat and not Curtis. He was starting to worry about his future prospects in the organization. Nick would handle this crisis as best he could without thinking of the consequences back in Washington.

The one thing that always bothered Nick was the fact that political appointees were allowed to have so much influence. He had specialized in the region and spent years living in it, when out of the blue some ass could come and become your boss. Nick had to laugh about that. He hoped that Curtis would at least get reprimanded for leaving in the middle of a crisis.

Nick left his office to visit Sami. Sami had an office outside of the main embassy building but inside the walls of the compound. It was where he coordinated the local guard force. Sami was on the telephone when Nick arrived. "Any more news?"

"No, and that's the problem. Usually I am able to contact my friends, but many have not called me back. It must be getting worse."

"I have decided to order an evacuation for all Americans in the country to take place at 1800 tomorrow. I figure since it's the Muslim holy day, it

117

will be a good day to leave because it should be quiet. I hate to leave here but I have to think about the Americans' safety."

Sami was quiet for a moment. "Of course, Nick, I understand. You are only doing your duty, and you must think about the welfare of the embassy. I will miss you, but do what you must. If you want to know, even though I hate to see you go, I believe that you are doing the right thing."

"I will miss you old friend, but if the situation improves I will be back."

"Insh'allah (God willing)," said Sami.

"Do you have your passport on you?" Sami reached in his bag and took out his passport. Nick knew he would have it under the current conditions. "May I see it?" He handed it to Nick. "I will give it back in an hour. I want to put an American Visa in it so that if an Islamic State is established and you must leave, you can be my guest in America."

"Shokran, Nick, you are truly my brother."

"Sami, I want Mariam to leave tomorrow. Do you think she will? Members of the FLN want her to help the nationalist's movement. They want her to stay. She is having a hard time deciding to leave."

"You have to understand what her father meant to her. Her father was one of the heroes of the war of independence and a leader in the now-struggling government. She idolized him. That is why she got into politics and became an activist herself. Her father, mother and brother were brutally taken from her. She is going through more pain than you and I can imagine. When I worked in the violent crimes unit, I saw this often. Instead of running away, some people would fight back and do things that we would think irrational. You know Mariam is a fighter. She will have a hard time leaving."

"But what about Fatima?"

"Well, that may help her decide to leave. Now Nick, I know she loves you, but she has been through a lot and may feel that leaving would be letting her father down. I know you love her and want her to leave. So do I. I think the best thing she can do is to leave not tomorrow, but today."

"Sami, I need your help. Can you book a flight for Mariam for tomorrow night at 8:00 p.m., leaving out of either Oran or Annaba?"

"Sure, Nick, but it will be expensive because many people are trying to leave now that the airport is closed."

"Don't worry about the cost. I will cover it. Just arrange it."

"No problem."

Nick next decided to see Carmen. Since she was an FSN, her office was downstairs outside the CAA. Carmen greeted Nick as she always had, very warmly. Nick always marveled at the Arabs' sense of composure and sincerity. Regardless how bad anything was, Arabs always greeted you

118

pleasantly. When Arabs asked how you were, they were truly interested in the answer, unlike Americans.

"Mr. Nick, I just want to thank you for your decision to issue visas to all the FSNs and their family members. After the diplomats leave, it will be bad for the rest of us. Arshad told us it was your idea."

"I am just doing what's right."

"That is why everyone here likes you. Since you have been here, you have always respected the locals. I started working for the embassy when the fighting broke out. It has not been easy for me. I have had to hide where I worked from people for fear of being hurt. My brother was actually beaten up in school last year because someone had said his sister worked for the Great Satan."

"Are you serious? I had no idea."

"I did not want to tell you because I knew that you would have taken it personally. You know why I continued to work here after my brother was beaten up?"

"Why?"

"Because of you, Nick. As long as you were here, I wanted to help you. I would have quit after Hasan was assaulted in school, but I didn't, because of the way you treated me. You came in and immediately asked for my help. You enacted the changes I recommended and I felt like more than a secretary. I felt like I truly made a difference here. I believe that the Americans should be here. It is necessary that you be here. I wanted to make sure that you stayed by doing everything I could to assist you."

"You know I think of you as more than a secretary. I could not function without you. If we leave, what will you do?"

"I don't know. If the government falls, women will have it rough. The Islamists have already stated that women should not work or be out alone without a male relative. I will stay for a while until it gets too unbearable, then my brother and I will probably go to America."

"Well, you know you and your brother would be welcome at my house."

"Thanks, Mr. Nick." Nick left her office to go to the conference room for the EAC meeting.

Nick looked at everybody around the table. He could tell that most did not get much sleep last night.

"I am glad to see everybody here. As most of you know, I have ordered an evacuation at 1800 hours tomorrow. I have received reports from the Ministry of Interior that the violence has been escalating and that the government will probably fall in a week. I do not want any of us to be around when that happens. If the government can contain the situation then we will be back in a few weeks. I know that this will be the first time any of you have been evacuated. It is simple. The Navy helicopters will come here and load all the Americans on board. The trip should only take about two hours. I have ordered John to be in charge of destroying all classified material. I want everyone to help him. Go through your office today and shred everything that is classified or sensitive. By now you have heard that I want all personnel records destroyed but copies sent back to the Department. There will be no room for anything except the most essential items. You know what the restrictions are, so don't make me the bad guy. I don't want to throw things out myself."

Nick continued but could see the sadness on everyone's faces.

"I think everyone should know that they will probably sack the embassy once we leave. So most likely all personal items will be destroyed. Tomorrow will be a long day and I want your help with the American citizens. They will be here by 1400 hours. We will still conduct business hours until 1630 hours in order to complete the arrangement for the evacuation. Everyone should be at the staging area in the center of the compound by 1700 hours. I think if we all do our jobs and stay calm, it will go smoothly. Any questions?

"Thank you." Nick got up to leave and thought, *Well, you wanted to be in charge. How does it feel?*

-Twenty-Six-

Nick returned to his office and the telephone immediately rang. It was Sami. "Nick, I booked a chartered flight at the airport in Oran. It's west of Algiers near the Moroccan border. The guy will fly her to Tunis for 3000 American dollars, cash."

"That's steep, but book it. At what time?"

"At 8:00 p.m."

"Thanks, Sami."

"Afwan (you are welcome)."

Nick called Mariam. "Allo. How are you?"

"I am fine, but busy. I have been on the telephone all morning and most of the afternoon."

"So, what were all the phone calls about?"

"Well, I talked to Sulaiman again. He has gathered support from all the remaining FLN leaders. They are gathering Saturday for a secret meeting. They have support from many of the army core commanders. The FLN wants to put this revolt down once and for all. They know that various Berber tribes are helping the Islamists. It's going to get bloody over the next few weeks. The FLN are not sure that they can win, but they are determined. They have asked me to attend that meeting on Saturday and want me to be a member of the parliament."

Nick was stunned. He had thought that Mariam had decided to leave, and now it sounded as if she had decided to stay.

"So you are staying?"

"No, I am not saying that. I am just telling you what has been going on. I am flattered that they want me in parliament. They feel that I can draw on my father's supporters. As I said before, the FLN are looking for symbols to re-energize the party and they believe if I was vocal and stayed, it would garner a lot of support for the party. He told me that many are confused and any symbol of continuity would be well received."

"So what do you want to do?"

"I am not sure. What has been going on at the embassy?"

"Well, I have ordered the evacuation for 6:00 p.m. tomorrow. It seems as if things are deteriorating, according to Sami. I had him book you a flight out of Oran for 8:00 p.m. tomorrow. It will take you to Tunis. I can imagine what's going on in your head and I don't want to pressure you, but if you stay you know your life will be in danger."

"I know, Nick, but I was supposed to die yesterday with my parents. I am alive and so is Fatima. I don't want to throw away my life, but I still want to make a difference here, too. Nick, I love you no matter what. Don't think because I was considering staying that my love for you has changed."

"Should I have Sami cancel the flight for you?"

"No, keep the flight as planned. I need to talk with Sulaiman again, but I will be on that flight and meet you Tunis."

"I am glad to hear that. I will call you later this evening. I love you."

"I love you, too."

Nick sat back and thought about Mariam. She was always so stubborn, but he knew that she had undergone a major shock. He was happy that she decided not to stay. He could understand why Sulaiman would want her to be a member of parliament. She was intelligent and a well-known female activist. She was young, which would put a different type of face in the parliament. Being attractive did not hurt either. Mariam was pretty without being dainty. She had olive skin, long brown hair, and a unique eye color that was a mix between brown and green. Her eyes were the shade of color that could only come about by a mixing of Berber, Arab, Roman and French heritage. Men always responded positively when they saw her, but she never used her looks as a means to take advantage of them. What Nick had found attractive about her was that she did not act as if she was attractive. Mariam was also a very good athlete who gave Nick a tough time on the tennis court.

-Twenty-Seven-

Walls have mice and mice have ears.

— Arab proverb

Abu Fahad received a telephone call. "All is set. I was able to have them pull fifteen of the local guards from the embassy to other locations. They had no problem believing that the threat was not so much directed at the Americans as at the government. One of my senior men decided to stay on the VIP detail. He threatened to have his relatives leave their positions with the police, so I had no choice but to keep him on the detail."

"What else is happening there?" asked Abu Fahad.

"The American ambassador left yesterday. Nick Phillips is in charge. They are very worried about the situation."

"Who is the man who decided to stay?"

"His name is Sami Bouteflica and he is good friends with Nick Phillips, Chargé D'affairres. If anything happens at the embassy, he will call me directly."

"Thank you, Allahu Akbar."

"Allahu Akbar," said Husayn Al-Shami.

-Twenty-Eight-

Nick sat at his desk, realizing that he had not eaten since breakfast. It was almost 3:15 p.m. and he needed to eat before the meeting at 4:00. He decided to walk to the snack bar. On the way, he saw Bassam, one of the janitors.

"Maharba, kaifak (hello, how are you)?"

"I am well, Mr. Nick, but I fear that the country is falling apart."

"How is your family?"

"Al-Hamdillilah (they are fine)."

Nick always made it a point to be friendly with everyone regardless of his or her job. He knew that many diplomats snubbed the janitors, but Nick felt that they had a tough job.

Bassam said goodbye and walked back to main building of the embassy. Bassam liked Mr. Nick because he always took time to speak with him. Bassam had worked for the embassy for 15 years and had seen many officers, and none had been as respectful to him. To Arabs, respect was important, just as the concept of wajh (face). Arabs were constantly worried about how they were viewed by their peers. Doing a menial job was not bad as long as they were not disrespected by those they worked for. A person's dignity, honor and reputation were of paramount importance, and no effort was spared to protect them, especially one's honor.

Nick got a sandwich and returned to his office. He saw a sealed envelope on his desk that said, "Eyes only Chargé D'Affaires." He opened it and saw that it was a response from Washington. The communications office must have left it here. It read:

Immediate for Embassy Algiers
From SecState Wash DC
Classified by Secretary of State

Post is authorized for an involuntary evacuation. We have dispatched the USS John F. Kennedy to move closer to the coast to assist you in your departure. Three helicopters will arrive at post at 1800 hours on 14 December from the aircraft carrier. Transit time will be ninety minutes. Post must inform the host government of the decision to evacuate, considering status of governmental authority.

Post's decision will be politically sensitive. Post should request the host government to accept the responsibility for safeguarding personal property of evacuees and vacant residences on the compound. Please remind all evacuees of proper NEO procedures. Although the Department does not take evacuating a post lightly, we agree that for the safety of the Americans in country, this is the best course of action.

Powell

Nick was relieved that his superiors agreed with his assessment. He knew that he now had to send a cable to the USS John F. Kennedy to summarize the political objectives and constraints relevant to the military's help, the nuances involved, and any impediments on the use of force. Nick knew that he was the accountable officer in charge of the evacuation. Once the military operation started, the military commander of the ship had the sole responsibility for carrying out the mission. He knew that based on his cable, the military would tailor its planning and action for evacuation according to the degree of hostility involved. He composed his cable:

Immediate for Commander in Charge, USS John F. Kennedy
From Embassy Algiers
Classified by Charge Nick Phillips

As you are aware, a serious security situation exists that poses a direct and immediate threat to the lives of mission personnel and a certain hazard to U.S. facilities. As such, we believe that it is necessary for the evacuation of noncombatants from Algiers. The longer the delay, the greater exposure to risk and the more visible the departure. We judge the environment as hostile. Rebel forces may oppose evacuation and/or military assistance. We anticipate 15 evacuees and will be in the designated staging area per the NEO orders at 1800 hours on 14 December 2001. We appreciate your assistance in this regard.

He knew that he had to send another cable to Tunis to let them know what was going on, but he decided just to relay his last few cables. He noticed it was almost 4:00 p.m. He walked quickly to the conference room for the meeting with the local staff of FSNs. As he walked into the room, it became quiet. Nick began:

"Thank you for coming today. It's unfortunate we are getting together under these circumstances. As some of you may have heard, I have ordered an evacuation of all Americans from this post as of 1800 hours tomorrow. I understand that this is probably a shock for you, but we believe that stability of the country is such that it would be dangerous for us as Americans to stay in the country. I know that many of you are concerned about being associated with the American Embassy. Because of those concerns I have initiated two procedures: One, I will issue U.S. visas for all embassy employees and their families; two, I am having all employee records destroyed, so that if the embassy is taken over, the extremists will not have any of your names. Arshad from consular will supervise the issuance of visas. I apologize that I can't do anything else. Tomorrow will be a normal business day for us until 4:30. Per regulations, each of you will receive one month's pay for each year you have worked for the embassy. If it turns out that the country does stabilize and we return, then everyone will be reinstated as if there was no break in service. This will not affect your retirement benefits. Please turn in all embassy IDs by 12:00 tomorrow. This is for your own safety. I want to thank each and every one of you for your years of service. I know this will put a strain on many of your families, I am truly sorry that we can't do more. Now before John comes up to the podium to give you a brief about security, are there any questions?"

Abd Al-Aziz from procurement raised his hand. "Do you know how long it will be before the embassy is reopened?"

"The initial evacuation depends of the situation, but it will be at least for 30 days. At the end of that period, the Department in conjunction with the post will evaluate the status here in Algeria and determine whether the evacuation should be continued, whether employees should be reassigned, or whether to terminate the evacuation. If the status is not terminated, it must again be reviewed every 30 days. So the short answer is that I am not sure, but it will depend on what happens here. I know the U.S. government would prefer to stay in the country. We have to see how the situation plays out."

"Who will take care of the embassy when you are gone?" asked Imani from the general services office.

"Well, John will be in charge of that, but in brief, we will keep on a few local guards and cleaning staff to make sure the embassy stays in some sort of shape for when we return."

Shareen from public affairs spoke next. "Should we issue a press statement to the media that we are leaving?"

"No, I don't want let the public know that we are leaving because of how this can be construed. It may seem as if we think the government will fall, and I don't want it to appear as if we believe that. If there are any inquiries, you should say that we support the FLN government and fully believe that they will be able to stabilize the situation. I will be informing the Algerian Ministry of Foreign Affairs (MFA) today of our decision to leave."

Nick answered a few more mundane questions, after which he left the room. He hated having to make that speech because of what it meant to his staff. If they were already concerned about the situation, this would make them even more uncertain. He returned to his office.

-Twenty-Nine-

A thief is a king til he's caught.

— Arab proverb

At Post One, Gunny waited for all his Marines to arrive before starting the meeting. He trusted all his men but wanted to give them a motivational talk. Gunny knew from his experience that although they were leaving tomorrow, things could go to shit quickly, and he wanted his men to understand the conditions they were under now.

"I want to talk to you guys about the next 24 hours. I know you guys are squared away and have your assignments locked on, but stay alert. If anything is going to happen, it will take place before we are evacuated. I know your chain of command says Nick, then John and then me, but for the next day it's Nick, then me. In case of an incident, call John last. I don't trust him, but I do trust Nick. Of all the State Department guys I have worked with, he's the best. If John orders you to do anything, you stick to procedure, our procedure, and I will take the heat for it. That's why I am here." Gunny asked if there were any questions; there were none, and he left the Marines to their duties.

He walked out of Post One and to the RSO's office. Gunny wanted to talk with Michael about what was happening. He thought Michael was a good kid and probably would be a very good agent if only he didn't have to work under John. He also wanted to see what John had done concerning the deteriorating security situation.

"Is John in?"

"No, he stepped out," replied Michael.

"Hey Michael, I wanted to know what John has done to handle the latest developments."

"He still doesn't believe that there is a real threat."

"In other words, nothing." Michael did not answer. "What do you think?"

"Well, John's the RSO and he's responsible for all security matters."

"Okay, I know John's your boss and he writes your evaluation. What do you think is the threat level here?"

Michael thought for a minute before saying anything. "I think it's a wise decision to get out of here. These terrorists are serious and kill people without hesitation. I joined DS for action but not to get hacked to pieces."

"It sounds like at least one person is thinking in this section. If you need anything, let me know." Gunny left the section to go see Nick.

At 4:30 p.m., all the embassy employees left the compound to return home. Because of the violence, not many people were on the streets. Too many people were afraid of being caught in the crossfire between the terrorists and the government forces, least of all Bassam. He left the embassy in a depressed mood. What would he do about a job? He had five kids and a wife who depended on him. Like most traditional Algerians, his wife did not work. He had been lucky to get the embassy job in 1985. He remembered the night before the interview, he had prayed to Allah for His assistance and he was rewarded with a good, steady job.

Although he was a janitor, Bassam did not mind the work. He earned more money than most people in Algeria who had college degrees. The embassy paid well and allowed him to save money for his kids' educations. He actually enjoyed the work. He had been a clerk in an office before and was treated poorly because he was uneducated. Many of his fellow Muslims treated him worse than any of the Americans. He was not a very religious man, but he knew the Qur'an like all Arab men his age. He remembered reading the passage that said there were no differences among Muslims except the faith in their heart. He thought about how many individuals only used Islam for their own purpose or when it suited them, instead of using it as a daily guide. Islam should be used to better society, not destroy it like these maniacs were doing now.

The GIA and the Islamic Army of Salvation (AIS) called themselves Muslims, but they were just another terrorist group. How could Muslims commit these types of violent acts against other Muslims? He thought about the people living in Bab el-Oued, the city stronghold of the GIA. They lived in a constant fear of the terrorists. Everyone's actions were under a constant scrutiny that meant life or death. If someone was deemed a Kafir then he or she would be killed by one of these terrorists. His father had explained to him the beauty of Islam, the name itself meaning submission to the will of God. People who believed in Islam were "ones who submitted." The doctrines of the Islamic religion are viewed as a summation and completion of the previous revelations to the Jewish and Christian prophets.

At the time of the Prophet, the Muslims were engaged in a war against the other tribes. Islam represented a disruption of their way of life. Consequently, there were many battles between the Muslims and the non-Muslim populations. Because of the conditions in seventh century Arabia, Allah sent down guidance to the Muslims stating how they should fight the unbelievers at that time. The Qur'an actually recognized the "Ahl al-Kitab" (people of the book), meaning other monotheist religions. Indeed the Qur'an and the Bible had much in common: the necessity of faith, reward for good actions and punishment for evil deeds on the day of Judgment, concept of Heaven and Hell, existence of angels who communicate between God and man, and the existence of Satan. Both religions also recognized many of the same prophets, such as Adam, Noah, Abraham, Ismael, Isaac, Jacob, Moses and Jesus. Bassam thought that any true believer would recognize that Muslims and Christians should have no problems getting along. These terrorists were taking passages from the Qur'an and distorting the meanings for their own purposes.

Bassam headed home from the embassy to his house. He dreaded telling his wife about the embassy closing. She would be upset, because they had wanted to buy a new car. He parked his car on the street as he did not have a garage. All the houses in his neighborhood were made of concrete and block. He liked his small villa. He bought it seven years ago after living in apartments all of his life. With his job at the embassy, he was solidly middle class. As he approached the door, he took out his keys.

He removed his shoes as was the custom in his house. He walked into his house and was immediately struck in the face. Bassam fell down. He had never felt such pain before. He felt wetness on his face and thought, *Why do I have water on my face?* Bassam was grabbed by his shirt lapels and thrown across the room. He landed at Tareq's feet.

"What do you want?" He was kicked in the ribs repeatedly. Bassam looked up. He noticed that the wetness on his face was blood. His five kids were sitting on the floor with his wife.

Tareq picked Bassam up. "Do you want to die, kafir?"

Bassam could only manage a weak, "No."

"Your daughter is very pretty. Do you want us to have our way with her?"

His eyes widened and tears started to run down his face. "Please sayyidi (honorable one), don't hurt my family. They are all I have. Oh Allah, protect me."

Tareq slapped Bassam in the face again. "How dare you use Allah's name. A kafir like you does not deserve Allah's mercy."

He knew they were going to kill him. Why else would they be here? He had read about the terrorists killing people in their homes.

"You may live yet. We will give you a choice: help us or watch your family slowly die in front of you." Bassam saw that his wife's face was already very bruised, and he nodded. Tareq explained what he wanted him to do. Bassam agreed to help them enter the embassy.

"What else can you tell me about the embassy?"

Bassam explained that fifteen of the local guards were reassigned and other details about security. The last fact that he mentioned got Tareq's attention. "They will be evacuating the embassy at 6:00 p.m."

Tareq kicked him again before going into the other room. He dialed the number on his cell phone. "Salaam Alaikum (peace be onto you)."

"Wa Laikum Salaam (and onto you peace)," Abu Fahad replied.

"My brother, it is done. One thing you should know: our friends will be evacuated from their homes at 6:00 p.m. by military helicopters."

"Shokran (thank you)." Abu Fahad put down the phone. He had received the two other phone calls about fifteen minutes earlier. So the Americans were leaving the country. Too bad no one would be alive when the helicopters arrived.

-Thirty-

Nick sat at his computer and composed the note for the MFA:

13 December 2001
To: His Excellency Mahmud Al-Abdallahi
Minister of Foreign Affairs

From: Nick Phillips, Chargé D'Affaires
American Embassy Algiers

It is with great regret that I write this letter to his Excellency. First, I want to express my condolences for the loss of your Prime Minister. He was a statesman of vision and conviction. We recognize that this must be a difficult time for the Algerian government. The United States of America fully supports your government and expects that this disturbance will be put down shortly. Unfortunately, because of the escalating violence, we believe that the degree of danger to the American community in Algeria is such that we can not guarantee their safety. On 14 December 2001, the American Embassy will evacuate all official and non-official Americans from the country. We believe our two countries have a long history together which we believe will only continue to grow. We fully except to return to the embassy once the situation has been neutralized.

We request that the Algerian government accept responsibility for safeguarding the personal property left on the compound until we return. We understand that under the current circumstances it may be difficult for the government to undertake such action, but it would make our return much smoother. Thank you again for your efforts.

Sincerely,
Nick Phillips

He did not know if Mahmud was still alive or not. He would have had Muhammad send it to the minister, but since he had gone into hiding, Nick would have a messenger take it over the MFA in the morning. He thought that the government would probably be the one who would loot the compound after they left. It was procedure, so he wanted it documented that he requested assistance.

Nick was finishing the letter when Sarah came in. "Nick, I am going to walk home and start packing."

"I have a letter to send to the foreign ministry. Can you have it sent there tomorrow morning?"

"Sure, Nick."

Nick noticed that it was already 6:30 p.m. "Okay, is everything all right?" Nick sensed that she seemed a little upset.

"I hate to ask you anything since you have so much on your mind, but I was thinking about my cat." Nick had forgotten that Sarah had a cat. "Is there any way I can take her with me? I have had her for five years and I can't imagine leaving her here."

Nick felt bad because the rules were explicit. "You know what the regulations say about animals."

"I know, I know, but I thought maybe you could do something."

Nick took a moment to think about it. "Well, here's how I see it. You are allowed one small bag. If a cat happens to get into that bag and no one knew about it, then who could say anything? Now this is all hypothetical because I can't advise you to bring an animal aboard."

"Thank you, Nick." She walked around the desk and hugged him before leaving.

Nick thought that Friday would be a long day, especially if he had to worry about every little thing.

Sarah was sitting at home looking at her books, arts and other collectibles that she had brought to Algeria. She was sad to leave them behind. Her cat came up beside her and rubbed against her leg. "Well, are you up for this journey? It may be tough." Her cat purred and went into the other room to eat her dinner. This would be her first evacuation in almost 15 years with the Department. She did not want to leave, but knew it was the right thing to do. She had not enjoyed working for the ambassador, but she did enjoy working for Nick. Sarah had spent all of her career overseas and had seen her share of diplomats but she had come to respect Nick in a way that she had no other officer. She decided to listen to some of her CDs and have a glass of wine, thinking that it would be her last night in Algeria.

John was in his office going through the weapons locker. "That ass Nick thinks he knows everything," he said to Michael. "He will see when two weeks after we leave everything is back to normal and we come back here."

"I hope that's the case, because I like it here and don't want to leave. But considering everything I have heard, I think it's a good decision," said Michael.

"That's why you are the assistant Regional Security Officer and I am your boss. You better start learning from a professional instead of listening to fucking amateurs like Nick and the Gunny. Now, make sure you record all the serial numbers of the weapons as you go through the safe. We will have to take all these weapons with us. I am accountable for them and I don't want any mistakes," said John.

Michael went through the weapons and thought about what an ass John was. Sometimes he wondered how John had lasted in the DS service for so long.

Gunny was walking around the perimeter of the embassy. He called Post One on his radio. "Vegas, Vegas do you copy? Over."

"This is Vegas, we copy."

"I hope you can see me on the camera."

"You are in my field of vision."

"Good, I just wanted to make sure that this camera was working. It didn't look too good. I will see you back at Papa Oscar in a few." Papa Oscar was the radio name for Post One and Vegas was the call sign for the Marine on duty. Gunny went back to the embassy thinking that maybe they would get through this in one piece.

Sami decided to call Mariam. "How are you? I just wanted to check in with you."

"I am fine, just getting bored. When I am not on the phone, I am playing with Fatima. She is keeping me busy. I never knew it took so much work to entertain a seven-year-old."

"So, Nick told me that you decided to go tomorrow."

Mariam hesitated for a second, "Yes."

"It's for the best, Mariam. This place is about to blow and you should not be here."

"Are you leaving Sami?"

"No, it's my job to fight these guys, so I will stay, but you are not me."

"I know, but this is my country, too. I told Nick I would leave, so I will be ready to go tomorrow. How will I get there?"

"I will take you once I see that Nick is safely aboard the helicopter. By the way, are you all right to stay by yourself tonight?"

"Sure, Sami. It's been quiet."

"Good, because I would feel better spending the night here with Nick just in case something happens."

"Thanks, Sami. Promise me you will help watch over him."

"Ta'ban (of course). You know how I feel about Nick."

"Tell Nick to call me later."

"Fine, ila la'qa (see you later)."

"Ciao."

Sami walked over to see Nick. The CAA was open. He decided to call him on the phone instead of walking in. "Come on in, all the classified material has already been shredded, so it's not much of a classified access area." Sami walked back and saw Nick pulling out files and destroying them. "It appears our esteemed ambassador kept a lot of personnel records in his office. I am just making sure that everything is gone before we leave."

Sami gave Nick a rundown of the conversation with Mariam.

"I am glad you talked with her and gave her your opinion about staying."

"I thought I ought to let her know that she was doing the right thing."

"Thanks Sami."

Sami helped Nick for the next hour to destroy the rest of the files. Nick took special care to destroy all memos produced in his office. He deleted all e-mails and made sure the cache portion of his memory was clean. Nick didn't want anyone to be able to obtain the data from his computer to use against anyone associated with the embassy. Sami and Nick left the office at 9:00 p.m.

"Can I stay at your apartment tonight? I thought it would be best if I stay at the embassy until you leave," said Sami.

"Sure, you think Mariam will be fine?"

"No one knows she is there, so she should be all right."

Nick and Sami walked to his house. At home, Sami decided to take a shower and read a little before going to bed. Nick went for a walk around the tennis courts and dialed Mariam's number.

"Hi, honey, how are you?" she said.

"I am fine, but tired. I am trying to make sure that everything is taken care of for tomorrow's evacuation. Sami tells me you are all set."

"Yes, I told Fatima that we would be going on a trip to Tunisia. She is so excited. She has totally forgotten about the plans to see our parents yesterday morning. I will let her know about our parents once we are in Tunis. I miss you, Nick."

"I miss you, too. Just think, we will be together in a day or two. I love you."

"I love you, too." Nick and Mariam talked about taking a vacation together and other plans before ending the conversation. Nick thought she seemed like her old self. He started to think of ways to surprise her in Tunis with the marriage proposal. He thought himself a lucky man to have someone like Mariam. He walked back to his apartment.

-Thirty-One-

"I cry to the Compassionate (Allah), be praise to Him, for fortune's fickleness and hostile rancor. And for calamities that have shattered my rock, and overthrown my frame and it's foundations, have broken down my stem, and woe to him whose boughs adversities pull down and break."
— King of Samarkand (12th century)

Friday
14 December 2001

Abu Fahad woke up at the sound of the Idhan (call to prayer) and thought the day would be a glorious one. He went through the ablutions before going to a nearby mosque. After prayer, he sat on the floor of the mosque and thought about the upcoming activities of the day. He thought that since the Americans were being evacuated, they will probably be preoccupied for most of the day. Allah was smiling on him and his cause. His men should be arriving in about an hour to the house. Someone sat beside him.

"Salaam Alaikum (peace onto you)," said Mahmud.

"Wa Laikum Salaam (and onto you peace)."

"How are you my brother?"

"I am well. Today is important for us. Our tribesmen, in conjunction with the GIA, will start random attacks around the city around 12:00. This will send the police in a frenzy. We must be poised to take advantage of this situation not matter what the cost."

"I understand my brother, I am prepared to die for the cause of Allah," said Mahmud.

"I know you are. I am proud of you, and our father would be proud of you as well. You have become our best warrior. If something happens to me today, I want you to take my place. You know the old man and he respects you. You are ready to lead. If by Allah's mercy we survive today, then you will have a high position in the new Islamic State."

"Thank you. I am only trying to do Allah's will. I will make the Americans pay in blood."

"Yalla, let's go to the apartment," ordered Abu Fahad.

Back at the apartment, the tribes starting arriving. Abu Fahad began speaking, "Ya shabab (oh men), today you will do something that hasn't been done since the Arab conquest in the seventh century. Usama Bin Laden may have blown up two embassies in Africa, the World Trade Center and the Pentagon on September 11, 2001, but that does not compare to what we will do today. That was not the attack of a mujahidin (Islamic holy fighter). We will go into the center of the devil's lair and take their hearts.

"Are you ready to go into history, my brothers?" The group agreed enthusiastically.

"I will check with our men at the hostages' houses to make sure all is fine before we leave. If everything is going as planned, then we will proceed. We will take three cars and stagger our approach to the embassy's compound. The first group will meet outside the embassy's compound at 11:30 a.m., that will be Amir, Muhammad and Ahmad. The second group will be Mahmud, Abdallah and Khalil; they will arrive at 12:00 p.m. Mahmud will be in charge in case something strange happens; call me on the radio and we will abort. I will arrive there at 12:30 with Ammar. Now it's important that everybody remembers the plan. There are two large dumpsters outside of the compound. Once you arrive, approach the dumpster one at a time. I want four men in each large dumpster. Because the smaller ones will be brought from the inside, only two people will fit. It will take four trips. Mahmud obtained us a map so I want everyone to memorize the layout. When I am there, we wait for them to take us inside and when we are in, we split into two groups. I will lead one and Mahmud will lead the other. We will attack the main embassy building from both sides. Our first goal is to take what they call Post One. Once we have that place, we can let the other men inside. Along the way, kill everyone you see and then we can leave. Mahmud, tell me about the other group."

"I have coordinated with the secondary group. We will have twenty men waiting about ten minutes away from the embassy. After we are inside the embassy, I will signal for them to approach. We have to take Post One first, which will allow us to lower the barriers and gates. I decided to station them further away from the embassy so as not to draw attention to the group."

"Good, Mahmud. We should be able to get in, gain access to the main building, and let our brothers inside within twenty minutes. I believe that we are ready. I will call the others who are staying with the hostages. Also, I have an extra special device that will help us succeed. It will be a total surprise to the Americans."

Bassam sat on the floor of his house. He was made to sleep on the floor with his family. He barely got any sleep. He could not believe what was happening. These men had entered his house and threatened to kill them if he did not help them. He could not help these terrorists, but when choosing between that and saving his family, how could he say no? After the leader left, the two men had taunted him and his family most of the night.

"Get up! You will be late if you do not leave now." Bassam got up and went into the bathroom. He was followed by one of the men. He quickly brushed his teeth and got dressed. He was so tired, but knew that he had to get through today if he wanted to see his family again. Before he left the house, he was reminded of what he must do and the consequences if he did not. His wife was slapped again in the face. Bassam shakily left his house for the embassy.

Bassam drove to work as he had done for the last fifteen years. He arrived and changed into his uniform. All janitorial staff wore orange jumpsuits. He went to the closet to get his equipment. He heard some noise and saw Hamza. Hamza looked bad; he obviously did not sleep much the night before. Kamal and Jamil came in a few minutes later. They stared at each other and knew they were all in the same predicament. Bassam was the first to speak since he was the oldest. In Arab culture, age was respected, so Bassam was always seen as a leader. The Arabs often said, "Older than you by a day, wiser than you by a year."

"Did each of you have visitors waiting for you last night?"

"Yes," said Jamil and Kamal. "You know I was out sick yesterday; they came to my house when I was in bed. What should we do?"

Bassam was thoughtful for a second, "The Americans have given us a good job and life. They have treated us fairly, but what can we do, as the terrorists have our families? I know they will kill them if we do not help them."

"You know they will kill all the Americans in the compound. Can you live with that?" asked Kamal.

"Can you live with the death of your families on your conscience? Let's go to work and do our jobs today. We have no choice. Now I want everyone to act normal and tonight we shall see our families." Bassam picked up the broom and left the room. The others gathered their supplies and followed him out.

-Thirty-Two-

No lamp burns til morning

– Arab proverb

Nick woke up at 0700 hours to begin his day. He thought that if he could get through the next eleven hours, everything would be good. He went into the kitchen and put on some coffee. Nick saw a note on the kitchen table; apparently Sami had woken up about thirty minutes earlier and decided to go to his office. Nick picked up the phone to call Mariam.

"Hi, habibti (sweetheart), I dreamt about you last night."

"I hope it was a good dream."

"Any dream about you is a good dream. How did you sleep?"

"I slept fine. I have a lot of calls to make today since I am leaving. Sami told me that he would take me to the airport after you leave. He's a good friend."

"Sami's the best. Today will be hectic, so I may not be able to call you until after the embassy closes. If something comes up, page me. I love you."

Mariam told Nick that she loved him and rang off. She decided to call Sulaiman to tell him that she decided to leave. "Hello, I have some bad news for you. I have decided to leave tonight because it's getting too dangerous. I don't intend to stay away forever, just until it settles down."

"Mariam, you can't leave now. We need support from people who have lost loved ones. The remaining FLN leaders need you. How can you abandon what your father spent so much of his life fighting against? He fought against the French and for the last eight years he fought against the Islamists. If you go, it could be weeks or months before you return. The country could be lost by then."

"What about Fatima? I can't let her stay here."

"I am thinking about Fatima. She, like you, is Algerian. That means something. If the extremists take over the country, the core identity of Algeria will be destroyed. We want you to carry on your father's legacy and serve as a leader of this country. The leaders who have decided to stay are like you: they are scared, but they are determined to fight. We will have a meeting on Sunday December 16. The Army will be there to protect us and your presence would bolster our chances of increasing our popular support

143

within the military and police. People are joining these religious fanatics only because they are afraid of them. They believe it's better to join them now so they will not be killed if they take over. The people have lost confidence in the government. Everyone knows you are here. If you leave, it gives the extremists more ammunition to say that they are the only ones who care about this country."

"I have to go. Good luck." Mariam rushed to get off the phone.

"Wait, just think about what I have said. We are meeting Sunday night."

"Bye." Mariam rang off and went to wake up Fatima.

-Thirty-Three-

Abu Fahad was on the phone talking with Tareq. He had already talked with the other three teams. Abu Fahad felt that today he would make his mark on the world. Abu Fahad had ambitions and he felt he was being guided by Allah's hand. He not only wanted to create an Islamic state in Algeria but he wanted to re-vitalize Islam across the Middle East. If he could pull this operation off, it would give him the bona fides to be a leader in the Arab world. Hadn't Usama Bin Laden done that? He had gone to Afghanistan and made a name for himself internationally. Every Muslim would know his name, as they knew Abu Nidal's name.

He would succeed and take his brother with him. He had to be careful today not to lose sight of the immediate goal. He remembered that smug American he had met in the Consulate. He could not wait to watch the blood drain from his face.

-Thirty-Four-

Nick put on his clothes and made sure that the gun was securely seated in the holster. He did not like the idea of wearing a gun, but under the circumstances he thought it was appropriate. Nick was reminded of one of the problems with the DS agents. They were special agents, like the FBI or DEA, but they were sort of the step-children of the federal law enforcement community. They weren't as hard-charging as the Bureau or the drug agents who routinely kicked in doors. Theirs was a world that centered around diplomats and foreign locations. Many agents would have an air around the diplomats that said, "Watch out, I carry a gun." It was called "gun envy" by people who knew the phenomenon. Nick thought that it was probably not prevalent among agencies that carried guns on a daily basis. The DS agents only carried weapons for specific assignments and never under routine circumstances in embassies. He thought that John probably had gunfight fantasies where he played out an image in his mind of himself facing an armed killer. Every time John wore his weapon, he always made sure that Nick saw it.

He walked over to his office and tried to think of all the things that had to be done today. It wasn't like leaving your home; he was responsible for everything, and many people would scrutinize his actions after he was back home, maybe even Congress. He laughed at that thought. Congressmen were notorious for conducting fact-finding trips overseas with their wives. He always wondered why they chose places like Rome, Paris, London, and Madrid. Ironically, our country leaders never chose cities like Riyadh, San'a, Muscat or Algiers. The problem with the congressional visits was that all projects were supposed to stop to baby-sit these people. When Nick was in D.C., he was chosen to brief Congressional members about the region. He was never amazed at the lack of knowledge our leaders had about the world.

Nick decided to do a walk through every section. He went to the Public Affairs office located outside of the chancery. He saw Shareen putting her things in a box. He asked her how she was. Shareen said that she was "Kwiysa" (good) but Nick knew that she was not. "I know that it's a sad day, but we may not be gone for long. Has anyone from the newspapers asked what we thought about the crisis?" Nick asked.

"No, that's the problem. If it was any other crisis we would have been flooded with phone calls for the U.S. official position. That makes me feel that the threat against the FLN is greater than they are admitting. The people are probably so consumed with just trying to survive. This same this happened in early 1992 when the military first took over and decided to nullify the elections. I was working here at the time; no one cared about the U.S. position when so much was going on with the Algerian affairs."

Nick thought about that and it made sense to him. He made a sweep of the section but he did not have to worry since Public Affairs did not contain any classified materials. He asked Shareen if there were any personnel records or other records that identified the section's workers; she said no. Because this was a small post, the embassy did not even have a Foreign Service Officer supervising the section. In most larger embassies, there was a Public Affairs Officer (PAO) who was the official spokesperson for the embassy. There was an official position designated for a PAO at the embassy, but no one applied for the position. Nick knew no PAO would come to this place because they were usually very knowledgeable people who knew what was happening in the world and would be hard to con. Nick laughed at that thought of management asking one of those guys to come to Algiers and them responding, 'wasn't that the place where people were being cut up into pieces and beheaded on a daily basis?'

Nick went inside the hard line, the area where Post One was located. It separated the visitors area from the main offices of the embassy. He decided to check out Post One. Sergeant Peter Clark was on duty with Corporal Jeff Swafford. He was buzzed into Post One. "How is everything?"

"Fine, Sir," replied Peter.

"Tell me about the security posture now."

"Sir, Gunny is walking the perimeter at this time. Jeff is near the back gate with the local guards and Hank is walking through the embassy making sure all classified has or is being destroyed. All the Marines are on duty at this time and will stay that way until we are evacuated."

"Good job, Peter." Nick did not have to worry about these guys; they knew what that had to do. "If you need me page me or call me on the radio." Nick left Post One. Ever since he arrived in Algeria the Marines were the best run section at post. Gunny made sure that everyone knew their duties and that each man could do any job on the security detachment. Nick was impressed with their efficiency and thought that they were the best group he had seen out of his two other tours.

He walked into the consulate to a flurry of activity. Many of the FSNs were there helping Arshad with visas. Nick was accosted by one of the Americans. "Are you in charge here? I need to talk to you about bringing more of my belongings when I am evacuated. This foreigner told me that I could only bring one small bag. Now, I am a taxpayer and I have my rights. You work for me and I demand that you allow me to bring additional luggage."

Nick had dealt with enough irate Americans in his career to last a lifetime. He had been threatened with lawsuits, congressional action and other unspecified penalties for just doing his job. Almost always the Americans had no clue as to their rights. They usually started by bullying anyone who refused their requests.

"Sir, we have explained the requirements for evacuation. These requirements come from the military who have made a joint agreement with the State Department. The Secretary of State has overall responsibility for the protection and evacuation of U.S. civilians and designated aliens abroad, but works with the appropriate military command in their theater of operations to affect an evacuation. There are no exceptions, and if you interfere or cause problems for my staff, I will have you confined by the Marines in one of the holding rooms. This is a difficult time and we have a lot of work to do. It's your decision. Will you cooperate with us or not?" The American looked cowed. Nick thought he was one of those corporate types that was accustomed to ordering people around and bypassing the rules. He told Nick that he would cooperate. "Thank you. Please go to the waiting room so you can be processed."

Arshad came up to Nick. "Thank Madir, he was upsetting everyone. We explained the regulations to him, but he started cursing at us and demanding to speak with an American. It's becoming a zoo and it's not even 9:30 yet."

"You did the right thing. Be polite but do not let anyone disrespect you. I am giving you permission to be forceful. Don't let anyone try and push you around today. We have a lot to do and have no time to be nice with people who are rude."

Arshad was very soft-spoken and always polite. He hated getting angry and telling Americans what to do. He had told Nick that as a Muslim, he always tried to be respectful and humble to everyone. Nick knew that it would be hard for him. "I will try, Madir. Can you approve the visa applications?"

Nick sat down at the computer and logged on to the system. As the Consul, he was the only officer legally authorized to issue visas. He was also held accountable for every visa he issued. After the blind Shaykh Omar Abd Al-Rahman obtained a visa in Khartoum, Sudan and subsequently went on to be the mastermind behind the World Trade Center bombing in 1993, the Department had instituted reforms within the Consular Affair's Bureau.

Every time Nick issued a visa, an audit trail was created, so that if he did issue a visa to a terrorist, the records would indicate he was the issuing officer. Not even the ambassadors at embassies could issue visas. Congress authorized specific individuals with that responsibility.

Nick went through the batch of passports, making sure to check the computer for any hits on the name. He recognized all of the applicants as embassy employees. He issued about 50 visas, and once he knew that he was finished, he went to the office to open the safe. He went inside and took all the blank visas and passports out of the safe. The passports and the visas were worth thousands of dollars each on the open market. He knew these things were like gold. Fraud was rampant around the world. Most of the criminals who sold fake U.S. passports specialized in photo substitution. They would acquire a real stolen American passport, cut the photo out, and put another person's in its place. Another ploy they did was to peel off the laminate and replace the photo and re-laminate the passport; all of those techniques were detectable. A valid blank U.S. passport was worth upwards of $20,000 U.S. dollars. A real U.S. visa was worth about half that. Ever since the State Department changed to the new machine-readable visas with computer generated photos, counterfeiters were having difficulties forging them. Nick made sure that these items were accounted for. He placed them in a diplomatic pouch and locked it with the key. He put the consular seals and stamps, biographic and investigative files, visa/passport fraud files, visa refusal files from the real bad guys, and pending immigrant visa petitions in a large bag. He would take these items outside and burn them. Even though these items were unclassified, they were sensitive and needed to be destroyed.

He went back inside the consulate and saw Arshad. "Are all the Americans here?"

"Yes, they were all here by 9:00 a.m. I guess they were scared of getting left behind and decided not to take any chances."

Before Nick left the section, he heard some shouting coming from the back of the consulate. He noticed a short, unattractive, blond woman in her early thirties yelling at one of his FSNs. He walked over to her. "How can I help you, miss?"

"My name is Lisa Hopper and I am the director of production of Mobile Oil Company. I don't feel as if your employees are treating me with enough respect. I demand that I see someone in authority now."

"I am the consul. What's the problem?"

"I am tired of waiting and I don't feel as if I should be made to wait."

Just what Nick needed, another spoiled American who felt entitled.

"Miss, you have to wait your turn. There are procedures here that everyone, including you, must follow. If you will get in line, we will get to you shortly."

"I said I am the director of production for Mobile. I want to see the ambassador."

"He is not here. I am in charge, Miss Hopper, and you will have to sit down and wait for your name to be called." Nick could tell that she was the type of women who could not handle being out of control, and the current crisis was definitely a situation she could not control.

Nick did not know which was worse, these crazy Americans or the extremists trying to take over the country. Nick left the section wondering what other problems he would have to deal with.

He went to the administrative section next. That department had the most files to shred. It was as if everything in the State Department had to do every piece of paper in triplicate. Thomas Burton, the head of the section, was a typical bean counter. He was an oafish man in his fifties. It was as if every post had a clone of this man. The admin side of the State Department usually drew people who wanted to work overseas but who had very little personal skills.

"Thomas, how is it going? Are all the personnel file destroyed?"

"Well, Nick, I thought that maybe we would keep the most important ones in case we return. I decided to have one 20-page document that summed up everyone's employment record."

"No, I want no paper documents to go out with us. I want that shredded immediately. I will not jeopardize anyone's life because we want to make things easy for you. I'm sorry but that's the way it has to be. The only records you can keep are building history files, contract files and equipment inventories." Thomas sheepishly agreed to shred the rest of the paper holdings. It was like Nick was a father who had to deal with wayward children. "Thomas, how much money is at post at this time?" Every embassy had American and local currency for payment of the embassy's bills and for changing money for its staff.

"We have about $20,000 in U.S. and about $10,000 in local currency. What should I do with it?"

"By law, if there is danger that monies, especially U.S. currency, could fall in the hands of a unfriendly power or group, we should destroy the currency in accordance with procedures to destroy other sensitive documents. If we do that, we will need at least three American officers to perform and witness its destruction. But I personally have a hard time doing that. At this time, I am making you the custodian for those funds. I want you to lock it up

ANDREW M. WARREN

in an approved diplomatic pouch and keep it on your person until we are
aboard the ship."

Thomas agreed. Nick walked through the rest of the section; it was as if
a storm had hit. Papers were thrown everywhere. Desks had been moved
around to make sure nothing had fallen behind them and pictures had already
been taken off the walls of the cubicles. Nick noticed the FSNs were working
at their desks feverishly to finish whatever they were working on. He was
impressed with his foreign workers' dedication.

Nick went outside to the burn container. He would usually burn visa foils
every month. This was the first time that he ever destroyed articles that were
still valid. He put the consular seals and stamps, biographic and investigative
files, visa/passport fraud files and visa refusal files in the barrel. He lit the
pile from the bottom and saw the flame catch. By law he had to wait until
everything was destroyed before leaving. He even had to sift through to make
sure that nothing escaped the fire.

He walked back to the chancery. He felt his pager vibrating; he read
Sami's number. He dialed his number from the closest phone. "Allo, my
friend, what's up?"

"Nick, I wanted to update you on what I heard from my ministry. Where
can I meet you?"

"Meet me in my office in five minutes." Sami agreed. Nicked walked
upstairs to his office.

Carmen was outside the CAA. He had not talked with her in a while. "Hi,
Nick, can I speak with you?"

"I have a meeting with Sami now. Can I come down in about 15
minutes?"

"Thanks, Nick."

Nick was opening the door to the CAA when Sami started walking up the
stairs. "My friend, I hope I didn't run you out the house with my snoring,"
joked Nick.

"No, I am having problems sleeping at this time."

"Let's go to my office."

Without preamble, Sami began, "I just talked with some friends in my
ministry. There have been several small attacks this morning, mostly car
bombs. This seems to be isolated, but it has us running around from
Boumerdas to Tipasa to Mostaganem. It's stretching our resources very thin.
I don't think it means anything by itself, but I am worried because it says that
they are still conducting operations."

"Well, at least they are not taking out targets in Algiers. I wasn't sure if
it would be worse today or not."

152

"Nick, it's still very serious and we are having troubles containing the rebels, but nothing of large proportion occurred last night."

Nick was relieved.

"Actually, my boss Husayn called me today and said that he believes that the threat against western targets may be decreasing. Who knows? Maybe you will be back in time for the New Year." Sami was only joking; he knew that the situation wasn't going to be changed that quickly, but he wanted to be positive. "Nick, although it's not getting worse, therein lies the problem – it should be. The MOI should have been able to crush these people as soon as the problems started. Since they haven't, that tells you that it is more serious than the MOI is admitting."

"Well, if we are back before New Year's Day, then dinner is on me," said Nick. "I have to see Carmen. I will stop by your office later. Hey, how come you never thought about dating Carmen? She's divorced, pretty and available."

"Well, it's been less than a year since the divorce. She is "jathab" (attractive) but I don't know." Sami was hurt so bad after his divorce, it was hard to think of being with another woman. He did want to meet another woman. He didn't want that experience to forever change him, but he was scared.

"Sami, I can put in a good word for you. I know she respects you."

"Fine, but don't push it. Maybe she and I can get together for a cup of coffee." Sami thought he would at least make an effort if Nick thought it was a good idea.

Nick thought Sami was a good-looking man. He was in better shape than most Arab men because of his job. Most Arabs did not like to work out and had poor diets, which contributed to their being overweight. He was a little under six feet and weighed about 185 pounds. His features were rounded, which gave him a perpetually jovial look on his face. He had a full head of black hair and was clean shaven, except for a thin mustache. Sami was 38 years old. One of first things Sami asked Nick when he met him one year ago was how old he was. In Arab culture, age is important. He wanted to see where Nick should be placed in his world. Was Nick junior or senior to him? Most Arabs do this without even making an effort. They have seen their fathers do it before them. Sami was actually shocked when Nick told him he was only 33. He was surprised that someone so young would have a position of such power. Nick knew that all Arabs respected authority from the day they were born. An Arab's world revolved around increasing his position and status, which was one of the most important goals in his life. When Arabs met people of position who were actually open and friendly and who sought to make friends with them, while they were genuinely interested in making friends because they liked the person, they saw it as a way to increase their social status in life by having a powerful friend.

Nick knew that he would be worried about Sami after he left. "Oh, I almost forgot. Your passport, sir." Nick handed him the passport with the visa inside.

"Thanks, you did not have to do this."

"La shokran alla wajab (no thanks is necessary because it was a duty)," replied Nick.

"I will stop by your office after 1:00 p.m." They said goodbye and Nick headed to Carmen's desk.

"Carmen, how are you?"

"I am fine. I wanted to thank you for the visas for my brother and me. I brought you something. She handed Nick an inlaid box made by the Berbers. The box was beautiful and seemed like an antique. "I just wanted to thank you for everything. I have enjoyed working for you."

"Carmen, that was not necessary. The box, it's amazing. I like it."

"I am glad, Nick. I have enjoyed working for you." Carmen's eyes were moist and he could tell that she meant what she said.

Nick asked Carmen what she thought of Sami. He knew that she was not seeing anybody. "He's a nice guy and seems karim (generous, kind). Why do you ask?"

Nick explained in Arabic that he thought they would make a good match. Arabs generally were receptive to matchmaking. "Have him call me and we will get together for coffee." Nick left the section to see Gunny.

He caught up to him outside of the embassy near the front gate. Nick noticed that Gunny had his sidearm on. Usually, as the detachment commander, he was never on duty at Post One, so he never wore a weapon. Gunny was in an even sterner mood than he was normally. Nick felt that he was doing what he liked best, being a Marine.

"How is everything going?"

"The same, but at least everyone is awake. I have been roving all day to make sure that all the guards are sharp. I have all my men working today and I requisitioned Michael to help us as well. He is making rounds through the embassy. I haven't seen John this morning but he came by to check on Post One this morning."

"Sami told me that his ministry believes that the possibility of violence against western targets is abating."

"Let's hope so, but until I leave this place, I will keep my men on their toes."

Nick walked back to main building of the embassy. He returned to his office. Sarah was at her desk completing some of the forms. "Sarah, have you updated the log for today?"

"Yes, Nick. I have received confirmations from all sections that all classified or sensitive documents have been destroyed. Gunny reported that he has inspected all the physical security controls. I have opened up a line with the Department's Operations Center and given them an update." The Operation's Center maintained a 24-hour global watch over all areas under threat conditions. Sarah continued, "Your log will be completed by 12:00 p.m. and ready for any of the reviewing authorities back in Washington."

Nick thought that this was why Sarah was one of the best secretaries in the Department. She was thorough and extremely competent. "Sarah, you have the duty until 1400 hours. I am going to see John. He has been rather absent from today's activities."

"I know. Usually he would have stopped by to check on everything. It's strange that we haven't seen him this morning."

John sat in his apartment thinking that since Nick wanted to be in charge, he should be able to function without him. He went through his belongings, thinking how he hated leaving his effects behind. "It's because of him that I will probably lose most of my belongings," he said to himself. John thought it was bad enough that his ex-wife took most of his property in the divorce settlement. He had spent the last year acquiring art, bric-a-brac, statues and other things, only to lose them because of one rash officer's decision. He hated Nick; his smugness and his arrogance pissed him off. He could not wait to return to D.C. where he would report to his superiors how Nick was totally out of his depth and had botched the situation. John thought about the complaints he would lodge against Nick. That would show him.

"Treat me with disrespect. Well, fuck him. He can handle this whole evacuation on his own."

Nick walked to the RSO's office. Michael had just returned from his rounds. "Where's John? Nobody has seen him."

"Sir, I think he is at his apartment."

"Why is he not supervising the security like Gunny?"

"I don't know, but I think he has decided to leave most of the arrangements to you and Gunny."

"Well, until he returns to this section, you are acting RSO."

Nick was shocked. So John wanted to try and distance himself from the whole evacuation process. Nick went over to John's house. He was going to have it out with this guy once and for all. Nick crossed the yard to where the embassy housing was located. He found John's apartment and did not bother knocking.

"Why aren't you outside supervising the last minute security arrangements on the compound?"

John's reply was terse. "Don't you know how to knock?"

"I asked you a question. You are about five minutes from becoming the former RSO."

"All of the classified material has been destroyed, and since you are in charge, I figured I would stay out of your way."

"Per State Department regulations, you have a responsibility to oversee all arrangements related to the evacuation of noncombatant personnel. You are not doing your duty and can be terminated. You should be reviewing the threat plan and working with the local guards on what they should be doing now. Your behavior is unacceptable and will be noted."

"You're the hotshot; you've called this thing from the start. You are fucking up everybody's life based on your hunch. Well I, for one, will tell you that you are an ass, and it will come out that you have ordered this evacuation precipitously. I think your behavior is unacceptable and will report it to my superiors. I am tired of your shit." John stuck a finger in Nick's chest as he said the last line.

Nick could not believe this guy. He had just jabbed his finger in his chest. Several recourses came into Nick's mind but he decided not to hurt him at this time. Instead, he would teach him a lesson. Nick grabbed the hand and twisted it in a outside wrist lock. As he put pressure on the wrist, he jerked it down and to the right, and John fell to his knees in pain. "A piece of advice: never stick your finger in someone's chest unless you are prepared to back it up. I want you to collect your things, get outside and do your job. Do you understand?"

John nodded but could not speak because of the pain. Nick saw his eyes begin to water and he let him go. Nick left John on the floor of the apartment holding his wrist.

Nick hated resorting to violence, but he'd be damned if he let this guy try to bully him. He wanted to tell Gunny about what happened just so that he would know the atmospherics of the situation if John tried anything again. Nick saw that it was 11:25 a.m.

-Thirty-Five-

The falcon does not struggle when he is caught.

— Algerian proverb.

Amir, Muhammad and Ahmad had arrived outside the embassy with a few minutes to spare. Amir called Abu Fahad on his cell phone.

"Hi, how are you?"

"We are fine. How are the kids?"

"They are well; they send you their best." Amir clicked off the line. Abu Fahad knew their message meant that they were in position and that all was clear. His biggest worry was the first team and whether the embassy had made any radical changes the past few days. This is why Abu Fahad decided to visit the embassy only a few days ago instead of weeks earlier. Also, being at the embassy, he liked the thought of the risk he was taking. He was not going to hide like Usama Bin Laden behind proxies, he wanted the Americans to recognize him when he killed them. "Mahmud, Are you ready?"

"Yes, my brother. I am ready." Abu Fahad kissed him on both cheeks as was his custom. He wished his brother luck and reminded him to call in before they got into position. Mahmud left. Abu Fahad knew the trip would take about twenty minutes, which would give them ten minutes to get into the dumpster. His brother would take the same route as Amir, Muhammad and Ahmad since they knew that no roadblocks were up on those roads. He didn't think there would be any roadblocks since all the actions from his other groups were being conducted outside of Algiers. They had purposely decided to only mount minor attacks over the night so as to lull the army and the police into a false sense of security. The other group would not start setting off car bombs in Algiers until after he left the apartment around 12:30 p.m. and would continue throughout his attack on the embassy. He looked at the box at his feet and could not wait until he took it with him to the embassy.

Bassam, Hamza, Kamal, and Jamil went through the day in a daze. All of them were worried about their families. Hamza had taken the worst beating among the group. The tall one's words kept coming back to him. He would do what he said so that his family would live. He hated being in this position, but was glad he was not alone. At least he was going through this with his friends.

Bassam knew what he had said to his friends earlier was true. They did not have a choice. But he had doubts as to whether he was doing the right thing. He could not let them know that he felt that way. Would Allah want him to sacrifice one group of people for his family? This could not be God's will. He was torn. He could not live with himself if he allowed his family to die. He was mopping the floors of the main entryway as he thought about his dilemma.

Jamil was collecting the trash in the offices while he thought about his family. *Bassam was right: we will do our jobs, let the men in and our families will be safe.* He thought Kamal a fool for even considering any other option. What did he owe these Americans? They were interlopers in his country. His family came first. He would do what he must and sleep well knowing that he saved them.

Kamal carried a trash bag to the small dumpster. He was having problems with the decision to have the Americans killed instead of his family. He knew that they would kill the Americans without remorse. He believed that the American presence was a good thing and that they should stay. These terrorists were trying to take over the country and if everyone gave up, it would be like Afghanistan where the Taliban ruled. Everyone would be forced to grow beards and women would not be allowed to hold jobs or be in the streets without a male relative to escort them. Could he be a part of that, he wondered, or was he too weak to do what he knew he must do?

Kamal decided to see if he could talk to John; since he was the Regional Security Officer maybe he could help him. Kamal hoped he had the courage to do the right thing. He saw John coming from his apartment building. He caught up with him as he went toward the embassy.

"Mr. John, how are you today?"

"Busy, what's up?"

"I was just thinking how sad it is that all of you are leaving today."

"This country's fucked up and the people are crazy. They are getting what they deserve. I have work to do. Leave me alone." John walked away and without saying goodbye or thinking about the consequences of his actions. Kamal was shocked. In his culture, one was always respectful and nice. In the rules of etiquette that Kamal was raised under, John may as well spit on him because the offense was great in Kamal's eyes.

Kamal stood where he was in the grass and watched him walk off. "And I actually thought that these people were worth the lives of my family." He still knew what he was going to do was wrong, but he would live with that fact later.

John walked away thinking of how he could get Nick back. He passed the back gate and saw Jeff, one of Gunny's Marines, there with the local guards. He went into the embassy to go to his office.

Nick sat in Gunny's office telling his story to him. "I wish I could have seen that," laughed Gunny. "That prick deserved it. He is lucky he didn't do that shit to me. I would have kicked his ass from here to Tunisia. Okay, you must lodge a formal complaint with me that he assaulted you."

"What, are you serious?"

"Very. By saying that he assaulted you and you defended yourself, it will be on record and appear as if you are not trying to hide anything. He will surely file a grievance against you so you should get yours in first and I will add a comment saying how he had acted toward you during the last year."

Nick thought that this was ridiculous but he knew Gunny was right. He looked at his watch. It was almost 12:00 p.m. and he had to do this bureaucratic crap. He began filling out the form.

Mahmud's group arrived at the site. He looked at Abdallah and Khalil and thought that they were about to move into history. He had for so long wanted to be a part of his brother's plans. All those years when his brother was training in the desert and traveling in Bosnia, he was left back at home to take care of their mother. He did not mind, but he had felt that his life was being squandered. Every time Abu Fahad returned home, he would tell him to be patient because his time would come. He kept reminding Mahmud, "Patience is beautiful and that he was like a tree giving shade to the outside." He had explained to Mahmud by helping their mother at that time, it would allow him to do other, more important things in the future. He knew now was the time. He dialed the number.

"Allo."

"How are you?"

"I am well."

"I just arrived at the store. I have purchased everything that you wanted me to buy. Was there anything else you needed?"

"Thanks, but I have everything I need. See you soon." Abu Fahad smiled to himself. They were in place.

Mahmud ordered Abdallah and Khalil to walk to the dumpster one at a time. Each person carried a small sack with their weapons in it. Abdallah went first and climbed inside the large container. He saw Amir, Muhammad and Ahmad and his heart settled down a little. They had their weapons and looked focused. Khalil came inside next and nodded to his tribesmen.

159

Mahmud looked around the area and saw no one. He decided that it was safe to head toward the dumpster. He walked slowly as if he had nowhere to go in particular. He jumped inside and saw his men. He had helped Abu Fahad pick these men; they were the best. He asked if they had seen anything unusual. They replied no. He settled back and waited for his brother. It was 12:10 p.m.

Abu Fahad and Ammar got in the Range Rover. He had picked this car because the security services never pulled over people in cars of this caliber. He had stolen it from one of the first families he killed. His friends had the title and license changed so that it was legally registered to his name, "Muhammad Abdallouwi."

Ammar drove. "What is the box for sayyidi?"

"It is a special surprise for the Americans. It will aid us in our cause."

Nick finished the form. "How's everything, Gunny?"

"Good. I have Jeff at the back gate with the local guards. Peter is on duty at Post One since he is my assistant. Jim is at the front gate and Mike is roving. We are all in radio contact and they are instructed to check in every 30 minutes. I will either be in Post One or roving. You have a radio, so if you need me just call me. My call sign is 'magnum.' You know I was in Panama." Nick nodded. "Well, we thought that would be a cakewalk. It wasn't. Many of my men were killed because we thought it was some banana republic that would just fall down when they saw us. We were overconfident, Nick. Be careful and stay alert. We are in the home stretch. Another six hours, we will be in the Med catching some rays."

"Thanks, Gunny."

Nick went back to consular to check on the how everything was proceeding. "Mr. Arshad, is everything calming down?"

"Yes, we have processed all the Americans and they are sitting in the waiting room. I didn't want them roaming around so we brought them snacks and sodas from the cafeteria."

"Thanks, my friend. Are all the visas done?"

"Yes, but two." He held up his wife's and his passport.

"Oh, I can't believe it. We were so concerned about everyone else that you were overlooked. It's a good thing I did not destroy all the visa foils." Nick went back and got two visa foils. He logged on the computer and approved both cases. He put the visas in the passports himself.

"Here you go, multiple entry and maximum validity."

"Thank you, madir. I hope your time away from here will be short. I will miss you." He put his hand over his heart, which showed the sincerity of his words.

"Arshad, I couldn't have done my job without you. You are not only a superb employee, but a friend." They shook hands. "I will be at my desk if you need me. I will come down about 4:00 p.m. to check in with you. Thanks for taking care of the Americans. I know they can be a headache. Here's fifty dollars; treat them to dinner in the cafeteria on me." Arshad agreed and Nick left.

Abu Fahad pulled up to the site. They had already gone by twice to look for anything out of the ordinary. They parked the car. "Ammar, I want you to walk to the dumpster and get in. If everything is fine, then call me on my cell phone but do not talk, just leave it open for a few seconds before hanging up. If you do not call, then I will assume that there is a problem and will leave." Ammar left the Range Rover and walked to the dumpster. It took him about seven minutes. Abu Fahad waited.

Ammar made it to the dumpster and climbed inside.

Mahmud said, "Is he here?"

"Yes," replied Ammar. He picked up his phone and dialed his number.

Abu Fahad waited and then heard the familiar ring. He answered but heard nothing before the call hung up. He exited the truck, picked up his bag, which contained the box and his weapon, and walked to the dumpster.

Bassam, Kamal, Jamil and Hamza sat in the lunchroom at the back of the embassy. This room was only for the janitorial staff. Jamil said, "Are you ready? It's about 12:45 p.m. We should start rolling the small dumpster outside. I want to get this over with so I can go home to my family."

"Relax," said Bassam. "I want Jamil to go first, then Kamal, followed by Hamza. I will go last. Agreed?"

They group nodded to Bassam's instructions. Jamil left the room and started toward the small container on rollers. It was full and he began pushing it toward the gate. He waved at the local guard and the Marine guard as he pushed the cart past them. The terrorists had told him to make sure the plastic top was flipped over on the container to cover the contents, so when they returned and the top still covered the container, nothing would seen amiss.

Jamil waited as security lowered the barrier and the gate rolled back. Once that was done, he pushed the dumpster through the maze of three foot high jersey barriers. He had heard from his friends that the embassy installed those barriers because of the truck bombing in Africa; no vehicle could even come close to the embassy now. He always hated the long push from the embassy to the dumpsite. At least it would be a lighter push on the way back.

Nick was in his office talking with Sarah. "So I think all the little problems have been worked out. Call the operations center and tell them that all is well."

Sarah left to make the call. Nick decided to check in with Mariam. He called her and they spoke for a few minutes about all the things Nick had to do at the embassy and about her day.

Nick asked her about whether she was ready to go. "Yes, I am ready. I spoke with my FLN contacts and told them I was leaving." Mariam explained what Sulaiman had said.

"I know this is tough for you, but I think it's the best thing at this time. We have heard that there were more attacks in the west last night, mostly car bombs. I have a lot to do here but I will call you in a few hours. I love you."

"I love you, Nick. I know how busy you are and I appreciate you checking in on me. Ciao."

Nick rung off and called Sami. "Hey, my friend, you want to grab a quick bit to eat in about 30 minutes?"

"Sure, I will meet you in the cafeteria at 1:30 p.m."

Nick went back to cleaning everything out of his desk and making last minutes notes in the log.

-Thirty-Six-

Abu Fahad walked slowly to the large dumpster. He had waited until almost 12:45 p.m., because he did not want to take any chances that a trap was set. He had to put some faith in Allah's will, but he would also be cautious. He reached the dumpster and climbed inside. All of his men were there. He instructed Amir and Muhammad to go in the first dumpster.

Jamil pushed the dumpster outside of the compound and finally reached the main dumpster outside of the embassy. He slowly took the garbage bags out and placed them inside of the larger container. Amir and Muhammad got inside of the small dumpster. "Remember, if you make a sound or otherwise cause any trouble, your family will die. This had better not be a trap," said Amir.

Jamil pulled the two large flaps over the dumpster. Amir noticed that it was very cramped inside. The two had to almost sit in each other's laps. They barely had enough room for their weapons. Each carried two nine-millimeter pistols, one AK-47 with a folding stock, a long combat knife and several grenades.

Jamil had a little trouble pushing the cart at first, but once it got rolling, it moved easily. He thought that if he just got them into the embassy, everything would be fine. He pushed it through the back parking lot and past the first security check. As usual, no one said anything to him. His heart was beating fast and he thought they would be able to see how nervous was. He finally made it to the gate. He noticed the local guards and the one Marine Security Guard. They waved him through as usual. He waited as the gate rolled back into the wall and the barrier went down into the ground. Jamil thought that the wait was intolerable. "Relax, relax, they don't know," he said to himself. Finally, the security measures had finished and he started pushing the cart into the embassy. He pushed the cart to the section of the embassy where they usually stayed until they were ready to be moved.

Kamal left the room as soon as he saw that Jamil had made it inside the embassy. His steps seemed heavy. At least he tried to do something earlier, Allah had to know that he had tried. He began pushing the dumpster to the gate. Kamal walked past Jamil but he avoided his gaze. Kamal reached the gate and waited for the guard to lower the barricade and open the gate. He made his way through the main security point to the outside of the embassy.

He pushed his dumpster through the maze of barricades as he had done for so many years. He saw the large dumpster sitting in the field.

Abu Fahad told Mahmud that he wanted him to go next. "Now, if something happens unexpected, you and the other men can still inflict some damage. I will go after you with Ammar. Once I am inside, we will wait for the last group, Abdallah and Khalil. Abdallah will tell the last janitor to push that dumpster into ours; that is signal for us to climb out. Mahmud, take four of the men to the far side of the embassy and I will take the other four to the near side. I will set my magic box off right when the last dumpster hits mine."

Kamal made it to the dumpster. He began taking the trash bags out and throwing them into the dumpster. He heard them move inside. "Take care, place the bags inside carefully," whispered a voice from inside. He continued to place the bags inside. When he was finished, he saw two men emerge and get inside his dumpster.

Mahmud and Ahmad got inside and tried to get comfortable. It was small, Mahmud noticed. His brother did not tell him how little the dumpster would be. He was 6' 2", tall for an Arab, and weighed almost 220 pounds. He had spent years working out while waiting for his brother to return to the house. He settled inside and put his legs on either side of Ahmad. He had been on numerous other missions but he knew that this was the most important in his brother's eyes and he did not want to let him down.

Gunny left Post One to go to the main entrance of the embassy. He wanted to check on Jim and the local guards. He walked around the fountain to the go the front gate. "Corporal, report?"

"Sir, nothing unusual. We have canceled all deliveries as you ordered." Gunny thought that one of the ways a group could try to attack the embassy was through the routine delivery trucks that came everyday. For that reason, all trucks were turned away today. He thought, *fuck 'em, security comes first.*

"Good job. I think we are winding down today but I wanted to check." Gunny left the gate decided to roam around to inspect the outer perimeter.

Kamal pushed the dumpster back toward the embassy. It was not hard. Years of pushing trash made his legs strong. He steered the contained through the barriers and made his way to the gate. He hoped that they would just open the gate as usual. The gate started back and he waited. After the gate opened, he pushed it to the barrier and waited for that to lower. He was through the security and he pushed the container beside the other one there.

Hamza rushed to the container. "Slow down and relax," whispered Kamal. Hamza pulled the container out of the row of other dumpsters and started to make his way to the gate. Kamal was worried about him because of the beating he had taken. He was really shaken. Kamal decided to go to the front of the embassy to pick up trash. He would slip out once it started.

Hamza was shaking. He tried to calm himself, but he had trouble not thinking about how they beat him last night. He made it to the gate. He thought the guards were looking at him in a strange way. He lowered his head and waited. He was through the gate in only a few minutes. He pushed his dumpster to the site. He knew he was going too fast, but he wanted to get it over with. He arrived and accidentally bumped the larger container. Hamza looked inside because he did not want to throw trash on them. They had hurt him so bad that he did not want to upset them. "Is everything fine?"

"Shut up and put the rest of the trash inside." He finished and the two men got inside of his dumpster. One had a small bag in his hand.

Abu Fahad and Ammar climbed inside and knew that Allah was with them. He pulled the box out of the bag. Ammar looked at it curiously. Abu Fahad started to set up the device. It was called the Vanguard Emissions Protector, a device used in hospitals and on planes to stop all radio transmissions within a specific radius. In hospitals, many of the technically advanced machines such as the kidney dialysis machine would not function properly if radios or cell phones were used in the same vicinity, and many of the devices on planes also did not function if radio emissions were present. He had learned about it from the Bosnians. He would activate it before they started the attack so the Marines could not communicate on their radios. They would be operating without information. He laughed to himself, it was actually made by the Israelis. He thought how funny it was that a Jewish device would help kill Americans.

Hamza pushed the dumpster into the embassy without any problem. Abu Fahad sat in the dumpster thinking that in only a few more minutes, the fun would start. His toy was ready. All he needed to do was to push the button. Hamza walked away quickly as Bassam came out of the rest area.

Bassam approached the dumpster and thought about how it was the last time he would be doing this job. He had decided to help this terrorist's group, but he was regretting it now. He thought, *What happens if they don't succeed and I am caught by the police? They will surely torture and imprison me if the Americans don't.* He now understood the complex situation he was in. He pushed the container to the gate. As the gate opened and the barrier lowered, he wracked his brain for a solution. Every step he made felt like a ton of bricks. He slowly made it through the barricades and started for the large dumpster. Once there, he tossed the trash in the large dumpster. The two men climbed out and entered his container. He pulled the top down and began the long trek back to the embassy.

Bassam finally made it to the gate and waited for security to open the gates. The first gate rolled back and he pushed it into the middle zone in front of the barrier. He looked inside the guard booth and waved to the guards and the Marines. They waved back. He knew that he had to do something. He said a silent prayer asking Allah to watch over his family. The barrier started to lower and he waited. He looked inside the booth and fixed his gaze on the Marine Guard. The Marine waved him through but he did not move. The Marine became anxious and came out of the booth. "What's up? Move it along." Bassam looked at him and at the dumpster. Bassam noticed that everything seemed as if it was going in slow motion.

Abdallah and Khalil sat in the dumpster. Why weren't they moving? They grabbed their weapons and prepared themselves for the worst. They heard noise outside of the dumpster. Abdallah took out his pistol and aimed it upwards.

The Marine guard walked over to the dumpster. He unsnapped the restraint on his holster, pulled out his weapon, and opened the lid of the dumpster.

-Thirty-Seven-

Abdallah jumped up and fired a single shot into his forehead. The Marine did not even have a chance to fire a round. His lifeless body fell against the dumpster before hitting the ground. Bassam was awakened from his trance when he heard the gunshot. He ran outside the gate.

Abu Fahad had been waiting and thought that the dumpster should have arrived by this time. He heard the single shot and hit the button on the box.

The two local guards were not paying attention until they heard a shot. Abdallah and Khalil sprang out and ran into the guard house. The two guards both grabbed their radios and tried calling Post One. Abdallah entered the room and took out his knife. He shoved it into the first guard's stomach and pulled upwards. The guard screamed as his intestines fell out of his body. Khalil hit the second guard in the face with the butt of his gun before cutting his throat as he killed him. He said, "bismillah (in the name of Allah)."

Abu Fahad jumped out of the dumpster and saw that Abdallah and Khalil had already shot the Marine and taken care of the two local guards. His men came out of the dumpster and broke up into two groups. Abu Fahad looked at Mahmud and pointed him in the direction of the west entrance of the embassy. Abu Fahad took his four men and went to the east entrance. He had hoped that no one heard the gun shot.

Gunny was on the farthest end of the embassy near the outside perimeter when he heard a shot. He had heard enough gunfire in his life to know what it sounded like. He pulled out his radio and called Post One. "Vegas, Vegas do you copy?" He heard nothing but static. He tried again, "Vegas, Vegas do you copy?" Gunny knew something had to be wrong. He ran back to Post One.

At first, Abu Fahad moved slowly through the embassy compound. Although he had planned the attack for months, he was amazed that he was inside so easily. He and his men moved quicker once they noticed that no one was in the yard. He thought that everyone must be inside getting ready to be evacuated. They eased towards the doors on the east side of the embassy.

Sami was in his office near the back of the embassy. He thought he heard a loud noise but wasn't sure. He decided he would walk to the cafeteria early. It was only 1:10 p.m. and Nick said he would meet him at 1:30 p.m., he would check on security at the back gate before heading for lunch. He

167

walked the length of the lot to the back gate. He didn't see the local guards in the booth. They were always undependable, so he went to the side door and walked inside.

Mahmud's group had a longer walk since the west side of the embassy was much farther away. They crept along the side of the embassy so that they would not be seen by the security cameras. His brother had told him to avoid shooting anyone until they blew the doors to main entrance of the embassy. Surprise would be their greatest weapon. He continued along the path to the main embassy doors.

Sergeant Peter Clark sat on duty at Post One. He was Gunny's assistant and thought to be the best Marine in the detachment next to Gunny. He had been in the Marines for seven years. This was his last post before he went back home to North Carolina to finish college. A radio check had just occurred about fifteen minutes ago so he just had to check the cameras around the embassy and make sure none of the alarms had been tripped. Post One, as the nerve center, controlled all the security measures inside the compound. He made sure that he looked at every light every few minutes.

Gunny ran for all he was worth. He was at the farthest end of the compound when he heard the shot. He raced toward the east entrance when he saw the group moving along the wall. There were four men with AK-47s. He stopped and decided to take out as many as he could before they made it in to the main building. He pulled out his pistol but was too far for a clear shot. At each post there were rules on the amount of force you could use against intruders, but he wasn't about to consider not killing these guys. They had entered his domain and as far as he was concerned, he would use everything at his disposal to take them out.

Abu Fahad saw the east wing door. They were about 10 feet away. He ordered Ammar to get ready to throw a grenade. He pulled out the pin and got ready to throw it.

Gunny saw the man pull out something from under his vest. It could be a grenade or something else. He was still too far for a good shot but decided to shoot at them so as to at least discourage the group and to warn Post One.

Ammar tossed the grenade at the same time shots came from another direction.

Sami could not believe his eyes. The two local guards were dead along with the Marine Security Guard. He grabbed the radio and tried in vain to contact Post One. He decided to go to Post One to tell them. He pulled out his gun and ran at full speed toward Post One, when he heard an explosion.

He did not want to be rash and moved cautiously the rest of the way.

Nick was in his office when the explosion occurred. He didn't even think, he reacted. He leapt up out of the chair and went outside the office. "Take the log and try to contact the Operations Center in Washington. After that I want you to go to the safe haven!" Nick shouted at Sarah.

"What about everyone else?"

"They know the plan. I don't know why the alarm didn't go off but I will check it out. Do those things then leave!"

"Be careful Nick."

Nick took the gun out of its holster. He checked it and made sure that it was not on safety mode. He grabbed his cell phone and embassy radio. He tried to raise Post One but did not get an answer. He tried using his cell phone to call the Marines through the switchboard; the phone registered no signal. He proceeded slowly down the corridor. He could hear his heart beat as he walked.

Peter was looking at the cameras in Post One when he heard the explosion. Seven years of training took over his next movements. He hit the button to secure all entrances. The magnalock doors sealed, which meant no one was entering or leaving the embassy without his permission. He hit the alarm, a screeching alarm sounded inside and outside the embassy. He picked up the radio to call Gunny or Nick, but all he heard was static. If Gunny or Nick did not hear the explosion of alarm, then they were dead. He didn't know what the threat was or how many were outside, but he was prepared for this. He put on his flak jacket and pulled the M-16 out of the weapons locker. He tried to call the police but the lines were dead. He decided to make an announcement to tell everyone to head toward the safe haven, when there was another explosion.

Mahmud heard the grenade go off. He started running to the west entrance. His men followed him. He tossed the first grenade himself at the door to the main building of the embassy. The doors blew off and a gaping hole loomed where the entrance once was.

John was in his office when he heard the first explosion. "What was that?" Michael did not answer. He went to the weapons locker and opened the safe. John tried to call Post One but no one answered. Michael opened the safe and pulled out two M-16s. He put on a class-2 Kevlar body armor vest and got up to leave the office. John sat there trying to call Post One.

"Forget it. We have to go to Post One," said Michael.

John got up and took the M-16. How could this be happening? What was going on? They heard the alarm go off. Now he knew that it could be nothing other than an attack on the embassy. "Well, if we are going to go, then I will lead." Michael uttered a silent curse.

Mike was roving outside of the embassy's main perimeter when heard the thunderous explosion. He tried the radio first before rushing back to the embassy. He pulled out his weapon as he ran. He heard the attack alarm at the embassy and a second explosion went off.

Arshad heard the explosions and the alarm. He told the people in the waiting room that an attack had occurred and that should go to the safe haven. There were screams and he yelled, "We are under attack. Calm down and follow me."

The group got up and began following him. Nick was at the door of the CAA when he heard the second explosion. He hoped that Gunny was around because he knew that John would be of no use.

When Abu Fahad went into the main embassy building, he saw a few local guards running from behind; his men shot them before them could come any closer. He heard the second explosion as he entered. He saw Post One as they went further into the embassy. He rolled a grenade to the door.

Gunny heard the second explosion as he was creeping closer. Before he had moved much further, he heard a third explosion and knew he was outclassed in the weapons department. He entered where the door was destroyed. He saw the group near Post One. He started firing at the group and instantly hit one of the men several times. Gunny squeezed out a few rounds in their direction but the men moved further inside.

Abu Fahad saw that Ammar was hit. He slumped and Abu Fahad knew that he was dead. He uttered a prayer for him. They started firing at the gunman who was shooting from outside while at the same time shooting at Post One.

Peter heard the explosion. He fell toward the panels. Wood and glass fragments peppered his face. He could feel the blood ease from the slight wounds. He saw his adversaries. He began firing the M-16 at the group. While he was alive, they would not take his position.

Mahmud's group had now entered the main embassy building and they saw Abu Fahad firing at Post One. The Marine inside was firing at his brother.

Gunny fired back at the first group. He did not want them to take Post One. He finished one magazine and hugged the wall as he put a fresh magazine into the weapon.

Nick saw the gun fight going on. One group of four men was at the east end near Post One. There was an exchange of gunfire between the Marine and the group. There was also gunfire from outside, probably from Gunny or the other Marines. He noticed that another group had just entered the west wing and would probably overwhelm Post One shortly. He saw the leader of the group near the west wing moving closer into the embassy. He exhaled, took aim and fired several rounds at the person leading the group.

-Thirty-Eight-

Mahmud started toward Post One. He believed that they would be able to take it now. Then all of the wind left his body and he could not breathe. He felt a sharp pain in his stomach, then in his shoulder and finally in his head. He fell on the ground dead.

Abu Fahad knew they would have control of the security nerve center shortly, now that his brother's group was inside. He had lost Ammar, but they still had seven men against two. Abdallah fired at the gunman who had shot at them from outside. Abu Fahad looked up and could not believe his eyes. A splotch of red appeared on Mahmud's stomach, then shoulder, then his head exploded. His brother's body fell heavily to the ground. He looked up on the stairs and saw a man he had seen before.

It was at that point he screamed like an animal. "La'a (No)!" He could not believe the American killed his brother. This great Mujahid warrior had been killed by the infidel. He cursed at the American and ran up the stairs. He did not care about Post One anymore. This was family honor. He began firing at the American at the top of the stairs. The American now had a blood feud on his hands. In tribal life, the murderer is held personally responsible for his act and the penalty is a life for a life.

Nick shot the man and began shooting at the other members of the groups when automatic gun fire tore up the wall near him. He backed up into the CAA and secured the door. He knew that his pistol was no match for automatic gunfire. He ran deeper into the CAA.

Sami made it to the embassy and saw Gunny shooting at something inside the embassy. "Gunny, it's me Sami, don't shoot." Sami ran up beside him and they both starting shooting at the group. One had been killed, and it looked like Nick had killed one from the other group. They kept firing at the two groups. One of terrorists took off up the stairs after Nick.

Mike made it to the west entrance and begin firing at the Arabs there. Amir and Muhammad ran towards Post One and rolled another grenade into the booth. Fortunately the glass was impact resistant. Peter was thrown around in the booth but continued firing out of the door. Ahmad kept firing into the door until a round caught the Marine in the leg. Peter fired at them until he ran out of ammunition in the M-16. He took out his pistol and began firing while bleeding from the leg. Khalil ran to the door and threw a grenade inside. Peter saw the grenade fly inside. Without thought to his personal safety, he took careful aim at Khalil and shot him twice through the head. The grenade went off and the shrapnel shredded Peter's body to pieces. He was dead.

Ahmad entered Post One and staring firing from there. Muhammad entered behind him and starting sweeping the embassy floor with AK-47 rounds.

Abu Fahad made it to the door. He fired an automatic volley into the hinges and the door fell backwards. He went slowly down the hall. Abdallah decided to go with Abu Fahad. He ran upstairs into the CAA. Abu Fahad almost shot him as he ran through the door. "What happened out there?"

"Ahmad and Muhammad have Post One."

"Good, help me find the American that killed my brother." Abu Fahad wanted to see him bleed.

Amir turned back and started firing at Mike, who was still firing from the west entrance. As he only had a pistol, it was no match for the AK-47. Amir shot Mike several times as he continued to fire back with his pistol at the Arab. Mike died outside the west entrance.

Arshad led the Americans through the commercial section to enter the safe haven from the other entrance downstairs. But he knew that he would have to cross the main entry hall of the foyer to get to the safe haven door. He heard gunshots from outside and stopped the group.

The FSNs that heard the explosions, alarms and gunfire made their way outside of the embassy. At the sound of the first gunfire the local guard tried to the call the police. After not being able to get through to the police or army, they heard the explosions. The local guards did not carry any weapons and decided that since they could not help, they would leave the embassy. The procedure in an attack was that if possible, all noncombatants tried to either make it to the safe haven or leave the embassy if the security conditions permitted.

Because all the shooting and explosions occurred inside the embassy, Carmen and Shareen both went toward the front entrance. Carmen tried her cell phone, but it did not work. She hated leaving but would try to call for help from the outside.

Amir went to Post One to join Ahmad and Muhammad. "Where are the controls to open the gate?"

"I don't know, hit all the buttons," said Ahmad.

Nick passed John and Michael in the hall. "What's up?"

"John, we have roughly 5-6 armed men outside of Post One. I think they took Post One."

"Let's go, we can go down and give them a real fight," said John.

"Negative, I killed one of them and another one is coming this way. We have to get the Americans in the consular section to the safe haven. I want you to follow me. We will take the back way to consular and bring them to the safe haven." John was hesitant but went with Nick.

Jim ran up behind Gunny and Sami and began firing at Post One. "I am out of ammo, give me a clip," said Gunny. "The problem is that our weapons are no match for theirs."

"What's the situation, Gunny?"

"They killed Peter and Mike and two headed into the CAA. They now have Post One."

"Gunny, they also killed your man at the back gate." Gunny counted that he had three shooters with him but with less fire power than the three in Post One. "Okay, I want you and Sami to go to the safe haven. I will cover you. I think our best defense is going to be from there and then we will figure out what's next."

"Yes sir," Sami agreed.

Nick, John and Michael made their way to the back stairway. They walked through the lower hallway and came to the door. They heard shooting from outside. "We have to get those Americans to the safe haven area," Nick said.

"It's impossible, too much gun fire," John blurted out.

"I don't give a shit. Those are Americans and they are my responsibility. Michael are you with me?"

"Yes."

Nick looked outside the door and saw that three Arabs were in Post One shooting at the east entrance. He saw Gunny, Sami and Jim by the entrance of the door. He waved and they saw him. Nick gestured to the doorway to show Gunny what he was thinking, making a run to the commercial sector.

Gunny saw Nick. When he glanced at commercial, he saw Arshad peeking his head out of the section. Gunny thought that the Americans must be with him. Gunny nodded his head to Nick.

Nick knew that Gunny understood what he wanted to do. "Michael, I am going to the commercial section. I want you to cover me. The Americans are there and I want to bring them in here."

John came up. "I will also cover you."

"After I get there, I want you to start firing everything you got into Post One so we can come back here." Nick looked at Gunny and focused his mind.

Amir and Ahmad kept watch while Muhammad pushed all the buttons.

They did not know when all the entrances had been secured. All the security measures had to be reset by an authorizing officer like Gunny, John or Nick. They decided to stay there and wait for Abu Fahad.

"We will wait here until they come and get us. They know that we came this way because I just saw the Gunnery Sergeant. The other path would have put us right near Post One, which would have gotten us killed," explained Arshad. The group sat there not saying a word.

Abu Fahad and Abdallah saw several offices in the CAA. They started checking all the offices. They did not know that there was a back stairway which led back toward the front of the main lobby.

Nick ran out to the commercial sector. Ahmad saw him run and begin immediately firing. Gunny, Jim and Sami started firing at Post One along with Michael and John.

Nick heard bullets hitting the floors and wall near him. He prayed that Sami and Gunny would be able to provide enough cover fire for him. He tried to stay low, but it slowed him down. He made it to the door and plunged inward. He fell on top of Arshad as he entered. "Madir, you are alive?" yelled Arshad.

"I am still here my friend." Nick looked at the frightened Americans and knew he had to assure them that they would be safe.

"Everyone listen. I know you are afraid and don't know what's happening. Here's what we know. A group of armed men have broken into the embassy and are attacking us. We have killed several of these people, but we have also lost some very good men today. Our primary concern is your safety. I am going to take you to the safe haven and then we will have you evacuated. You will be fine. I guarantee it. Now you have to do something that will be tough. We have to cross the lobby to get to the safe haven. You will hear some gunshots, but keep on moving. We have to go now. You have no choice." Nick checked his gun to make sure he still had some ammunition in the pistol. He peeked out and signaled Gunny.

"Arshad, I want you to run the safe haven door and I want the five of you to follow him in a single file line." Nick assigned the order of who would go after Arshad and told them to get ready.

The one woman who had been a bitch before spoke up. "I am not going to run out there and have people shoot at me."

"Fine. If you don't go out there, they will come in here and kill you, but before they do, they will rape you repeatedly. Now, this is not a request. Get your ass ready to go now!" That seemed to stir her into action. Arshad peeked out and started to run.

Gunny, Sami and Jim began shooting at Post One. John and Michael followed. The two M-16s from John and Michael were enough to keep the three inside Post One from doing any damage.

One by one the five Americans ran to the safe haven door. Nick was the last. He took a deep breath and sprinted toward the doors. He could tell that Gunny, Sami and Jim had run out of ammunition because suppressing fire was only coming from John and Michael.

Ahmad and Amir fell back to the floor under the barrage of fire power. The five Americans began firing a flurry of shots into Post One. They waited until the gunfire subsided. They saw the American diplomat run back to the other door. They started to fire again.

Nick felt marble chips hit his face as the bullets glanced off the marble tile on the wall. The 100 feet seemed like 100 yards. He ran as fast as he could. He didn't even try to stay low. He burst through the doors. "Okay guys, we have to lay down fire for Gunny and the guys." Nick nodded to Gunny to make a run for it.

Gunny looked at Sami and Jim. "Sami, you go first, then Jim and I will bring up the rear."

Sami looked at Gunny and shook his hand. Sami took off for the door. Post One started firing. Michael, John and Nick fired back as Sami came in. Jim burst in next and Gunny made his way in last.

"It's good to see you guys," said Nick.

Gunny replied, "You too. What's the plan?"

"We now go to the safe haven." Before he left, Nick turned and secured the doors. He led and was followed by Michael and John. The five Americans were in the middle with Gunny, Sami and Jim watching the flank. They made their way to the safe haven hoping that they did not run into any other terrorists along the way.

-Thirty-Nine-

Ahmad, Muhammad and Amir watched the last of the Americans go into the downstairs door. They knew Abu Fahad would be mad at them, but they still held Post One. If only they could find out how to open the gates.

Abu Fahad and Abdallah went through every office upstairs. They could not find anyone so they decided to head back to Post One. Abu Fahad was seething with fury. He thought about Mahmud and what he meant to him. Abdallah sensed his mood and put his hand on his shoulder. "We will get them, especially him." Abu Fahad remembered the name Nick Phillips. He was the man that he had to destroy.

They made their way back to down the hall, careful to be leery of an ambush by the Americans. Abu Fahad sent Abdallah out of the upstairs door to check on the situation.

Amir, Ahmad and Muhammad saw Abdallah look out the upstairs door. Amir whistled to Abdallah and he went back inside the door. "Everything is fine. Our men still have Post One." Abu Fahad and Abdallah went quickly down the stairs to Post One.

"Why aren't our other men here?"

Amir said sheepishly, "We can not open doors that were locked by the Marine. I have tried, but it appears that he locked out the computer system after we came in."

Abu Fahad looked at Peter's lifeless body on the floor. "Get him out of here." Ahmad and Muhammad pushed his body into the hallway. "Abdallah, you know computers, take a look and try to figure out how to open the gate."

"Na'am, sayidi." Abdallah went to the computer and was amazed that it was still intact. He began to hack into the system that controlled security.

"We will wait here for the moment. They are in this embassy some place. Abdallah will get the gates and doors open. I want Amir to watch over him. Since no radio emissions came out of the embassy during the attack and our men have created havoc all around the country, I doubt we will have any trouble from the security services. Ahmad and Muhammad will come with me. We will make a comprehensive sweep of this embassy, floor by floor, room by room until we find them. Once we do, they will not die quickly."

-Forty-

Nick led the group to the safe haven area. The group seemed to be under control but it was hard to tell. Nick knew that stress would be a factor and he would have to maintain control of the situation and be someone everyone looked up to. He didn't want anyone to panic. The door to the safe haven was reinforced with concrete that was secured with heavy steel beams across the back. It was locked. He had figured that at least Sarah had made it there. He knocked on the door with the butt of the gun.

Sarah, Thomas Burton, and Rick Williams had been in the safe haven for what seemed like forever. Sarah was the first to make it to the room, and on her heels were the other two. They immediately sealed the doors and waited for the others. They heard the gun fire and the other explosions and had thought the worst. Sarah was worried about Nick. They heard the knocking against the door and stood up.

"Sarah, Sarah, it's Nick. Open the door. I have the Americans with me along with our guys."

"Don't open it. It could be a trick from the terrorists. They could have coerced him to cooperate," said Thomas.

Sarah had known Nick for a year and knew him to be an honorable man. He would rather die then to be used as a tool by some terrorist group to hurt other Americans.

"Now, I know Nick and he wouldn't have come here if they had caught him. It's not in his character. I am going to open the door. If you get in my way, I will hurt you." Sarah was about 45 years old, 5'6" and a 140 pounds, but she would not let this geek endanger the lives of Nick or the other Americans.

"You could get us all killed."

Sarah was determined and started moving toward him. Thomas backed down and allowed her to open the door.

Nick heard the latches slide back, and the heavy door opened up. "Thank God you are all safe," said Sarah. She hugged Nick.

Nick walked in along with Arshad, John, Michael, Gunny, Jim and the five Americans. "This is all that's left?" asked Rick.

"I'm afraid so," answered Sami.

Gunny and Jim resecured the door and went to the ammunition stores to

181

resupply their weapons. "Give me your guns. We will reload the magazines," said Gunny to Nick and Sami. They passed the guns to them.

Nick asked the group to sit. "Okay, how is everyone? Is anyone hurt or in need of medical attention?" No one in the group indicated they were hurt. He knew his first course of business was to reassure the five Americans. He faced them. "Everything will be all right, we will get you out here safely. Just calm down and take a seat. I need to talk with the embassy personnel. We are prepared for this contingency. I know you are afraid and want answers, but they best way to help us is to let us do our jobs." Nick hoped that they would do as he said.

Nick walked over to the embassy personnel. He did not want the Americans to hear what they were going to discuss. "Sarah, do me a favor. Go over to the Americans, reassure them and keep them away from us. I know they will be pushy and want to talk to me but we need to keep them from getting mettlesome or excitable." Sarah agreed it was important and went over to make sure they were not going to bother him.

Nick addressed his staff, "This is the situation we are facing: they have Post One, it's only 1:45 and the NEO will not be here for another four hours. Gunny, what's the ammo situation?"

"We have enough rounds to fill two magazines for each pistol, but we have several magazines for the M-16s."

Nick continued briefing the group. "Gunny, what's your assessment of the crisis?"

"Well, we have an unknown number of hostiles who have taken control of Post One. We don't know how many are outside the perimeter. I don't think we can hold out here if they try to take the safe haven."

"The computer system was locked out once your Marine secured the doors. They will not be able to unlock the doors to let anyone in," John said.

"You want to bet your life on that, John?" said Gunny.

"The helicopters will be here in four hours. We should wait here and then we will be fine."

"John, we know they have explosives but we don't know how much or what type. This room is not made to withstand a prolonged attack. Nick, you wanted my assessment. We are dead if we stay here and wait for the NEO."

The group watched the exchange between the three. Michael spoke up, "Gunny, are any of your men still alive?"

"No. I lost three good men today. They fought well, but were overwhelmed by firepower."

"Sami, what do you think the response will be from your ministry?"

"It depends whether or not the Marines or local guards called for reinforcements, and also on other terrorists acts happening around town."

"Communications are out. Right after the attack, I tried to call Post One and only received static. I decided to check the signal strength. Someone is jamming us. I don't know what type of device it is. It's probably localized, but I am sure your ministry did not receive any calls from the embassy," explained Rick.

"If that's the case, I can't say how long it will be before we receive help from the police or army. I am sorry Nick, but I don't think it's likely to be anytime soon. As I told you this morning, there were many attacks going on west of Algiers. I am sure that they are swamped."

"So, Nick, I think our options are limited," replied Gunny.

"I think so, too. I think it would be best for us to evacuate the embassy and call in the exfiltration team to meet us someplace outside of this area. I agree with your assessment, Gunny, that it's a matter of time before they find us and break in here. We can get the Chevy Suburbans from motor pool – they are bullet proof – and take everyone to a new evacuation site. Once we are away from the embassy, we can call in our new pick-up site to the Operations Center. It will only be a ninety minute wait for the helicopters. What do you think, Gunny?"

"Are you fucking crazy, leaving the embassy? I am not taking any part of this. We have to stay here and wait for the NEO. We would be jeopardizing these people's lives if we left here," said John.

"I think it's our best option," said Gunny.

"Michael what do you think?"

"I think it seems like our only choice."

"He's a fucking rookie, he doesn't know shit," said John.

"Sami, what do you think? Can you guide us to another evacuation site?"

Sami looked at the group. He knew that John hated him, but he didn't care at this point. Nick was his friend. He would not let him make the wrong decision. "I think it's suicide to stay here. We can't expect help to arrive. It's best to leave. I know a few places that could serve as an evacuation point."

"Now you are listening to a fucking foreigner. It's his people that are trying to kill us."

"John, I am tired of your shit. Sami put his job and his ass on the line to save our lives. I won't have you saying anything about him," yelled Gunny. John could see from Gunny's eyes that he was serious and should not be challenged.

"Fine, I won't say shit about Sami but I will not let these people leave this safe haven." John stood up confrontationally.

"Gunny, we are going to leave this safe haven. I want you, Jim and

Michael to devise the best plan to exit the embassy. Sami, give us three options of the best places to be evacuated from."

"I am not going to let you take these people out of here." John moved closer to Nick and Gunny. He placed his hand near his pistol.

"Gunnery Sergeant Johnson, if John in any way interferes with our plan or the security recommendations that I have laid out, shoot him," ordered Nick.

Gunny racked back the slide of his nine-millimeter, chambering a round into the barrel of his weapon. "Yes, sir!"

-Forty-One-

Abu Fahad searched the consular section for signs of the Americans. Ahmad and Muhammad were going through the nearby offices. They made their way into the commercial section and then into the procurement department.

Ahmad called out for Abu Fahad, "Shuf (look), what do we have here?" Ahmad saw that one of the local staff was still in the embassy. "Stand up, dog," ordered Ahmad.

Abu Fahad came into the room. "What is your name?"

"Abd Al-Aziz, sayidi."

"Well, where do you work and what are you doing here?" asked Abu Fahad.

"I work in procurement and was too scared to leave because of all the shooting."

"We will not hurt you. You are a Muslim. Just help us. Where could the Americans be hiding?"

"I am not sure because if they are not gone, then they are probably in the Classified Access Area or CAA. We are not allowed to go there, so I do not know where they could be inside."

"Do they have a special area in case something happens?"

"Yes, sayidi, but I do not know where it is. It is definitely in the CAA. On the eyes of my children, I speak the truth."

"Very well, I have faith in you." Abu Fahad looked at Ahmad and nodded. Ahmad pulled out his knife and sliced through the man's stomach. He grabbed his stomach in an attempt to keep his insides from falling out. "You have served the kufar (infidels) for too long. We will release you to a better life."

Ahmad slid the knife into Abd Al-Aziz's kidney area. He yelled in pain before falling to his knees. Ahmad had been taught by Abu Fahad in the best methods of making people feel pain before they died. Abu Fahad had learned from the Bosnians, who had practiced on the Serbs. The last cut was across the femoral artery located at the upper part of the thigh. He bled to death in 10 seconds.

Ahmad wiped his blade on the old man's shirt. "Let's go to this CAA to find these people. You still have your grenades?"

"Yes, sayidi."

They left the section and went into the ground floor of the CAA.

-Forty-Two-

Nick knew that all the arguing was hurting morale among his staff. He had hoped that now since John would not be a problem, all would go smoothly. Gunny, Jim and Michael worked on the plan to leave while John sat in the corner. Nick was not worried about him since everyone knew he was an ass at this point. They knew if they listened to John, he would get them all killed.

Gunny spoke up, "Nick I think we should leave here ASAP. They are bound to come after us and once they start attacking this place, we will not be able to leave."

"I am with you, Gunny. Give me a plan."

"Okay, we open up the back doors to this safe haven and exit through there. We take the back stairs to go up to the second floor of the CAA. On the second floor, there is an access shaft going to the roof. We climb through the shaft and go to the roof. From there it's easy. We climb down the ladders on the other side of the embassy and go to motor pool for the trucks. The best thing about it is that there are no cameras in these areas, so the guys at Post One will not be able to see us. It's the best we got and I think it's doable."

"Michael and Jim, what do you think?"

"We both think it will work," replied Michael.

"Good, we will go with it. Sami give me a quick brief of your three sites, after that we all go. Everyone get up. We are moving in a few minutes."

Nick sat next to Sami on the floor to see the map. Gunny, Jim and Michael all stood.

Sami had pulled a map off the shelf after Nick told him to look for sites. He started by saying that going west would be bad idea because of the trouble there. "We are located south of the city center here in Biar. Our three options are this: One, we go south via N36 through Dria and Baba Hassan to Douera. It's a main road leading to a larger area with a large soccer stadium we can use for the evacuation point. I am sure it would be deserted. Two, we can go south-east via N36 to N1 through Birmannreis and Birkhadem to Baba Ali. The area is smaller because most people moved to Algiers a few years ago, but there is an old deserted water reservoir that is not in use any more. It would make a good landing field. Three, we go through the city on N5 passing Hussayn-Dey and Les Pins Maritimes to El-Harrach. There is an empty field outside of the area that is surrounded by trees. It would work. Those are our choices in the order of my preference."

"Thanks, Sami." Nick looked at Gunny and Michael. "I like the soccer stadium. It's secluded and a recognized landmark."

"Me too," said Gunny. Michael agreed with the two of them.

Nick went to the five Americans. "We have decided for everyone's safety that we must leave the embassy, because we can not withstand an attack from these people if they try to break in. The evacuation team is not due here for almost four hours. We will exit the embassy compound and move to an area where the military can pick us up. We believe that this is our only option. If we stay, we die; if we go, we live. Now, it could become rough as we move. There will be more shooting. I need everyone's cooperation. Listen to me and I swear you will get out here safely. Do I have your cooperation?" Nick looked at their faces. They were afraid and unsure but all nodded.

"Let's move, people," ordered Nick. Gunny had taken the M-16 from John and opened the back door. Jim and Michael were at both sides of the door. The group started out with Gunny in the lead, followed by Michael. The five Americans, Sami, Sarah, Thomas, Rick and Arshad came out next, with John following them. Jim and Nick were the last to leave. Nick pulled the door shut and prayed they were doing the right thing.

-Forty-Three-

Abdallah had tried all of the mechanisms that looked like they could control the doors, but it appeared as if they had been disconnected when the Marine closed the doors. He went to the computer and pulled up the central directory. He saw that it listed all the security systems. He tried to access the system, but he was told that he did not have access privileges. He decided to go to the disc cache to see if the computer memorized the features that it used most often. He went inside, but it was of no use. He decided to check the e-mail accounts in the hopes that the passwords were in an e-mail that one of the Marines sent to another. He scrolled through the directories until he saw an interesting subject line called "security passwords." He opened the e-mail and was rewarded with the password to the system. He called up the security system again and entered the password. "Access approved," it read. He called the system back on line. He got up and hit the various buttons again. He saw through the cameras that the doors were opening.

The twenty men had been waiting for more than 50 minutes. They were led by Mehdi, Abu Fahad's cousin.

Abdallah spoke into the microphone, "Ya shabab, we have done it. We are in Post One in the main entrance of the embassy. Meet us here."

They made their way through the embassy to the security center.

Ahmad, Muhammad and Abu Fahad had searched every office and found nothing. They went to the end of the hallway. "Where could they have gone?" asked Ahmad.

Abu Fahad looked around and could not see how they escaped. His two men started to go back in the direction they came when Abu Fahad noticed that the two side walls were not the same color as the back wall. He hit the back wall with the butt of his AK-47 and heard the sound it made. He hit the two side walls with the weapon but heard a different noise. He knew where they were.

"Ahmad, Muhammad, yalla (come here)." They walked over to where he stood. Abu Fahad asked them for three grenades. The secret door felt reinforced to him. He took the three grenades and put two on either side of the hallway. He took the third one and kept it with him. He told his two men to go into the nearby office. He knew that if one of the grenades exploded, it would ignite the other two grenades. Since he did not have any detonation cord or plastic explosive, this would have to do. He ran down the hall and stood in front of the office where his men were waiting inside. He pulled the pin and held the grenade in his hand for a few seconds to allow the internal fuse to count down. When he thought he had about two seconds left, he tossed the grenade and dived into the office. The grenade sailed through the air heading toward the back wall. As it touched the wall, it exploded. That explosion detonated the two other grenades. A deafening sound echoed throughout the hallways.

Abu Fahad and his men stepped out of the office and saw a huge back room with supplies. He thought that they must be inside. They approached the room and looked in. It was deserted. Abu Fahad saw the back door first. His prey had gone out through a back exit. He figured that they could not be far and his group would follow. He would follow, even into the fires of hell. He thought of his brother and moved toward the door.

-Forty-Four-

Nick was on the roof when he heard the explosion. He knew that they had broken into the safe haven and would probably be coming up fast behind them. "Gunny, I think they have broken through to the safe haven. We have to hurry." Michael had gone down first with John and Rick. The five Americans were climbing down now.

"Shit!" exclaimed Jim. He saw the twenty men going toward the front of the embassy. "There are twenty hostiles heading into the main building."

Nick cursed to himself. He saw Sarah climbing down in front of Thomas. They could only move so fast. The group had to stay together because they did not have much fire power. Nick ordered Jim and Sami to go next. Nick and Gunny aimed their weapons at the roof opening.

Nick had a thought. "Gunny, see that old air conditioning unit? Let's put it on the hatch." Nick and Gunny grabbed the unit and lifted it over the door. Gunny told Nick to start climbing down. "You go, Gunny."

He pushed Nick toward the ladder. "This is my job to do this shit. Now don't piss me off."

Nick rushed down the ladder. Once on the ground he told the group to move toward motor pool. Gunny threw the M-16 over his shoulder, grabbed the sides of the ladders and slid down the ladder without using the rungs. He hit the ground hard, but immediately sprung up. He saw the group moving to motor pool. Fortunately, it was located on the opposite side of the embassy from where the terrorists were coming.

Abu Fahad went upstairs and saw the second floor CAA. This was the section that they had searched before. The Americans had been deceptive before. Where had they gone? He ordered the men to check the walls for any fake passages. They searched the hallway for about five minutes before he saw the roof access panel. He called his men over and sent them up. They went through each level until the saw the door to the roof. They tried to open it but something was on top of it. "Push together!" They forced the panel open and climbed onto the roof.

The group had about 50 yards to go. "Michael, run inside and get keys to two of the Suburbans."

He took off to get the keys. The cars were inside of the garage and the keys were located on the main board in the office. He first ran in and saw the

191

two trucks he wanted. He checked the license plates so he would know which keys to retrieve.

Abu Fahad and his two men were on the roof. They looked over two of the sides before seeing the group of Americans. Abu Fahad noticed that there were two Algerians with them. One was thin and short but the other was surely a security type. He fired several rounds at the group as they entered the garage.

Nick and Gunny saw them before they started shooting. They shouted to the group to take cover inside. "The rest of you go and get into the vehicles we will hold them off," ordered Nick.

The group was inside when Michael came back with the key. He told three of the Americans to get in one truck and the other two in the other. He explained to the group that he would drive one and Sami would drive the other.

"You follow me, Michael," Sami said. The two groups piled into the vehicles.

Gunny and Nick returned fire and the men on the roof had to back off for a second. The garage doors went up and the two vehicles roared to life. "Nick, you get in with Sami. I will get in the other vehicle."

Nick climbed in the front seat. He saw the three Americans, Jim, Sarah and Thomas in the seats.

Gunny fired repeatedly with the M-16. He hit one of the guys in the center of his chest. On every yearly range qualification test, Gunny shot expert with the M-16. He had probably fired over 10,000 rounds through this weapon in his career. He loved the way it felt.

Ahmad's chest exploded and he sank to the ground. *Damn, that Marine is good,* Abu Fahad thought. He and Muhammad kept firing but they did not have any clear shots. He saw the trucks pull out and pick up the man that killed his brother. He saw that the Arab was driving. He started firing at the two vehicles.

Sami floored the car and weaved through the embassy compound, driving to the back gate. He sped as fast as he could under the circumstances. Gunfire peppered the hood of the car. "Keep your head down," said Nick.

Gunny jumped in the second vehicle beside Michael. In his Suburban sat John, Arshad, Rick and the two Americans. Michael did a standard J-turn and came up behind Sami. Gun fire also raked their vehicle.

Abdallah saw the two Suburbans on the camera, but he could not find the right switch to raise the barricade. "Amir, help me find the controls to raise the barricade before they leave." The two searched as the trucks approached the gate.

Because Abu Fahad's men did not have a chance to push the small dumpster through the back gate, the barricade was still down, although the gate was closed. Sami saw the gate. "What should I do?" asked Sami.

"Ram it. It's made to keep people from breaking in, not breaking out," Nick responded. Sami floored the Suburban.

A huge crash was heard when the vehicle hit the gate. It gave way easily. Nick thought they were lucky that the truck had a reinforced exterior. Michael's vehicle shot out of the gate after Sami's. Nick saw the two men on the roof and hoped he would never see them again.

-Forty-Five-

What is brought by the wind will be carried away by the wind.

– Arab proverb

Abu Fahad watched the vehicles exit the embassy. He cursed Nick Phillips and the people with him. He had to make a phone call, but the device was still activated. "Muhammad, go downstairs to the back gate. Look into the dumpster and bring me that box that I left inside." Muhammad agreed and left.

Abu Fahad made his way down to Post One. He felt a pain in his chest. He could not believe that Mahmud was dead. He walked back through the CAA hallway to the main lobby near Post One. He saw Mahmud lying on the ground. He walked up to him and cradled his head in his lap. Blood and brains were everywhere. He said a prayer for his brother and swore on his children's lives that he would kill the American.

Abdallah had found the switch too late to stop the embassy vehicles. He saw Abu Fahad hold the dead body of his brother. He knew that they had not done so well today. He told the other men to wait outside until Abu Fahad called for them.

He rose from his brother and seemed to be seething with rage. He asked Amir to bring the men into the lobby. "Ya shabab, today we drove the Americans from the embassy like cowards. But not without a severe price. We lost some brothers today who were truly mujahidin. Their reward will be paradise. I have lost something that was special to me today, but we will prevail. Amir, get me several large vehicles from the car section in the embassy. We are going after them. Mehdi, I want your men to burn this place down. Muhammad, bring me the device."

Abu Fahad turned off the device that had been so effective for them. Immediately, he heard the phones start ringing at Post One. He needed to call Husayn at the Ministry of Interior to get some information. "Husayn listen to me, that one officer who decided to stay at the embassy, what was his name and where does he live?" Abu Fahad pulled out a pen and wrote down the information. "I want you to find out where he's taking the Americans and let me know immediately."

Abu Fahad called for Mehdi. "I want you to pick three of your best men

195

to go to this address. I want them to find out who is there and have that person contact this guy Sami to find out where he will take the Americans. If he has family, kill his children. That should get the wife to assist you. After they learn all they can from her, your men may have their way with her before they kill her." Mehdi agreed and went out to bring back the men.

Mehdi returned, "These are three of my best men: Ali, Ra'id and Karim. They will go there and find out what you want to know. They will call you once they finish their mission. My other men have already started to blow up and burn down the buildings. We will destroy this building last. What else can we do, my cousin?"

"I want you to split up your group into four-man teams to look for the Americans. We know what they are driving and that they will probably try to leave the country. They will be looking for a place to evacuate. The rest of my men are conducting operations today. It's just us. We will stay in contact through our cell phones as we search. Amir, Muhammad and Abdallah will go with me. Don't forget this American killed your cousin." Abu Fahad described the vehicles they left in and Nick Phillips.

"My cousin, we will find this man and make him feel pain like he has never felt before." Mehdi kissed his cousin on both cheeks and whispered in his ear, "I am sorry for your loss. I feel it too." He walk out to see his men.

Abu Fahad thought about the old man. He had comforted him the first time he lost a loved one. He would not only kill this American, he would bring back his head for the shaykh.

Amir drove up, leading a trail of sport utility vehicles. Abu Fahad got into the vehicle driven by Amir. Muhammad and Abdallah climbed in after him. "We will try and catch the Americans." They pulled away from the embassy. The four other sport utility vehicles pulled away too. Each group had its own job to do. Abu Fahad watched in his rear view mirror as the embassy and the rest of the compound went up in flames.

-Forty-Six-

Sami drove out of the embassy at almost reckless speed. He stayed to the secondary road as he made his way south. He got on the N36 highway going south. The trip was about a 70 minute drive and he wanted to get there as soon as he could.

"Sami, tell me about where we are going," Nick requested. Sami explained exactly where the site was.

Nick tried his cell phone, and the signal bars showed that it was operating properly. He called the Operations Center in Washington. "Hello, this is Nick Phillips, Charge D'Affaires, calling from American Embassy Algiers. We have an NEO scheduled today for 1800 hours." The operator told him to give him his employee number so as to verify who he was. He stated his number impatiently.

"Yes, Mr. Philips how can we help you?"

"The situation has changed drastically since we last spoke to you." Nick knew what he was about to say would be recorded so he wanted to phrase his thoughts as though he was writing a cable:

"At 1300 hours today, unknown forces penetrated the American Embassy Algiers and attacked the compound. It was not known how the force gained entry to the embassy compound. A battle ensued between eight terrorists and the embassy staff. In the process three U.S. Marines were killed in the line of duty. The terrorists took Post One, and the embassy personnel along with five American citizens took refuge in the safe haven. Believing the degree of danger to be perilous, Embassy Algiers evacuated the embassy at 1400 hours. As the embassy staff left, another force of approximately twenty armed men broke into the embassy. We request immediate evacuation for fourteen U.S Citizens and one Foreign Service National who is under severe personal risk due to his U.S. employment. We are currently traveling south in two Chevrolet Surburbans on highway N36 toward Douera. The site is located 90 kilometers south of El-Biah. There is a soccer stadium in the north quadrant of the city which will serve as an evacuation point. Our situation is dire and we assess that hostile forces are trying to identify our location."

"Please hold for one moment while we contact the USS John F. Kennedy, which is standing by in the Mediterranean Sea."

Nick waited for the operator to come back on the line. "Mr. Phillips, the

197

aircraft carrier has confirmed that they will have two helicopters at your anticipated destination in 90 minutes. Can your party be at the location at 1530 hours?"

"We will be there, and tell them that the degree of danger is certain and that our evacuation will most likely be opposed by hostile forces." Nick gave them the phone numbers for his and Gunny's cell phones.

"We read you, Mr. Phillips, and good luck."

Nick hung up the phone. "Everything will be fine. They will pick us up at the new location in ninety minutes." He could see the look of relief on their faces. He called Gunny on his cell phone and told them the good news. Sami continued to drive south at a high rate of speed when his cell phone rang.

Nick heard only the end of the conversation.

"Allo. What is happening? I see, that bad, huh?" Sami listened for about ten minutes and then said, "Okay, I will deal with it. Be careful. Bye.

"That was a friend of mine who works in the west. He is a colonel in the army and helped arrange the ticket for Mariam. He told me that the west has been totally taken over by terrorists. They have taken over all the airports west of the city, including Oran. No flights are coming or going. Car bombs have been going off since last night but they have been coordinated. Many of the soldiers have gone over to the extremist's side. There is total anarchy in some parts of Western Algeria. He said that the extremists must have been feigning weakness to launch these kinds of attacks. It's bad."

"What about Mariam leaving tonight?"

"There is no way she can leave from Oran. Maybe out of Annabel, which is in the east near the Tunisian border. My cousin, Walid, works at that airport. I think you met him before. He should be able to arrange a flight for her. If not, we can arrange for her to be driven across the border." Nick remembered Walid, a young guy about 27 years old.

"Will it be dangerous, Sami?"

Sami did not want Nick to think that it would dangerous for him and Mariam to attempt to make it to the airport. "It shouldn't be bad. I am in the police so I should be able to get her there without any trouble."

"You told me that it's dangerous for all security personnel in this country. I can't ask you to risk your life anymore."

"It is all right. I promised her that I would see you safely evacuated. As we both said, you will probably be back in a few weeks. I will call my cousin and make sure the airport is open."

Nick decided to call Mariam to explain to her the new developments.

She picked up on the first ring.

"Hello, how are you?"

"Nick are you all right? I heard from a friend that the American Embassy has been bombed and is now on fire. I have been trying to call you at the embassy for the last hour but I couldn't get through the line."

"I am fine." Nick explained to her what happened at the embassy.

"Are you hurt?"

"No but three marines were killed."

She gasped over the phone and apologized to Nick about what had happened.

"I have some bad news, the airport at Oran is closed." Nick relayed Sami's information to Mariam and the plan.

"Nick, it sounds dangerous for Sami and me."

"It will probably be more dangerous to stay here, Mariam."

"I suppose you are right, but I still feel guilt for leaving. I love you, Nick."

"Mariam, I will see you in Tunis in two days." Nick gave her the details of where he would be staying in Tunis and the phone number of the embassy there. "I love you, Mariam." He hung up the phone.

Sami continued to drive to Douera. He was about 30 minutes away. He saw in his mirror that the other vehicle was still behind him.

Nick felt uneasy about having Sami undertake a difficult task for his girlfriend. He tried to put it out of his head because he didn't have time to think about that. He had to prepare his after-action notes for when he met the military mission leader. So many things had occurred quickly, in the course of only a few hours. No one had a chance to take anything, except Thomas, who did take the bag of money with him. At least he remembered to keep it on him. Nick had left the diplomatic pouch with the U.S. passports and visas in the embassy. If what Mariam said was true, then at least those items would be destroyed in the fire at the embassy. He knew that many people would be scrutinizing his actions today. He wanted to write down everything that happened so management would know how it unfolded.

-Forty-Seven-

Abu Fahad was riding around looking for the two large sport utility vehicles. He told his men that he would go east on N5 and sent the rest of his men in other directions. He knew that it would be difficult to locate the group like this, but he did not have a choice. He had called his tribesmen and GIA fighters in different parts of the country to keep a lookout for the vehicles, but he did not want them to abandon their missions for the search. This was a blood feud now, and while he didn't mind using his cousin's men to help, he would not take men off other assignments to help him. The shaykh had a plan and it was about to be carried out. He did not want to destroy it because of this one American. They had made the Americans leave and had burned down their embassy. They would be able to use that as an example to the other western embassies in the country.

Abu Fahad would wait to hear from the men sent to Sami's house, that traitor. He had helped the Americans. Abu Fahad would see him pay as well.

Ali, Ra'id and Karim drove in the truck looking for the house where that infidel lived. Ali was the oldest member of the group and therefore was in charge. He would enjoy hurting this man's family. He knew that Abu Fahad was upset at this man. If he did this job well, it was a possibility that he would be under Abu Fahad's group. And if he took over the country, he would remember Ali's contribution and give him a high position in the government. Ali thought that he had an amazing opportunity on his hands. He thanked Allah. He remembered the proverb his father had told him a long time ago: "It's all fate and chance."

He instructed Ra'id to turn down the Rue St. Augustine. This man's house was a short walk away. He did not want to park too close in case there was security at the building. He told Ra'id to park the car. They carried only hand guns and their knives. They got out of the car and began walking to Sami's house. Ali smiled to himself and thought how much fun he would have this afternoon.

-Forty-Eight-

For miles the roads were deserted. Nick knew that most people were afraid to venture out onto the streets because of the violence. Sami pulled the car off the highway into the city of Douera. Sami had been driving without saying much. Nick thought that he felt bad about what happened at the embassy and to the Marines. Nick understood that Sami always thought of Nick not only as his close friend, but also as his guest in his country. When John had said it was 'his' people who were trying to kill them, Nick knew that Sami took that personally. Arabs tend to have a greater sense of social responsibility than Westerners. If a child did something wrong in a neighborhood, it was the duty of the neighbor to punish that child, or at the very least tell the parents. Nick knew that Sami felt as if intruders had broken into his house and not the embassy.

"It's about ten minutes away," said Sami. Nick went back to writing his notes.

"Khara (shit)," Sami muttered. Everyone looked up and saw the roadblock. Ever since they left the embassy, Nick had been worried about the faux barrages (fake roadblocks), checkpoints resembling those of the army but in fact thrown up by the Islamists, who would order people out of the cars, murder them and then flee into the hills.

"Everyone relax," said Nick. He called Gunny on the cell phone. "I don't know, but stay alert. I will keep the phone line open so you can hear what's going on.

"Is it a real roadblock, Sami?"

"I am not sure because so many of these groups have uniforms like us. We will play it like it is real but if I sense something is out of the ordinary then I will run it."

"I understand, Sami. Did you hear that, Gunny? We will pull up and see, but be prepared to start firing."

Sami pulled the vehicle to the roadblock. He greeted the guard but did not pull out his police ID. Nick heard a heated debate that concerned them in the vehicles. Nick followed portions of the conversation, but it was tough to translate everything since it was in colloquial Algerian.

Sami told the man to wait a few moments. "These men are not real policemen, but they do not know that I know that. I told them that you were

203

oil company executives. Do you have any money, Nick? I mean real money, because that is the only way we will make it out of here without bloodshed. We have to pay them off."

Nick knew that bribing was common in many parts of the Middle East. The Egyptians were notorious for it. "Thomas, give me the 10,000 Algerian dinars you have."

"But Nick, that money is U.S. government property and I am the custodian for those funds. I can't just give them to some guy on the road."

Nick could not believe that he was hearing this. This guy was about to get them killed over money that was not even his own. "Thomas, this may be our only chance to get out of here. I will sign a receipt later. Give me those funds. Jim, please help him, now!"

Thomas begrudgingly pulled out the funds and handed them to Nick. He passed the cash to Sami. The guard's eyes widened when he saw the money. Sami started saying something is rapid Arabic that Nick could not follow. Whatever he was saying, Nick noticed his tone was very authoritative. The guy finally told the guard at the roadblock to lift the gate. Sami gunned the engine and put the gear into drive. He pulled away faster than was necessary.

"What happened, Sami?"

"As I said, those men were Berber tribesmen who had set up the roadblock on their own. I explained to them that I was the mandub or personal representative of the company and that the company knew that these things happen and were prepared to compensate the men for their efforts. I stressed that they should not see this as a one-time thing, but we would pay them for their continued protection and goodwill. I wanted to make sure that they did not changed their minds and kill us anyway, so I explained to them that I am Kabyle, a Berber like them, with a strong tribe. I told them that I only did this job for the money and that we could have a good business arrangement together. I, in fact, made a business deal with them. Basically, they agreed not to kill us today because they can get more money off us in the future. They only bought that story because my family's name is well respected."

Nick was amazed that Sami pulled it off. "Gunny, did you hear that?"

"Yes, Nick. Tell that guy I own him a dinner next time he comes to the States."

Nick told Sami. He looked at his watch and saw that it was 1520 hours. Sami saw Nick glance at his watch and explained that the stadium was a few blocks away. They pulled into the stadium, which was deserted. Nick called Gunny and told him to meet him at the front of the stadium. He wanted Michael, John and Jim to stay in the vehicles with everyone else. Gunny,

Nick and Sami approached the gate. A padlock was attached.

"Let's climb over," Sami suggested.

The three men climbed over and walked into the stadium. Sami told Nick he was going to the main office to see if anyone was there. Gunny and Nick walked around. "Well, we only have a few minutes before they arrive. It has to be this place. You told them to expect hostile contact, so the Marines will be armed accordingly. We should get the people in here ASAP," Gunny said.

"You're right Gunny, we can't wait."

Sami came back and told Nick that the place seemed deserted. The three went back to the gate and climbed back over. Nick waved the people out of the trucks.

Gunny told everybody to move away from the gate as he tried to shoot the lock. He placed several well-placed shots into the lock. The lock fell away. "Michael and Jim, pull the trucks into the stadium."

The group moved to the inner portion of the stadium. Sami was trying to place a call while walking with the group.

"I want everyone to move to the outside of the playing field. John, Jim, Gunny and Michael, I want you to set up a perimeter around the group. You can pick your sites. They should be here in a few minutes." The group followed Nick's orders and went to their positions.

"Nick, I haven't been able to reach my cousin at the airport."

"Do you think he's there?"

"He should be, but maybe he is busy with everything going on."

"Damn, I wanted to make sure that he would be there before we left."

"Keep trying, Sami."

Nick walked away and saw in the sky two helicopters heading his way. They swooped down and hovered above the arena surveying the site. After what seemed a long time, the two landed near the middle of the field.

"Gunny, come with me to the helicopters." The Gunny ran to where Nick was and the two approached the helicopters. Although the Gunny's uniform was dirty and disheveled, he still wore it in a proud manner.

Nick saw a captain in the Marines jump down, along with eight other Marines. The captain ordered the men to take up security positions around the stadium. "Who's Nick's Phillips?"

Nick said that he was. Gunny saluted the captain who returned his salute. "What's the situation sir?" asked the Marine officer. Nick nodded to Gunny.

"The embassy was attacked about two hours ago. I lost three of my Marines defending the embassy. We had to withdraw because we were overpowered. We escaped and evaded for the last 90 minutes on the way here. We arrived only a few minutes ago. We have thirteen American citizens and one FSN to be evacuated."

"I understand," said the captain. He ordered two of his men to start putting the people aboard the helicopter. They were stressed out and somewhat ragged, but Nick could see how happy the group was to walk toward the helicopter.

Nick had to speak with Sami. "So, did you get him?"

"No, the lines are down right now."

"Sami, we have to go. What do you think the chances are that the airport is open and your cousin is still there?"

"Nick, it's hard to say because everything has been changing so rapidly. I will take her there and make sure that she is safe. Don't worry."

Nick saw the last of the passengers get on the helicopters. "Sami, wait here."

Nick started walking toward the helicopter. He knew he had done a good job getting these people to this point without more loss of life. He had done his duty. At each step towards the open doors, he felt a calm come over him. He made up his mind and knew what he had to do. He approached the helicopter and called Sarah and Gunny to the door. "Take these notes. These are the logs that I have created. Make sure they get to management in Washington. Gunny, I am going to stay. I want you to witness that I am appointing Sarah acting Chief of Mission. Sarah, I want you to make sure that everything is relayed as it happened. I need to get Mariam out of the country. I have done what I had to do thus far. I've got all of you here safely and now I have to do this. Sarah, I will be at the American Embassy in Tunis on Monday."

"Sir, we have to leave now. We can't keep this location secure for much longer," said the captain. Nick told him he needed a few more minutes. The captain looked at Gunny, who nodded. "Okay, sir, but please hurry."

"Nick, you can't do this. Your career would be ruined," said Gunny.

"If he wants to stay, fuck him, let him stay. Let's go! We have to get out of here," yelled John from the back.

"Captain, that man back there hates Marines. He has given my men shit for two years. Three of them lost their lives today trying to help save his sorry ass. Do you think you can persuade him to shut the fuck up?"

"It would be our pleasure, Gunny. Lewis, Gobar, go back and teach that man some respect. Make sure he understands that this is a Marine transport and that he is riding this helicopter because we allow him to." The two men enthusiastically barked and went back to "talk" with John.

"I love her, Gunny, and I can't abandon her now. I once read this quote by Charles Dubois that said, 'The important thing is to be able at any moment to sacrifice what we are for what we could become.' I am willing to make the sacrifice for her. I will help her get to Tunis and then I will meet you at the embassy there. I will see you there in two days. I can't ask Sami to do something this dangerous alone. It's not his responsibility. It's mine. I will ask him to help me, but I must go with him."

Gunny looked Nick in the eyes. "You do what you have to do. Semper Fi." He handed Nick his pistol and a few extra magazines of ammunition. He held out his hand and they shook.

Sarah's eyes were watery. "I understand, Nick, and I will make sure that the facts are known in D.C. You did a hell of a job. I agree with Gunny. Take care of yourself and come back safe. Good luck."

Nick backed away from the helicopter. He saw Gunny tell them that they could take off. Nick saw them rise off the ground and hover for a few minutes before leaving the area. Nick walked to where Sami was standing. "Come on, let's get Mariam out of here."

-Forty-Nine-

Ali, Ra'id and Karim walked down the streets trying to find the address. Ali knew this guy lived on Rue Debbih Cherif, but he had a hard time finding the house. He lived in Bab el-Oued and never ventured out into the more expensive parts of the city. He looked at the address again and saw that he had found the right house. It was a small villa with a nice balcony. He walked up the stairs and rang the bell.

Mariam had been worried about Nick all day since she had spoken with him. These Islamists were seizing her country piece by piece. She could not believe that they would attack the embassy, of all places. Her father's country was falling apart in front of her. She heard the bell, but thought it strange that anyone would be at the door. She was expecting Sami, but he had a key. She walked to the door and saw three men outside through the peephole. She used the intercom. "Oui, what do you want?"

"We are from the police department. Sami told us to come and look after you. He is worried about you."

She knew that Sami was coming, but who were these men? She was sure that Nick would have mentioned if Sami decided to send men to watch over her.

"I am not sure of what you are talking about. Let me call Sami and I will come back in a few minutes." She rang off and started back to call Sami when she heard a crash.

Ali had tried to do it as he was instructed, but once she made the call she would know that Sami did not send them. "Break it down," he ordered the men. They kicked the door in quickly and ran inside.

She heard the men enter the house. The only thought that went through her head was Fatima's safety. She could not let them find her. She ran across the foyer and up the stairs.

Ali closed the door behind him and chained it. He told his men to look for the woman. He didn't know how many were in the house, but he wanted to find everyone quickly.

Mariam ran into the bedroom and grabbed Fatima. "Tima, listen to me. Some bad men have broken into the house and want to hurt us. You must hide. Okay? Whatever you hear, do not come out unless you hear my voice or Sami asking you to come out. Do you understand?"

"Yes, but why do the bad men want to hurt us?"

"I can't explain it right now, but if they find you, they will hurt you." Fatima was only seven years old, but she was precocious. Mariam had now wished that she had told her about their parents so that now she would understand what was going on. She held her hand and led her into the closet. She put her into the clothes hamper. "Now stay here until you hear from me or Sami. Think of it as a game. Don't make any sounds." Mariam put clothes on top on her. She closed the closet door, but left the room's door open to make seem as if there was nothing to hide. She went to the other bedroom and locked the door.

Ra'id was searching in the kitchen while Karim looked in the living room. Ali decided to go upstairs to check the bedrooms. He went into the bedroom that had the door open. He had his pistol out in front of him. He looked under the bed and in the closet but he did not see anything out of the ordinary. The next bedroom he went to, he noticed the door had been locked.

Mariam had been looking frantically for a weapon, any weapon, when she heard someone approach the door. The person did not wait; the door flew inwards. The man she had seen at the front door was in the room. She tried to throw books from the shelves at him, but he brushed them aside easily. He bounded over the bed and slapped her in the face.

Ali called to his men. "Ya shabab, I caught the shamuta. Come upstairs." He picked her up and slapped her repeatedly in the face.

Mariam did not know what he wanted. Whatever it was, she had to protect Fatima. She would die before she told this man where she was.

Ali dragged her by her hair to the bed. "Don't worry, we will not kill you yet. There are things that we must know first. Ra'id, hold her on the bed." Ra'id came and took out his knife and held it to her throat. Ali took out his mobile phone.

"Abu Fahad, I am in his house and I have his wife. I want to let you know."

"Good, my friend. Find out if she knows where her husband is and where the Americans are. If she doesn't, have her call him to get the information. I told Mehdi that you could have your way with her after you are done. Call me when you have some information for me. Salaam Alaikum (peace be onto you)."

"Wa Laikum Salaam (and onto you peace)," replied Ali.

Abu Fahad thought that now the plan was coming together. This was the first lead that he had. He had not heard from any of the other groups yet. He would know where the American was going soon.

Ali walked back into the bedroom. "We will start with the easy questions.

Do you want to live?" Mariam nodded her head. "Ra'id, please show her that I want to hear her answer the question." She was hit in the stomach very hard.

Mariam screamed in pain. "Yes, I want to live."

"Your husband has committed a crime against the Algerian people. He has worked with the Kufar to destroy this country's Islamic identity. The Americans are gone but those who committed sins must be punished. Do you want to be punished for his sins?"

These people were crazy; they thought Sami was her husband! They were probably in the same group that killed her family. She couldn't tell them who she really was. They would surely kill her if they knew who her father was. She would have to try and pretend to be Sami's wife so that they would not find Fatima.

"I don't want to pay for his sins."

Ali thought the woman was pretty. He would like taking her once he knew where her husband was. To him, she stopped being a Muslim when she married a man like Sami, a man who served the Americans as a guard dog. Since she was not a Muslim in his eyes, he could do whatever he wanted with her.

"Where is you husband now?"

"I don't know. He went to work this morning and I haven't heard from him since that time. I swear."

"I want to make sure that you are properly motivated. Ra'id and Karim, make her understand that the next few questions are important." Karim left the room for a few minutes while Ra'id slapped her in the face several times.

"I don't know where he is, I swear," Mariam pleaded.

Karim came back with a length of electrical cord that he obviously ripped off a lamp. Ra'id sat her on the bed and Karim put the cord around her neck and tightened it.

Mariam became light-headed and thought she had never felt pain such as this before. She didn't want to die like this, but knew that if she died, then Fatima would probably not be found. Ra'id pushed her on the bed and tightened the cord even more. Her face started turning blue.

-Fifty-

Sami drove and Nick sat quietly beside him. Sami knew that he gave up much to be in the car with him. Nick had not said a word since he told Sami that he wanted to get Mariam out of the country.

Sami felt honored to have a friend like Nick. He always did the right thing. Sami remembered the time when Nick told John that Sami should have an office at the embassy. Nick had argued that it was ridiculous for the head of VIP protection to not have an office on the compound. John said that since Sami was not a cleared American, it was forbidden. Nick fought and made it happen. His friends in the police had always made fun of him before that by saying the people he protected did not even trust him enough to let him have an office on the compound. Every other embassy with security had an office for the head of their protection detail. Sami laughed to himself about how trivial it was, but it meant something to him and Nick knew that.

Nick was in deep thought. He knew he did the right thing but believed that certain people like John would try to take advantage of the situation since he wasn't around. They would say that he abandoned them, but he completed his mission. He protected the lives that were entrusted to him. He was lucky that Sarah was a solid professional and well respected within the Foreign Service. She had his notes and would make sure that the story was told right. He would be in Tunisia in a day or two and could give them a complete debrief at that time. He had always taken calculated risks in his career that paid off. He knew that this time there would be hell to pay. What could he do? He could not just leave her here not knowing what would happen. He had always tried to live an honorable life. His father once said, "a poor man only has his word." He smiled as he thought of his father.

"Sami, you know why I stayed, don't you?"

"Ta'ban, I understand why, and you would have a hard time living with yourself if you did not come."

"I love her, Sami, and have never felt this way about a women before. I couldn't leave without knowing she was safe. I know the trip will be dangerous, and I couldn't ask you to take a risk that I, myself, would not be willing to take."

"Everything will work out. We should be at the house in ten minutes, then the four of us will go to the airport. You will probably be in Tunis before your staff."

"I hope you are right."

Mariam was awakened by a slap in the face.

"You are not going to die on us, are you?" The one called Ali was standing over her. "Now where is your husband?"

"I swear by Allah's name, I do not know."

Ali pulled out this knife. He ripped her shirt off and held her arm. He slowly cut a 12-inch long gash on her forearm from the elbow to the wrist. She screamed. He slapped her again. "You will not die. There are no major veins or arteries on that side of the arm but I know it hurts."

Mariam was delirious with pain. *Why don't they just kill me?* she thought.

Ali pulled her bra off and ripped her pants off. "Well, if pain is not something you respond well to, then maybe something else will motivate you to help us." Ali wore a traditional dishdasha, a long robe than hung from his body; underneath he wore light cotton pants. "Hold her, men, while I see if I can get her to talk to us," Ali ordered. He lifted up his robe and started puling down his pants.

Mariam believed she was in hell. She had saved herself for Nick and she was proud that she had only been with one man in her life. She had thought of her virginity as a gift that she wanted to give to that special person. The thought of these men raping her was too much to bear.

She kicked Ra'id between his legs and stuck her finger in Ali's eye. She may die, but they would not violate her while she was alive. Karim tried to cut her with his knife. She felt the hot pain across her stomach as he slashed at her. She got to her feet and pulled the door closed as she ran out. Karim took off after her and tackled her in the hall. She kicked, poked, punched, bit and screamed. Mariam would make them kill her here.

Sami and Nick drove along Rue Debbih Cherif to look for a parking spot. They got out the car and walk to Sami's house. Nick had noticed a long time ago that this part of town seemed unaffected by all the violence so prevalent in other part of Algiers. Sami was ahead of Nick and walked up the stairs to the door. He immediately saw that the door had be kicked in. He told Nick and they ran up the stairs.

Karim was tired of this shamuta. Ali did not know how to handle her. He hit her squarely in the face. She continued to fight. He hit her again and again. Ali and Ra'id were watching from the door. "Don't kill her yet, my friend. We need her to call her husband."

Nick burst through the door and heard the struggle going on upstairs. Sami was on his heels. He pulled out his pistol. Nick took the steps three at a time and saw her on the floor. A man was standing over her.

Karim heard the noise from downstairs and stood up to see what had happened. He saw a tall western-looking man running toward him.

Nick approached Karim as he went for his knife. Nick shot a quick Muy Thai kick to his left inner thigh and punched him with a right cross in the face.

Sami saw the two other men at the doorway and shot one in the chest. Ali saw Ra'id go down and dived into the room to get his gun. Sami ran after him in the bedroom.

Karim was stunned, but charged at Nick and shoved him into the other bedroom. Nick fell into the dresser and saw the man coming at him with a knife. Nick had a glimpse of Mariam before he was pushed into the room. He could not believe what he saw. Her face and hair were covered in blood. He focused on what he must do now. He would kill this man for hurting her.

Karim stepped in with the knife at his waist. He thrust it at Nick's chest. Nick counter attacked; while Karim was moving in, he pivoted his body to the side to make himself a smaller target. At the same time, he parried the knife with his left hand, trapped it with his right hand and struck him in the face with a left backhand. Karim dropped the knife but Nick continued his attack. He struck him across the bridge of the nose with his left elbow, and the nose broke on contact. He grabbed his hair with his left hand and pulled his head back. Nick concentrated and struck a right punch into his trachea. As he struck, he envisioned striking six inches through his opponent. Karim made a gurgling sound as he fell to the floor. Nick had crushed his windpipe; he was dead.

Sami rushed into the bedroom. He fired another round into the man on the floor. The other man must have gone into the bathroom. He raised his gun and approached the bathroom.

Ali lay against the wall of the bathroom. He would not let this kafir live. He was ready for Allah, but was the infidel? He made up his mind to run out of the bathroom firing his weapon at this infidel.

Sami had decided to back out of the room. There was no place for the man to go. There was a heavy metal screen over the window from the outside. It could only be opened from a central control panel by the bed, so he could not go out through the window. Sami heard the man run out shooting in the room. After he heard several shots, Sami bent down and got himself in a supine position. He had practiced this move numerous times in training. He called it survival shooting skills. He knew that he would not always face an opponent in a conventional firing position and had practiced shooting from a variety of unusual positions. He used his knees and feet to propel him into the room. As he entered the room, he saw the man, aimed squarely and shot him in the chest four times. He heard the man say the words "Allahu Akbar" before he died.

Nick left the room after he heard the last gun shot. He saw Mariam on the floor and ran to her; she was curled up in the fetal position. He approached her and said her name, "Mariam, It's me, Nick."

She could not believe she heard Nick's voice. She reached out for him and he lay on the floor beside her. He took off his shirt and gave it to her. She put it on. He hated seeing her in this condition.

"What are you doing here? I thought you left."

"Walid, Sami's cousin, the person who is arranging the flight for you from Annaba, can't be reached. Since Sami could not contact him, I was worried. I didn't want to leave without knowing you were safe."

"What about everyone else?"

"The helicopters took off about 30 minutes ago. Everyone is safe."

Mariam hugged and kissed Nick.

Sami came out and looked in the other bedroom. He saw the man on the ground and approached him cautiously. The man did not move. He rolled him over, he saw the broken nose and his tongue hanging out of his mouth. He knew he was dead. He had forgotten Nick knew some form of Martial Arts. He went to check for Fatima.

Nick helped Mariam get up. He was taking her to the bathroom, but after she took a few steps, she yelled "Tima." She left Nick and made her way to the guest bedroom. She saw that Fatima was still in the hamper.

"Mariam, are you all right?" She hugged her big sister, but kept asking if Mariam was fine.

"I am fine, it's nothing." Mariam hugged her for a few minutes.

Nick and Sami watched them. Nick was happy that both were fine. He thought about the man in the other room. Nick had never killed a man with his hands before. He was a little unsettled. He wanted to make sure Mariam wasn't hurt too badly before going to the airport.

Mariam walked out with Fatima. "Sami, can you watch her while I clean up?" Sami agreed and took her downstairs. Nick and Mariam went to the bathroom.

Nick sat with Mariam in the bathroom wiping her face with a towel. Her face was swollen and a few ribs were bruised, but he did not think anything was broken. There was a deep groove around her neck that was already turning black. "What happened here, Mariam?"

"They choked me with a electrical wire."

Nick was furious, but did not want to upset her. He wiped the blood from her face. He saw that most of the blood came from a long cut on her arm and a slash on her stomach. He wrapped a towel around the cut. "I will get a bandage for your arm." Nick got up and left for a few minutes. When he came back, he noticed that she was just staring at the wall. "What's wrong? Is there some other pain or wound?"

"No, I was just thinking about my father and what democracy meant to him. You know he fought in the war of independence."

Nick nodded.

"My father always told me that if something is worth having, you must fight for it. I know what he means now. I was ready to die to protect Tima."

Nick continued wrapping her arm in the bandage. He felt sorry for her. She had gone through so much in the last few days.

Sami was sitting downstairs when he received a phone call. "Allo, Husayn, how are you?"

"Busy, but I was worried about you when I heard about the embassy. Are you okay?"

"I am well."

"I called because I wanted to know what happened there. The government will get hell when this becomes public. Is there anything I can do?"

"No. We were attacked but we were able to escape." Sami relayed the whole story to his boss and the attack at his house.

"I am happy that you are well. What's your plan now?"

"I am with Nick, Mariam Al-Qana'i and her sister and we are on our way to the airport in Annaba. Nick and Mariam will go to Tunis and I will report after I drop them off about 10:00 or 11:00 p.m. tonight."

"Mariam Al-Qana'i, how did she get involved in this whole thing?"

"She and Nick have been dating for a while and after her parents were killed, I decided to bring her here. I thought it was the best thing to do since she was probably in danger also."

"You were right to bring her there. You did the right thing. Take care of yourself, Sami. I am sorry that your friends were attacked. I should have listened to you about putting more protection at the American Embassy. I want a full debrief later. Look on the bright side. You will probably get promoted out of this event. Good job." Husayn clicked off the line.

Sami rang off and thought about what his boss had said. It would be good to get a promotion. He had deserved one for the last few years, but the work he did at the embassy was not looked upon as real investigation work, so he had not been promoted.

Sami felt tired but decided to call his cousin again. His phone said the cell phone user he was calling was out of the coverage area. He thought that they would just go to Annaba and see him there. Sami was sure he could arrange another flight if his cousin wasn't there. Sami watched Fatima eat a bowl of ice cream. She seemed to have forgotten everything already. He was always amazed at how kids were so resilient.

Nick waited for Mariam in the room. She wanted to shower and put on some other clothes. After she had left her parents' home, she didn't have a chance to get any of her things at her apartment. Sami's maid had lent her some clothes. While she was in pain, she was also mad at these extremists. First they killed her parents, and now they had tried to kill her. She cleaned herself up and got dressed.

"Are you feeling better?"

"A little, but I need some aspirin."

"Let's get some ice on your face. It will be less painful." Nick and Mariam went downstairs.

Nick and Sami sat together while Mariam applied ice to her face. Her face was badly bruised, but otherwise she appeared fine for someone who was just assaulted. Nick always admired her strength.

"Sami, how do you think they knew she was here?"

"I don't know, but maybe someone at the scene saw me talking to her and figured out she came here."

"That's doesn't seem plausible. Mariam, did they say how they knew you were here?"

"Nick, they didn't know I was here. They came looking for Sami and assumed I was his wife."

Sami and Nick looked at each other.

"They kept saying that because he worked for the Americans he was an infidel and therefore must be punished. I knew they would kill me if they knew who I really was, so I kept my mouth shut hoping that they would not kill me. They wanted to know where Sami was and I told them I didn't know."

"Sami, it seems weird that they would come after you, right after they attacked the embassy."

"You're right, Nick. They obviously knew I was with you today while the embassy was being attacked. These guys have to be connected with the attack today. They were probably trying to find out where I was taking you guys to be evacuated. If they sent one group, they will send another. We have to get out of here now, Nick."

Nick agreed with Sami and got up. He told Mariam to get Fatima ready to leave.

Sami ran upstairs and pulled out two AK-47 assault rifles from his wall safe.

"Where did you get that?" asked Nick.

"I took it off of some terrorists we arrested. I thought it would be useful to have."

"My friend, you are always prepared."

Sami pulled out ammunition and told Nick to grab food from the refrigerator. They gathered their gear and went to the door. Nick asked Sami to pull up the truck. He would stand guard as they left the house. Mariam and Fatima went down the stairs and got into the Suburban once Sami brought the vehicle to the entrance. Nick pulled the door shut and ran to the car.

-Fifty-One-

Husayn Al-Shami sat in his office at the Ministry of Interior thinking about his conversation with Sami. He cursed to himself. He could not believe the Americans had already left the country. Abu Fahad would be upset and he hoped that it would not affect his plan. He had been trying to call Sami since he talked with Abu Fahad at the embassy. He figured that the cell phone network had become overloaded because of all the activity in the country.

Ever since Abu Fahad had propositioned him at his wife's house, he had decided to help him bring about a new government. As Abu Fahad was his wife's cousin, he always knew he was a devout Muslim who wanted to make some changes, but he had no idea what type of changes he wanted.

Abu Fahad had approached him one year ago and asked him for a favor. He was meeting with his group of friends and wanted to know if any police patrols would be around. Because he was his wife's relative, he felt obligated to help. After he did, Abu Fahad had come to him and asked him if he were the head of the Ministry of Interior, what would he do differently? He had spent hours explaining how bad the security services were and how they never listened to his suggestions. Abu Fahad had confided in him a few weeks later that he knew some people who wanted to reinstate the election results of 1991 and install an Islamic government. He wanted to know what he thought about that idea. Husayn explained that he did not have any problems with the idea as long as it didn't affect him. Abu Fahad struck a deal with him a few weeks later: if he helped his friends and the government fell, he would be appointed the Minister of the Interior in the new Islamic republic. Husayn was 50 years old with five children that he had to put through college. He wanted to better his situation and provide his children with a nice life. Husayn had agreed but never thought that Abu Fahad had enough influence to pull it off.

Husayn called Abu Fahad. Abu Fahad was upset. He had been calling Ali, Ra'id and Karim for the last 30 minutes with no answer. They should have called him by now. He called a few of his men to make sure the plan was still going along smoothly. The attacks had the government unsettled. After a few more days of this type of activity, the shaykh would come out and ask for the 1991 election results to be reinstated. He would join forces with certain military leaders to form a new Islamic government. He would hold elections but Abu Fahad was sure that the Islamists would win. The shaykh's plan rested on his ability to topple this current government. Now that the most important government leaders were killed, the void was open for the shaykh and his high Islamic council. The shyakh had been cultivating relationships with various mid-level military officers. He had promised them top positions of military units if they supported his cause. Most agreed to assist the shaykh for fear of being killed. The shaykh had picked his officers carefully, he chose only people who he thought would agree to help for promise of a much higher position later. Abu Fahad marveled at the old man's brilliance.

Abu Fahad's phone rung. "Allo, it's me. I have some bad news for you. The Americans have already left the country, but Nick Phillips, the American Charge, and Mariam Al-Qana'i are still here. Mariam and Nick are dating each other and that officer, Sami, is helping them. He took the Americans to a place to be evacuated and now he will take them to the airport. They killed your men at his house. I am sorry about the men, but now I know where they are going."

Abu Fahad hated this fat pig. Getting information from him was like skinning a sheep; it took hours. "Where are they going?"

"It's getting tough around here; people may suspect me. Is it possible to give me an advance on my future salary? I need a few thousand dinars."

Abu Fahad would kill this man when he was finished with him. "No problem. I will have someone drop it off at your house today."

Husayn knew he would be able to get some money out of him. "They are going to the airport in Annaba. They were just leaving his house when I was talking to them. It would probably take them about two hours to get there."

"Shokran (thank you)." Abu Fahad looked at his watch. It would take them about 90 minutes to make it from where he was. He could not believe that they had left, but it didn't matter because he would get the one who killed his brother. He thought of the bonus. Mariam Al-Qana'i, daughter of Ahmad Al-Qan'ai, confidente of the president, was dating this infidel. She would also be killed at the same time. "Alhamdilillah (praise be to God)," yelled Abu Fahad.

Amir asked what had happened. Abu Fahad explained that they would have a chance to get the American. He told them where they would meet up with him. He would kill the American, Mariam and the traitor Sami. He would cut his heart from his chest in front of the shamuta. He would be able to tell the story for years how he killed the American, face to face. His legend would grow even larger. He would use this act to raise his stature even higher in the eyes of the Muslims.

"Do you want me to have some of the other groups meet us there?"

"No, we will kill them ourselves. The four of us should not have any problem with two men and one girl."

Abu Fahad reveled in the thought of what he would do to the American when he saw him. "I told you we would meet again, Mr. Phillips."

-Fifty-Two-

"How do these work, Sami? I have never seen an AK-47 before, unless you count an hour ago when we were being fired upon."

Sami said, "That is funny, my friend. This is an AK-47 assault rifle. It is 7.62 caliber and has a muzzle velocity of 2,950 feet per second. It holds a 30 round magazine and it has a folding stock. Look on the right side. See that small handle? That's how you chamber a round in the barrel. Pull that back and you are ready to go. Just one thing, it fires fully automatic and semi-automatic. That switch below the charging bolt is what changes modes. Move the switch to the center position and the rifle will fire 600 rounds per minute on full automatic. Move it to the lower position for single round shots."

Nick had known that Sami knew weapons because of all the time he spent at the gun range every month. Nick became familiar with the rifle and made sure that it was loaded. He also reloaded Sami's pistol. He had fired guns before but he had never thought he would be in this situation. When he saw that man standing over Mariam's bloody body, the only thought that went through his mind was to hurt him. He had never felt that way before. He thought he had lost her and he wanted to make that man pay.

Nick thought about all the time he had spent training in Martial Arts. Nick remembered when his first instructor had asked him why he wanted to take Martial Arts; he had said he wanted more discipline and to compete in a sport that was not team-oriented. His instructor, Master Hiroshi, told Nick he was lying. He explained that Martial Arts was about one thing – fighting. He said no matter how much one philosophizes about developing character and walking in peace, if he's a true warrior then he began by learning to fight and planned to spend the rest of his life honing his combat skills.

He told Nick that it was all right to take Martial Arts to learn how to fight, but at least be true to the art and himself. He went on to say that peace and character development were important parts of learning the art, but strength and confidence were its foundations, and the warrior must learn to walk without fear. In every confrontation, he stressed that you must be willing to die if you truly wanted to prevail. Most people focused on not getting hurt, which limited their ability to defend themselves. He taught Nick that true power resulted from releasing your anxieties, which would allow one to fight at one's true peak. He told Nick that this released his true inner power, or chi.

Nick now understood what he meant. When he saw that Mariam may have been killed, he did not think about himself being hurt; he focused all of his internal energy on defeating his opponent. Nick silently thanked his instructor.

"Sami, how will we get to the airport and how long will it take?"

"It would only take about two hours normally, but that is if we use the main roads. I don't trust those roads. Once we get out of the city, we will take the back roads which will take us almost three hours. I know it's slower, but it's safer."

"I trust your instincts, Sami. You haven't led us wrong yet. By the way, Mushkur (it is appreciated). I know that you are doing this not because it's your job, but because we are your friends. I want you to know that I can't put my appreciation into words."

"I understand, Nick."

Sami concentrated on his driving duties because he wanted to get Nick and Mariam out of the country safely. He could not believe what had happened today. He looked in the rear view mirror at Mariam. She was talking to her sister. She seemed as if nothing had happened. She was a very strong woman. He knew that she hadn't had time to mourn for her parents or brother. It would hit her later, once everything settled down. He had seen this phenomenon before. As long as the adrenaline was still pumping, she would be fine. Since her parents had been killed, she had been taking care of Fatima, making calls to politicians, and talking to her family. He hoped Nick understood what type of stress she was under. She may seem fine, but she had undergone more traumatic events in 48 hours than most people see their whole lives.

Mariam was in the back with Fatima talking about what they would see in Tunisia. She had wanted to take the little girl's mind off of what had happened. She saw them drive out of the city by way of the Casbah. She thought how beautiful it once looked. They passed the Theatre National Algerien and the St. Augustine Monastery, two of the most beautiful sites on the Rue Ahmad Bouzrina. She could also see portions of the Palais de Justice. What shocked her were the burned out cars and barricades sitting along the road. She could not believe what was happening to her father's beautiful dream. The once glamorous Casbah looked like a war zone. As she looked out the window to see the Palais du Government where her father used to work and made his speeches, a tear ran down her face.

Sami left the Casbah and turned onto the N5. He had to drive on this main road for a few miles before he could take N24, which followed the coast until Annaba. He prayed that they saw no more roadblocks since Nick didn't seem to have another 10,000 Algerian dinar on him. He turned onto N24, hoping he was taking the best route.

Mariam liked the coast road because it had been untouched by a lot of development. It reminded her of Algeria of long ago. She thought about the outings her family used to go on when she was a little girl. Her brother always made her sit in the backseat because she was a girl. He was so young at that time, only 12, and thought that being a man meant that he was supposed to treat women as second class citizens. She laughed to herself. When her dad found out he was treating her that way, he had explained to his son that only backward desert nomads treated their women like that. He told her brother that a real man must protect the weak and leave those backward traditions behind them. He stressed that in today's society, he should help educate those who believed women were inferior. Her brother went on to become one of her biggest supporters in the women's movement. She tried to hold back her tears.

Nick tried to think about what he would say to his superiors in Washington. He would probably be posted to the embassy in Papau, New Guinea, if he wasn't outright fired. Nick laughed; he would have a lot of experience for Papau, New Guinea. That post was probably the worst assignment in the world because of all the violent crime that took place there. More divorces had come out of that embassy than embassies five times that size. As a way to improve the quality of life there, they started a program that would allow spouses to only spend six months a year there. Nick could probably be the ambassador there after this assignment.

Nick looked at Sami and thought that a person could not have such a good friend as him. He found himself wondering what would happen to him after they left. He saw Sami as his brother and could not bear the thought of him being killed. "Hey, Sami, I don't suppose I can convince you to come with me. We could probably give you some sort of asylum in Tunis because of the danger associated with being an officer in the Ministry of Interior."

"Nick, it's tempting, but as I said earlier, this is my country and I will not leave it without a fight. I have fought these people for the last eight years. I can't be like the ones who don't care enough about this country to stay. People are leaving in droves. How do you think that Iran became an Islamic country? First the people rose up and begin to demonstrate and protest. That activity went on for a few years. When it got too bad, on 16 January 1979, Muhamad Reza Shah left Iran. Less than two weeks later Ayatollah Khomeini arrived at the airport in Tehran. Within weeks of his arrival, Iranians from the intelligentsia, merchant class, scientific community and the government left the country. This was all before the Islamists changed the constitution or established their first Islamic high council. They gave the country to that maniac. I will not give my country to them. They will have to take it from me. Don't worry, Sami's no martyr. I still have your visa in my passport; if everything turns to khara (shit), I will go."

Nick always thought it was funny when Arabs spoke in third person. In the Middle East, it was done more often than in the West.

"I see your point and respect that. Well, if you change your mind, you have my address in the States. If I am not there I will probably be in a cardboard box on Pennsylvania Avenue, that's after I am fired."

Sami laughed, "Come on, Nick, they can't fault you for doing what you did. Your leadership saved fifteen lives at the embassy today. They can't dismiss that."

"They won't dismiss it, but they will probably look upon my not being evacuated with the rest of the embassy unfavorably. I am sorry I brought it up. Let's skip that subject and move on to something more cheerful, like whether or not we will see another roadblock of blood-thirsty nomads looking to chop us into little pieces."

"Nick! Don't forget Fatima's back here. You are lucky she doesn't speak much English, but be careful of what you say. Okay?"

"I'm sorry, I guess we are all a little out of sorts because of the day's events."

"I know what you mean. I am trying not to think about what could have happened to me. Thank you for saving me. I just think of what those animals could have done to me, and it gives me the chills. They had no remorse. They weren't raving lunatics; they were lucid and believed in what they were saying. What was even more alarming was that they did what they did because they thought it was what Allah wanted. You couldn't negotiate with them. They were there for a mission and either way they succeeded. I have heard their speeches; they say the shortest way to Jinna (paradise) is by Jihad. If they succeed, we lose and die. If they lose and die, in their eyes they still win. It's insanity."

Nick could tell that she was caught up it in the moment. He had been expecting some reaction to the week's events. She continued, "They blow up anything they want, kill anyone they please and justify it by saying that they were only carrying out Allah's will. That's not Islam; they are worse than those they call Kufar (infidels). You should have heard the conviction in their voices; they had no doubt or uncertainty. They were ready to die for their cause."

Nick leaned back to face her. "It's all right. You are safe now and will be even safer in two hours."

"Nick," she said, "with this phenomenon of Islamic extremism, we will never be safe. We are susceptible everywhere. Wherever you have people who take advantage of uneducated people, the possibility for type of violence can exist. They use most of the people to obtain their own goal. I heard Sami talking about Iran. Do you think those people in Iran today are better off now than under the Shah twenty-one years ago? The answer is no. The standard of living is worse now than previous thirty years. What is different? The people at the top who are making the laws and making the money." Nick knew she was right.

The three of them sat in silence after Mariam finished her speech.

-Fifty-Three-

Abu Fahad and his group would take the main road of N5 to get to Annaba. They were not concerned with the military or the police. His groups were doing so much damage in the west that the eastern part of the country was open territory for them. He had instructed his men to place periodic roadblocks to catch people who were leaving. Those who would escape Allah's justice would find that His arm has a long reach. After they consolidated their power in the new Islamic republic, Abu Fahad would send out teams to find those who robbed and stole money from the country. He would go after those who sold rights to the foreigners to pillage their oil and natural gas industries. Algeria was the world's largest producer of liquefied natural gas and had income from oil, mining, and agriculture. There was no reason that unemployment should be a serious problem as well as having a poor diet and living conditions for lower classes. There was no reason other than the nationalist's greed that kept the country poor. They would all feel their wrath. The new Islamic republic would take care of everyone. No one would be poor or rich. Everyone would have what they needed.

Abu Fahad was the sword of Allah, like Khalid Ibn Walid, the great Muslim leader. He would bring back the new glory days of Islam. He knew that the Muslims were capable of doing it. They had the greatest empire in the world from 711 until 1258. The world had never seen such an empire before. It spanned from Spain to India to China as well as North Africa. He had studied history under the shaykh; he knew that life was cyclical. The Muslims would be great again. Did they not perform the first successful brain operations, create algebra, introduce the alphabet and the concept of zero, and give the world Avicenna, without whom the West would not have been able to read Aristotle's work? The shaykh was right: Abu Fahad would help make the Muslims rulers of the world again.

After Abu Fahad completed his Jihad and they were in power, he would return home. His family lived in the southern desert near Tamanrasset. He had not been home for over two years. He was afraid of the security services following him home and using his family against him.

He thought about Fahad, his oldest son. He remembered the last conversation he had with him. "Ta'al Ibni (come here, my son). Your father must leave to exert the supreme effort for Allah. I must go and I may not come back again. If I do not return, then you will be the lord of the house. You should know that if I die, it will be for fighting in Allah's cause."

Abu Fahad had started teaching his son the Qur'an from a very early age. He could not understand the meaning of many of the chapters but he knew many sections by memory. Abu Fahad had instructed his son in how he needed to live even if he wasn't there to guide him. He had stressed the following values: that humans can't control all events; that some things depend on Allah; that piety is one of the most admirable characteristics in a person; that there should be no separation between church and state; and that religious tenets should not be subjected to liberal interpretations or modifications which can threaten established beliefs or practices. He had also warned his son about certain things, such as the Arab peoples having been victimized and exploited by the West. The Palestinian issue was one of the more painful and obvious examples. But the most important value he tried to instill in his son was that loyalty to one's family takes precedence over personal needs.

Abu Fahad had hoped that he taught his son everything he needed to know before he left home. He knew it was hard on his wife for him to be gone for so long, but at least she believed in his cause. He loved her and his three kids and wanted an Algeria he could be proud of, even if he would have to die for it.

"Abu Fahad, after we kill the American, what will be our next mission?"

"We will go to the house of the shaykh so we can be ready when the government falls. He will come out from hiding and he will need his most trusted mujahidin beside him to watch over him. You are my most trusted tribesmen, so you will be there with me. After we complete this act, we will one step closer to Jinna (Paradise)."

"Allahu Akbar (God is great)."

Abu Fahad sat back, thinking about the best way to ambush the American and his friends at the airport.

He knew this airport. It was very small with no real terminals. It was mainly used for private trips from very rich Algerians who kept their planes there. His men did not control many locations in the east, but it wasn't necessary because they would just go and wait for them in the main hangar. They would cause a disturbance such as an explosion and then in the confusion, he would kill them. The airport should be destroyed because only the rich used it. After they were dead, he would make sure that no one else could use the airport.

"So what does your cousin do at the airport?" asked Nick.

"He has been a mechanic there for three years."

"Do you think that he is still there and will he help us?"

"He is like me, he would not leave unless the situation became extremely bad."

"How close are you with him? You had told me that he's your cousin."

"Well, we are very close. You know in the Middle East we have no word in Arabic for cousin. We say either my paternal aunt's son or maternal aunt's son, like that. We only say cousin because it said in the west. But with us Kabyle, a cousin is just as close as a brother because he still shares the same bloodline. He will help us to get you, Mariam and Fatima out of the country."

Nick looked at Mariam and thought that she looked sad. He tried to put himself in her shoes, but it was hard. She had gone through so much. He had hoped that she could get over the trauma. He would propose to her in Tunis after he bought a ring. He thought about their life together in the States. She was a graphic artist. He knew a lot of companies in D.C. that would love to hire her. He would place the calls as soon as he arrived in the States.

He really didn't think that the situation would change back so quickly. He felt the country would become an Islamic state. He would be in Washington until they officially decided to close the embassy. The State Department would only say that the embassy was temporary closed because of a current unstable situation. If the problem existed for more than a few months, then the Department would have to make a decision: either recognize the new government and establish relations or officially pull its embassy from the country. Nick thought as it was, Algeria would need to pay reparations for the destruction of U.S. Government property. Nick laughed at that thought. We would demarche them by asking them to pay us reparations. The new Islamic government would probably say, 'Fuck you! Come and get it, infidel.'

Nick knew the government would try and carry out its normal diplomatic procedures, but he thought these people would not respond as the U.S. was accustomed to. Nick thought it was hard to have diplomatic relations with a country who sliced and diced Westerners into small pieces because they were Christians or Jews. Nick thought about Iran. *They took our embassy and held hostages and after 21 years, we were only now making some small gestures at diplomatic reconciliation.* Nick sat back, thinking about American diplomacy.

Mariam continued to look out of the window after her outburst. She could only focus on her father and his efforts in the country. If he were alive, he would be horrified at what was going on in the country. He was such a role model and statesman. How could they just kill him like a dog?

"Look!" said Mariam. About 200 yards ahead in the street was a military checkpoint.

"Sami, what should we do?" asked Nick.

Sami slowed the vehicle down and looked at Nick. "There are never check points on this coast road because it's not traveled much. I am sure it's not a real check point."

"Do you think you can talk us through it again?"

"Do you have any more money that we can bribe them with?"

"No."

"I think we should run it, because if we stop, we will be killed. Nick, take the assault rifle and fire a few rounds at them on fully automatic to let them know we are serious. Try to take out the vehicles so they will not be able to follow us." Nick looked at the men who stood along the side of the road in old fatigues. The men only had two wooden barricades across the road. Nick counted six men.

Sami gunned the engine and the car quickly picked up speed. Nick leaned out of the window and started firing the weapon on fully automatic mood.

Hussam saw the vehicle slow down a few hundred meters in front of their checkpoint. His group had already stopped two cars during the day. The first one contained a husband and wife who were trying to flee Algiers on their way to Tunis. They killed the man quickly, but the women gave them some pleasure before they sent her to receive Allah's judgment. The second car tried to run after they stopped it. An older man who said he was a colonel in the Army demanded to know the unit number of Hussam's unit. He tried to run the blockade when Hussam laughed at him. They shot out the tires and approached the car from all sides. They had pulled him out of the car and beat him before stabbing him in the throat with their knives. The arrogant ass thought that he could order him around. Well, he got what he deserved. This was the third. It looked like a large SUV, but it was hard to tell from so far away.

Hussam had set up in Jijel because he thought he would catch people who were trying to avoid the main roads. He was acting on his own, but his group was allied with GIA and the other tribal groups. The GIA leadership had allowed him to operate in this portion of Algeria, but he had to pay a portion of what he stole to the GIA. He didn't mind because they allowed him to operate semi-autonomously. Today was different because he had received a call from Mehdi, one of the Taureg tribal leaders and a commander in the GIA. He was honored just be talking to this man. Hussam had been instructed by Mehdi to keep a look out for a large SUV that carried Americans. Mehdi told him to call him immediately if they saw the trucks. He had explained that Abu Fahad had wanted the vehicle stopped and the people killed. Hussam was from a small tribe but everybody knew about Abu Fahad. It was said that he had the ear of the shaykh. If he could find the Americans, he could possibly join Abu Fahad's main group. That meant prestige and more money. He saw the car speed up, and someone leaned out of the window. He yelled to his men to take cover.

Nick fired the weapon at the men on the checkpoints; they scattered out of the way very quickly. He did not want to kill them, but just wound them and shoot at their tires of the vehicles. He fired repeatedly at the vehicles and the men but found it hard to aim properly from the window. A few fired back at Nick. Nick leaned back into the car. The bullets ricocheted off of the windows and reinforced frame. Nick was glad that they were in the embassy car.

"Watch out, Nick. The glass is bullet resistant, not bulletproof, and be careful not to lean out too much," shouted Sami. Nick stuck his hands out of the windows with the weapon but kept most of his body inside of the vehicle and started firing again.

Hussam dived to the ground but continued shooting at the vehicles. He only had a pistol and was outmatched by the man firing an assault rifle. The vehicle neared the checkpoint and crashed the wooden barricades without any trouble. Hussam's men got up and fired at the back of the fast moving vehicle. He cursed to himself. He called his men, "See which car is working and we will follow them," he ordered. He noticed that the man shooting looked western; it was probably the ones that Mehdi wanted. He didn't want to tell Mehdi that they had run past them, but he might still be able to get catch them.

"Are they following us?" asked Nick.

"No, Nick. They are trying to decide which car to use. You really took care of their cars."

Nick was still pumped up; he kept looking in the back window, knowing they would come after them. "Sami, I think we should get off this road for a while in case they decide to follow us."

"Good idea." Sami turned the car onto the unpaved gravel. The ride was rough and bumpy because of the uneven surface of the ground. Sami switched the gear into four-wheel drive, and it drove smoother.

"So, where are we and where are we going now?"

"Nick, when I was a child my father used to take me hunting around here. I still remember a lot of the terrain." Nick had seen that the forest paralleled the road they were traveling on. "We will go through this forest for a while on our way to Cheddia. It's a small town that specializes in agriculture. We can go around that city and get back on N43 near Taher. It will add about 30 minutes to our trip, but they will not think to look for us here."

"It's a good thing you know these woods from when you were a kid. Although it's not dense, it seems fairly hard to know where you are going." Before Nick had come to Algeria he had thought it to be a desert country. He was pleasantly surprised to learn that the country had numerous forests, marshes and saline lakes. The whole northern part of the country was covered with many wooded areas and streams. Nick and Mariam had gone on many picnics together and canoed down some of its small streams. Nick had discovered that some of best fishing in the Middle East came from the small lakes in the country. Nick had marveled at the vast geographic differences in the country. In the north the country was relatively fertile and mountainous, while in the south, the Sahara desert expanded for thousands of miles. Nick found himself staring out at the scenery as Sami sped through the woods.

Hussam called Mehdi. "Salaam Alaikum (peace be onto you)."

Mehdi replied, "Wa Laikum Salaam (and onto you peace)."

"It's Hussam. I saw the large SUV that the American was in. My men slowed it down and now we are about to follow him."

"Where is he now?"

"Well, he was on N43 about a few kilometers east of Jijel."

"Wait before you do anything, I will call you back in a few minutes."

Mehdi was excited. He called Abu Fahad. "Cousin, we have found the American; he is traveling east on N43 towards Skikda. Some of our brothers who were manning a checkpoint saw him and are about to go after him."

Abu Fahad thought about where the SUV was located. If the American was going east towards Skikda, then Annaba was only 75 kilometers further east of that city. Husayn was right; they were going to the airport there. He wanted to take them at the airport and not have some amateur mess up his plan. If they saw the group following them or thought it was a trap, then the American would change his plans. No, Abu Fahad thought, he didn't want them going after those people. He would see Mr. Phillips in Annaba.

"Mehdi, I know where they are going and I have a plan to stop them. Tell our brothers thank you, but do not go after them. Tell them that they have done well and will be rewarded, but under no circumstances are they to be followed. Think of some way to thank them."

"Hadar (it will be done), I will tell them right now."

Abu Fahad did not want the group to follow them to impress him. So many of the young Islamists knew of him and wanted to get in his good graces. He looked at the phone and knew that his plan was coming together.

"Brother, I have spoken to Abu Fahad and he appreciates your efforts. He told me to tell you that you will be rewarded. Come to my camp in Bab el-Oued tomorrow, we will talk."

"Shokran and Ma'salaam (goodbye)."

Hussam was elated. He would meet Mehdi and possibly Abu Fahad. "Ya shabab (oh men), we will not follow them. We have done our duty."

Abu Fahad was going to be ready when he met Nick Phillips. He had trained for years to be a holy warrior. No American would be able to defeat him. He had no fear of dying. He would cut the American, make him bleed and see how arrogant he would be then. He remembered the lessons taught to him by the Bosnians. They were the best at torture because they had suffered so harshly at the hands of the Serbians. Through that type of pain, one discovered ways of hurting their enemy that surpassed their own ordeal. He had watched several interrogations by the Bosnians. They would not even ask questions until they sliced off a piece of skin or cut off a finger. They called that process motivating the participant. Abu Fahad had brought those techniques back from Bosnia and introduced the techniques to his tribesmen. Although he had learned much in Bosnia, he had learned how to become a true warrior from the Arab Afghans who returned to Algeria in the early 1990s.

Many of the Algerians who left for the Jihad in the 1980s never made it back, but the ones who did were fierce fighters. Abu Fahad spent many nights hearing their stories. Most of the times they lived on nothing more than dry bread and tea. They only wore old worn out sandals, whether climbing mountains or walking through the desert. These warriors learned how to withstand the demanding nomadic life required for combating the Russians. They did not carry rations or canteens. They often had to get their water where they found it. Abu Fahad went through numerous camps run by these mujahidin in the Sahara Desert. At the end of his training, he was presented with an Afghan dagger, a unique looking knife with a t-shaped blade and a camel bone handle that was curled at the end. He touched his knife that rested inside of his robes and smiled; he had killed many with it, and he had a few more to kill before the evening was over.

-Fifty-Four-

Sami wheeled the Suburban expertly through the paths in the forest. He knew these trails would lead them out to the small back road near Taher. He drove through at breakneck speed.

"Slow down, Sami. I don't think anyone is behind us and I don't want us to run off the road. How are you doing, Mariam?" Nick was worried about her because she hadn't said much since the incident at the checkpoint.

"I am fine. I am more worried about Fatima." During the incident, she had put her hands over her ears and just screamed. She could tell that she was afraid. Mariam had been trying to calm her by telling her stories. Mariam had learned the Thousand and One Nights when she was a little girl and knew that Fatima loved those stories, too. Fatima at first had asked her why Nick was shooting at the men and why they were shooting back at them. Mariam gave her a quick answer before going on to the stories. Fatima wasn't paying much attention to her; she wanted to know why the men had tried to hurt her in the house and now at the checkpoint. Mariam knew that it was time to tell Fatima the whole story. She begin by explaining how their father was a powerful man in the government who wanted the people to be able to choose what they wanted instead of being told what to do by the religious fanatics. She described the colonial period under the French and how her father had fought against the imperialists and won. When the religious extremists tried to take over the country, her father had fought against them, too, but this time, he did not succeed. "The extremists killed him along with mother and our brother."

Fatima stared at her blankly for a moment before she started to cry. She kept asking Mariam why they had to kill their parents and brother. She asked who these people were and how they could be stopped so they would not kill anybody else's daddy and mommy. Mariam hugged her sister and tried confronting her. She sobbed and cried for almost 30 minutes before telling Mariam that it was not fair that they killed her parents. Mariam just sat there holding her. Nick tried not to look in the back seat because it was too hard emotionally to see this little girl learn a very harsh lesson about life. Fatima fell asleep in Mariam's lap. Nick looked at Mariam and he saw tears in her eyes.

Sami pulled the truck onto the road. He had just made it to Taher and was only two hours from Annaba. He looked at the gas gauge. It read half full. He knew the vehicle had two large fuel tanks and that they would have no problem making it to the airport without getting gas.

Muhammad asked Abu Fahad about when he thought the government would fall. He explained that it depended on the shaykh's deals with the military officers and how much chaos they could create in the next few days. "Once we create enough fear among the population, then anything is possible because they would do anything to stop the violence, even establish an Islamic state." This was one of the reasons that all of their acts were extremely bloody and heinous. The brothers wanted to send a message to those in charge: leave or die slowly and painfully. Their plan was working because already many were leaving the country. He knew not many leaders would stay at the possibility of being flayed alive. He laughed; he would let a few escape to talk to the press.

He had studied Afghanistan and the Taliban's takeover. Initially, the international community was outraged. After a while, the world stopped putting pressure on the country and the Taliban eased some of their rules. They would do the same thing. Initially the press would describe how many atrocities were being carried out. It would only keep people away from the country. After they consolidated their rule, they would ease up the restrictions so they could move on to running the country.

Abu Fahad knew that he was a part of something the world had never seen. He and the shaykh had studied history and knew how to use it to their advantage. They knew why the Islamic government in Iran was not doing well, why the Taliban was able to push the Mujahidin out of Afghanistan, and why the Islamic Group was not able to start a revolution in Egypt after killing President Sadat. The shaykh had told Abu Fahad early on that they would win because they would not forget all those historical events that had occurred previously.

Abu Fahad understood why the shaykh put so much trust in him. He believed in the Muslims' superiority over all others. He knew that the Muslims were the only group who once ruled and were now being targeted by extinction by the Western leaders, yet they still survived and would rise up. Did the Muslims not pull one of the biggest terrorist events in history in New York on September 11, 2001? He was happy for days when he read about the event and he had laughed when the Federal Building in Oklahoma City was blown up. They blamed Muslim terrorists and it turned out to be some American who had a grudge against the government. He laughed again.

"How much further until we are there?"

"We should be there in about 30 minutes," said Amir.

Walid Bouteflica stood underneath the engine of the Cessna 182 doing a pre-flight check. He liked the light twin-engine aircraft because it was easy to work on. The plane's owner had called and wanted to leave immediately. Walid had heard of the problems in Algiers and the West, and knew that more people would probably want to leave from his airport. He liked his job at the small airport. Work was slow and his employers were never around. He had been there for three years and had learned how to work on almost every type of plane in that time. His shop was located in a small hangar at the western end of the airport. He would pull the planes inside and work on them out of the sun. He had a nice workshop and all the tools he needed. After he raised enough money, he wanted to start his own business that specialized in working on planes. He would try and work out of the main airport in Algiers and Oran. He wanted to hire other mechanics and establish an office in Algiers, the center of everything in Algeria. Once he had half the money to start his business, he would ask his tribe to supply the other half. One of the good things about coming from a close tribe like the Kabyle was that everyone stuck together.

Walid would have to take special care with this plane since it hadn't been used in almost six months. When the owner had called and said he wanted it ready in an hour, Walid had laughed. He explained to the man that since it hadn't been flown in so long, he would need at least three hours before it was ready. It was already 8:00 p.m. and he had just started. He would miss dinner at his house. His family lived in El-Hadjar a small town about 30 minutes south of the airport. He would have to call his wife and tell her that he would be late.

Abu Fahad had the car pull up about 100 yards from the outside of the tiny airport. It was 8:30 p.m. and extremely dark. He was lucky that they got here at night. It would be easier to do what they had to do. Amir asked Abu Fahad about the airport. "It's not used that much, mostly rich Algerians who have private planes. They have one small terminal which is connected to a tower and the main hangar. I have been here before. I flew out of here the second time I went to Bosnia. We didn't want the Ministry of Interior to track me so I went out of here and there was no record of my trip because I didn't go through immigration. Now, there is one main hangar with several small hangars where people will work on the plane. Since the main hangar is connected to the terminal, I want to go inside and take over that area. We will kill who we have to and wait for them to come. When they arrive, they must go to the main hangar. When I left out of here, after I went inside, they told me to go to the main hangar. I do not want to take the terminal because although it's small, someone may notice that something is wrong and call the police out here. Our influence is not as great in this part of the country.

"After we are finished, we will kill everyone and set the building on fire to let them know we were here. But I think we can do this by just taking the hangar. There should not be many people here at this time. It's not a very busy airport. The American and the infidel should be here in about 45 minutes. We will wait to they come in and kill them, but do not kill the American. He is mine and I want to kill him with my own hands."

Nick had noticed how quiet Mariam was. She hadn't said anything for the last thirty minutes. "Sami, do you think that the extremists have taken this airport?" he asked.

"I don't, because it's so far west. It seems like the main objective of the extremists is to take the west and Algiers because those are the most important areas in the country. There is nothing in the east, and therefore that area will be easiest for them to take if they succeed in toppling the government. They have no reason to move this far east at this time. But I will call one of my friends to check."

Sami pulled out his cell phone and made the phone call. He spoke for five minutes and didn't seem happy when he hung up. "That was a friend of mine in the west. He told me that the Islamists are gaining groups and have also started moving south. They have not heard of any major disturbances in the east. There are still the random attacks, like the checkpoint we passed, but everything in all the east is relatively calm. That being the case, I think we should still be cautious until I get you on a plane."

"Tell me more about this airport, Sami."

"It's been around only for about 30 years but it's a small semi-private facility. All of the main air traffic goes out of the international airport or at Oran. I think I remember only one small terminal and a large main hangar. I want to try my cousin again." Sami dialed the number but was not able to get his number.

"Do you have the phone number of the airport?" Nick asked.

"No, I will try the operator to see if I can get the number." Sami attempted to get an operator, but those lines were busy. "Phone service will be like this until the crisis calms down. Our telecommunications system is not prepared for all the calls that are being made right now. Because the extremists had opposed having a western company installing fiber optics, we will continue to have problems getting through. I think we should just go there and see if he's there. He works late a lot. If he is not there, he will probably be at his home, which is not too far away."

"That sounds good, Sami, but I want to make sure that we don't get too overconfident, because we have already seen these guys do things that I never thought were possible. I thought the embassy was impenetrable. I still don't know how they got inside. Do you?"

"Nick, I think someone let them in. One or two of the local guards probably was bribed or coerced assist them. That's the only way. Gunny's men were monitoring everything."

"I guess you are right, but it's been bothering me for a while." Nick sat there think about what Sami said about the airport and how the men could get in.

Mariam sat in the back listening to their conversation. She was having so many emotions go through her. Her head was hurting, as well as all the cuts on her. She had pain all over her face and felt ashamed by the men seeing her naked. She was starting to feel sick, but attributed it to the attack. She looked at Fatima sleeping and thought how her life had changed so much. Her parents had been killed and her country would most likely undergo a political upheaval. How would her sister remember the country when she left?

Mariam took a few more aspirin but knew she needed something stronger. She was having problems keeping her mind from thinking about what had happened to her parents and herself.

"How far are we from the airport?" Nick asked Sami.

"We should be there within the hour. It's hard to see at night because there are not a lot of lights there. It's totally different than the international airport or the one at Oran. I think you will be surprised how small it is. Mostly wealthy Algerians use it to travel in and out of the country."

"Pull around to the back gate," said Abu Fahad. "We will kill the guard there. I don't want to kill the guard at the front gate because it may alert the American that we are here." Amir pulled the car around to the back of the airport. The four men got out of the truck. They checked their weapons. Each had an AK-47 and a knife. Abu Fahad was confident that they would have no problem killing the group.

Abu Fahad approached the gate alone. "Excuse me sir, I have an appointment with Muhammad." The guard asked where he worked. "He works in the main terminal, I have to work on one of the planes." The guard looked at his list. Abu Fahad grabbed him by the throat and shoved his knife in his stomach. The guard tried to strike Abu Fahad, but he easily parried the blow and slit the man's throat. He was amused at the man's attempt to stop him.

"Yalla (let's go)." His men came out of the darkness and walked toward the gate. They entered the back entrance and started walking toward the main hangar.

-Fifty-Five-

Walid had just called his wife to let her know that he would be late. She had told him that she had prepared his favorite rice and chicken dish. He told her to keep it in the oven until he got home. Walid was upset that he would have to work late. The owner of the plane had told him that he wanted to fly to Tunis tonight and would pay an extra hundred dinar if he rushed his pre-flight inspection.

"Do you think they will penalize you for not leaving with your staff?" asked Mariam.

"I am not sure. I will have to explain my argument to them in detail but the important thing to me was that you are safe. Don't worry, I was able to get my staff and the Americans to the helicopter to be evacuated. They can't dispute that fact. What I decide to do after that is my own concern. I can't imagine that they would fire me over that, but if they make too much noise, I can always go to the media. I can see the headlines now: 'Diplomat saves embassy only to be fired for attempting to save local political leader's daughter.' The State Department hates it when they look bad in the media." Nick didn't want her to think that he would get into trouble. The truth was that he didn't know what would happen to him. He would surely be brought in front of a review board to explain his actions. He thought about how John would try and take advantage of his absence. There would be hell to pay.

"Nick, I am happy and appreciative that you came back for me, but I hope that this won't ruin your career." Mariam had felt guilty earlier when she heard Sami and Nick talking about the problems he would have. She had so many thoughts in her head. She remembered what Sulaiman had said about what would happen if the extremists took over the country; the core identity of Algeria would be destroyed. She thought about her father's legacy.

"Nick, we should be approaching the airport soon. I have to take the main road of N44 for the last few kilometers, but I don't think we will have a problem because it's getting late."

"Okay, Sami. I want to check the weapons again and reload the rifles." Nick loaded the magazine in the AK-47 that he had fired and chambered a round. He checked the Beretta that Gunny had given him. He had almost forgotten about it. Sami passed him his pistol and Nick made sure that the magazine was fully loaded.

245

"You're getting good at this, Nick. A few more gun battles and you will be able to field strip the weapon."

Nick grinned and said, "No thanks. After today I think I have had my fill of weapons. I prefer the combat in the Martial Arts arena to this stuff." Nick watched as Sami pulled onto the main road.

Abu Fahad and his group did not walk through the airfield without hiding. They had changed into their indigo-dyed cotton robes and put on their veils. Abu Fahad had told the men to dress in normal Algerian attire for today's attack, but they had brought their own clothes for later. After they killed the guard, they changed before moving inside the airport. They were Tuareg, and their enemies would cringe before them. They continued toward the main hanger. Outside of the hangar, Abu Fahad told his men to gather around.

"Muhammad and Abdallah, you go to the back of the hangar. Do not be seen. Amir and myself will go through the front. In exactly five minutes, we will burst inside and take them. I want no mistakes and no gunfire. We do not want to alert the terminal staff what we are doing. When they get here, we want them to see activity inside the small terminal. When we have the hangar, if someone comes in, kill them. You are the best we have; we should be able to kill the staff without our guns. Now go! Allah Ma'ikum (God be with you)."

Muhammad and Abdallah went slowly around the side of the building to the back. They trusted their leader and knew that he was the best warrior among them. Muhammad eased around the side of the building first. They saw two men outside smoking cigarettes and speaking about a woman that they had seen earlier that day. Because of their dark blue robes the two men never saw them. Muhammad sprang first. He pushed the point if his blade into the first man's throat while Abdallah kicked the other man in stomach and came up behind him. He slit his throat from ear to ear. The two men fell on the ground.

The group kept moving because they had a schedule to keep. Abu Fahad would be upset if they were even a minute late. He demanded perfection and tolerated no excuses. They saw the back hangar door and looked at their watches. Two minutes to go.

Abu Fahad told Amir to go to the side door and he would come in through the front of the main hangar. Abu Fahad saw Amir go to the side of the building. He knew that it would be easy to kill those inside. He had been envisioning how he would kill Nick Phillips. He knew he had to do it up close because it was a matter of family honor now. This man took his brother's life. Nothing other than his death would satisfy him. He would not kill him quickly. He must experience pain as he never had before. Abu Fahad looked at his watch. Five minutes had elapsed. He burst into the hangar at the same time Abdallah and Muhammad came in from the back and Amir from the side door.

Tamer was sitting at his desk sorting out which flights were scheduled to leave this evening. He thought that there would probably be more people requesting to leave later tonight and tomorrow. He had heard from friends at the airport in Oran that the extremists had taken over the airport and the main one in Algiers. He knew that they weren't set up to accommodate a large number of travelers. They offered only small charter services and services for private airline owners. He had two flights leaving in one hour and another at 10:00 p.m.

He was called in from home about an hour ago. He normally did not work on Friday, but because of the anticipated number of flights that management expected, he was called in. It was Friday, his only day off. Because he was poor, he worked six days a week and looked forward to Friday as the day he spent with his family. His wife was upset that he had to leave, but he explained to her how jobs were scarce and that they needed the income from the airport. As most traditional Algerians, his wife didn't work outside of the home. He had hoped that he could leave before 11:00 p.m. At least he could see his children before it became too late.

Tamer was shocked to see the men crash through the door and run into the main hangar. They were dressed in blue and their faces were covered and they had rifles. He was frozen with fear and he could not move.

Abu Fahad led the charge. He was surprised to see only a few people around. He saw the short fat man sitting at the table and correctly determined that he was in charge. He directed Amir to make sure that he did not call anyone or do anything rash; he instructed him not to kill the fat man yet.

Abu Fahad saw a young girl writing flight numbers on a large board. He pointed to Muhammad to kill her. She turned around when she saw him approaching her with a knife in his hand. "Please, no, whatever you want you can have. Don't hurt me." She screamed and Muhammad saw the fear in her eyes.

"Bismilliah (in the name of God)," he shouted as he ran to her and grabbed her hair. She tried to get away but to no avail. He stabbed her in her heart, and she died instantly. He laughed. *That was too easy*, he thought.

Abu Fahad saw a tall, young man of about twenty who ran for the door. He was dressed as a cleaning person. Abu Fahad yelled to Abdallah to get him. Abu Fahad spoke only in a dialect of Berber called Chaouia; no one other than the Tuareg tribe could understand what he said. Abdallah pounced on the young man and pushed his blade into the man's kidney, and he fell.

Abdallah asked him, "Do you believe in Allah?"

"Yes, yes, I do believe in Allah, he is the Lord of the worlds. Yes, I do." The young man was afraid of what would happen if he said he did not believe in Allah.

"That is a good thing, for you shall see him shortly." Abdallah cut his throat and watched his body convulse on the floor.

"Muhammad, check the offices. Abdallah check the bathrooms." Both left and begin checking the other rooms.

Abu Fahad stood with the AK-47 in his hand, making sure no one came in or tried to leave. He walked around and surveyed the hangar. It was large and open, which would make it hard to surprise them. He didn't have a lot of time to come up with a plan, so he would make it simple. He thought that he would sit at the desk and his men would be in the offices and bathroom when they came. They would shoot that kafir first and then the woman; he wanted the diplomat himself. They would have no problem with them. Earlier today, they had the Marines to help them escape, and now they were alone. There were four of them and only two men in the other group. He thought it would be easy.

Abdallah returned from the bathroom and said that no one was there. Abu Fahad ordered him to find a tarp so that they could cover up the blood on the floor. He did not want them to be scared off before coming into the hangar. Abdallah went off to find something to cover the floor.

Muhammad came back and said the place was empty. "Muhammad, go and remove all the bodies, and take them into one of the back offices. Also make sure that there are no large bloody areas that can be seen as you walk inside; when Abdallah returns, I want to discuss our plan."

Abu Fahad walked over the fat man. "Did you see what happened?"

He nodded his head and appeared to be in shock. Abu Fahad hit him in the face and he fell out of his chair and onto the floor.

Tamer lay on the ground bleeding from the nose. He knew he would die. He could only think about his wife and four children. He should not have been here. He said a prayer to Allah to himself.

Amir pulled him off the floor and sat him back in the chair. Abu Fahad looked at the fat man. "If you want to live, then you will answer my questions truthfully. Is there anyone else here?"

He told Abu Fahad that there were only five people working tonight inside the hangar.

"We killed two before we came inside," shouted Abdallah.

"Tell me the procedure at this airport and whether anyone will come in here."

"Well, well, there are two people inside the tower but they never come out here. The terminal is small. There are a few private guards that wander through the tower and terminal, and one person at the main desk inside." He stuttered as he spoke because of his fear.

"What happens when a passenger wants to leave?"

"They will usually go to the terminal first before coming in here to coordinate with me on the times. Since this is a private airport, the planes basically leave when the passenger wants to leave. I tell them when a runway is available for them and they will either wait here or inside, depending on the weather."

Abu Fahad noticed that the fat man was sweating profusely. "These private guards, how many are them, how often do they come in here, and are they armed?"

"They usually only come in every hour or so. They were here about ten minutes ago. They make rounds over the whole airport. There are about five of them: one at the back gate, two at the front entrance and two that roam. They carry handguns."

Abu Fahad was happy to hear that the security was so poor. "Are you expecting anyone to come here within the next 45 minutes?"

"No, Sayidi, I swear no one is expected to be here."

"Amir, take him in the back and tie him up." As Tamer turned, Abu Fahad indicted that he wanted the man killed. Amir nodded and took him away.

He noticed that Abdallah was covering the bloodstains with tarps. He walked around to get a feel for the place. Muhammad had removed the bodies and was also covering up the bloodstains. Amir came back from the back room. "How was it?"

"No problem, he died quickly."

Abu Fahad saw that everyone had finished their tasks. "Ya shabab, ta'al (oh men come here). The American who is coming has killed my brother. By our law he belongs to me. Kill the policeman quickly but try not to kill the woman. If you have no choice, kill her, but the American is mine, do not shoot him. If the woman lives then we will kill her slowly at the end. After we complete this last act, then our part will be finished. We will go to the shaykh's house and wait for the remaining groups to do their parts. Our main goals have been achieved; we have killed the prime minister and several of the senior FLN leaders, and we have pushed the Americans out of the country. I want Amir and Abdallah to each wait in one of the side offices. When I start shooting, then come out. Muhammad, I want you to keep a watch until you hear that they are coming. When they get here, go to the restroom on the other side of the hangar and wait for the same signal. Once we finish with them, we will go into the terminal and kill everyone else. You are my best mujahidin and we will have this country in a week, Allahu Akbar!"

"Allahu Akbar!" The group replied and left to their positions.

Nick and Sami looked around as they approached the airport. Sami had driven around first to survey the outer perimeter to make sure that nothing appeared out of the ordinary. "Nick, be ready for anything."

"I'm ready." Nick had put his pistol back in the holster and had the AK-47 by his leg.

"I am going to pull up to the guard at the gate." Sami eased the car to the guard shack. Nick noticed that his pistol was in his right hand.

"Salaam Alaikum," Sami said to the guard.

"Wa Laikum Salaam," the man replied. Sami held up his police identification card. "My name is Sami Bouteflica. My cousin Walid works here. Do you know him?"

"Yes, I know him."

"Is he here tonight?"

The guard looked at his list inside the shack. "Yes, he's here. Check in the main hangar. If he's not there, then they should know where he is."

"Shokran," replied Sami.

The guard opened the gate and told them they could drive to the lot in front of the hangar. Sami pulled the car through the gate and went toward the main hangar.

Muhammad ran inside the hangar. "I see some lights coming this way." He went to the restroom on the other side of the hangar. Abu Fahad pulled his robes and veil off and sat in the chair where the fat man was sitting. He held the AK-47 under the desk toward the front of the hangar. He would wait until they were inside the hangar, and as they approached the desk, he would start firing at them.

-Fifty-Six-

The world has not promised anything to anybody.
– Algerian proverb

Sami pulled the truck into the lot in front of the main hangar. "I see someone coming. Hold on for a second. It looks like security. I will explain the situation to him." Sami got out of the car and approached the guard. Nick saw him take his ID out again and explain to the guard why they were there. The guard and Sami shook hands and walked to the truck. "He knows Walid and will take us to the main hangar. We can call him from there and he will come from where he is working. Nick, grab the AK-47, because we don't know how long before you take off, and we want to be prepared." Sami slung the rifle over his shoulder and Nick did the same.

Nick, Mariam and Fatima climbed out of the Suburban. Nick noticed that Fatima stayed very close to her sister. The poor little girl must have been afraid of losing her one family member left. Nick's heart went out to the little girl, but he knew that once he and Mariam got married, that would help provide a more stabilizing force in her life. Nick thought that they would have to improve her English before she started school in the States.

They started walking toward the hangar with the guard. Sami and the guard were in a deep conversation. The guard was Kabyle and they knew some of the same people. Sami and he reverted to Berber, and Nick did not understand a word. Nick looked at Mariam.

"How are you feeling?" Nick was worried about her.

"I am very sore and can use a rest, but otherwise I feel fine."

"Hopefully, we will be in Tunis in an hour. I look forward to leaving this place."

Mariam was quiet as she walked toward the entrance. Fatima held on tightly to her as they walked. The five walked through the main entrance.

Abu Fahad saw them but there were five, not three, and a little girl. It didn't matter to him because anyone with the American was his enemy. The other man wore the same uniform as the guard they had killed earlier that night.

Abu Fahad pointed his AK-47 toward them under the table. He had already put a round in the chamber. All he had to do was to tighten his finger around the trigger. He saw the American; he was the tallest among the group.

Sami had switched back to Arabic and Nick was able to follow the conversation better. They were talking about Sami's cousin, Walid. As they entered, they saw the desk with the man sitting at it. They started walking toward him.

Abu Fahad caressed the trigger. *A little closer,* he thought.

At about 50 feet away, the guard saw the man sitting behind the desk and said, "I wonder where Tamer is?" At that same time, the phone rang on the desk.

Abu Fahad saw the light on the phone light up and heard the ring. Both of his hands were under the desk holding the AK-47. He couldn't answer the phone and keep a steady aim on them. He tried to look like he was busy studying some paperwork on his desk. The phone was hooked to a bell, which informed people who were on the other side of the hangar that the phone was ringing. Abu Fahad cursed under his breath.

The guard said to Sami that he was just here and Tamer was sitting behind the desk. Sami asked how he could tell from so far away. He explained that the man was so fat that you could see him a mile away. They walked closer to the desk. All along the phone kept ringing.

Nick noticed that the guy at the desk did not pick up the phone; with all the noise that it made, it seemed weird that he wasn't answering the telephone. He scanned the room with his eyes. The hangar seemed pretty deserted. Sami saw that the guy had his hands under the table.

Nick finally got a good look at the guy sitting down. He was studying something on his desk. Then the man looked up and Nick saw his eyes. They burned with hatred. Nick's mind flashed back to the embassy and the guy who screamed after he shot the one terrorist – it was the same man.

This didn't feel right to Sami. He raised his arm to grab the AK-47. Nick pulled out the pistol from his holster.

Abu Fahad saw that the American had recognized him. He threw the desk back and pulled the trigger.

Sami fired as the desk went up. He felt the round go past him. Nick had jumped in front of Mariam to protect her. It seemed like all hell broke loose then.

From three other rooms within the hangar, gunfire erupted. Three men came out and begin firing their automatic weapons at them. Abu Fahad fell behind the desk and used it as a shield against Nick's and Sami's shots.

Sami yelled to Mariam, and Nick to run to the other side of the hangar while he covered them. They were about 40 feet away from their assailants but they were in the open.

Nick heard Mariam scream and looked over at her. His first thought was that she had been shot, but Nick could not see where she had been injured. She screamed as if she was in agony. Nike continued to return fire but followed Mariam with his eyes. He saw the little girl's body on the ground, lifeless and bloodied. Nick heart jumped. He grabbed Mariam and ran toward the side of the hangar where tool dollies, work tables and benches were. He put his right arm around her while shooting with his left hand. They ran to the right side of the hangar.

Sami covered them as they ran. He fired on full automatic mode to the four men. The guard had begun firing with his handgun. When Sami saw that Nick and Mariam had made it to the wall, he shouted to the guard to follow him.

Abu Fahad saw the round that went in the little girl's head. He fired after the American and the women. He yelled to Amir, Muhammad and Abdallah to go after the two men while he went after the American.

The three moved closer to Sami and the guard as Abu Fahad went after Nick.

Sami made it to the side of the left wall. He had lost track of Nick and Mariam but he saw Fatima on the floor, blood oozing from her head. He fired at the one man near the bathroom. Sami was behind a tool cart and the guard was at a tool counter next to him. Sami switched the AK-47 to semi-automatic. He saw the man shooting from the bathroom. He knew he needed to lower the odds. The two others fired at them as well, but they were farther away from them. "Fire at the two men over there while I take this one. I have a plan." The guard agreed and started firing at the two men. Sami knew that this guy wanted to come closer. Sami began shooting much farther ahead of the guy.

Amir was the closest to the two men, but he could not get any closer because one guy was firing at him with an assault riffle every time he moved.

Sami continued to fire in front of the man.

Amir noticed that the shoots were not that close to him. He decided to run toward them firing. He started out of the doorway.

Sami continued to fire in front of him. As he came out of the bathroom, he centered the sight between the man's chest. Amir came closer, feeling that his assailant could not put any shots near him. Sami squeezed off three rounds. All three hit Amir in the chest in a small grouping.

Walid heard the gunfire from the main hangar. He wasn't sure what to do. He tried to call the terminal but could not get anyone. He tried the police but the phone was also dead. He reached in his tool chest and pulled out a Llama pistol. His cousin Sami had given it to him in case he was ever in trouble. He decided to head toward the hangar to see if he could help.

The two front gate guards heard the gunfire and tried to call the police on their radios, but they could not raise anyone. They locked the gate and headed toward the hanger. They took out their guns as they ran.

Nick and Mariam headed into a back hallway. Mariam was still screaming, "They killed Tima, those bastards killed Tima!"

Nick shook her, "Mariam, pull it together or we won't get out of here." The door flew open and shoots ricocheted off the walls. Nick pulled Mariam down, his AK-47 falling when he grabbed her. Gunfire ripped above his head. He had to move further back into the hallway. He had to make a choice: either grab the rifle or her.

Automatic gunfire roared in the passage and hit the walls near him. He and Mariam moved into the hallway and went into an office. More automatic rounds ricocheted off the tile in the hallway. He fired back with the Beretta. "Stay low and back against the wall in this office." He fired down the hall again, but a return of shots was the response.

Sami fired at the two men. Abdallah saw the man kill Amir, and he would make sure that he paid for that. The guard continued to fire until he was out of ammunition. Muhammad saw that the guard was reloading. He fired at the tool dolly and ran toward the guard. The guard panicked and had a hard time putting the clip into the well of the pistol. Muhammad fired a volley into the guard. Sami could not do anything except take careful aim and fire back at Muhammad. He hit him in the leg and arm. Sami changed clips and switched back to fully automatic. Muhammad tried to dive behind a tall tool cabinet but Sami shot him in his back as he dived. He did not move; he was paralyzed.

Nick reloaded his pistol with his last magazine. He knew that he was going to run out of ammunition soon. The man firing at him was using an assault rifle against his pistol. He only hoped that Sami was able to shake the three other men and make it to him and Mariam. They were trapped in the office without an exit.

Abu Fahad kept firing into the small office. He saw the American drop the assault rifle and thus far had only fired back with a pistol. He knew he had him now. He walked toward the office firing multiple round bursts into the wall.

Sami looked at the dead guard beside him. He heard the pistol shots from the back hallway and knew it was from Nick's Beretta; he heard a volley of automatic rifle fire and knew that Nick was in trouble. If he wasn't using the AK-47, something had to be wrong.

Nick fired a few rounds out of the office. He had pulled the heavy metal desk down, and he and Mariam were using it an a buffer against the automatic gunfire. The fury of the assault was becoming much stronger because the man was coming closer. Nick tried to conserve ammunition but he knew he would run out before his assailant did.

Abu Fahad was almost to the office. He fired three round bursts into the room. The American was firing only a random round now and again. He peeked his head around the corner and saw them behind a large metal desk. He continued to shoot into the room.

Sami was trapped. The last terrorist had him pinned against the wall behind the tool dolly. He heard Nick's pistol fire fewer and fewer rounds. He knew that he had to make a move soon or Nick would run out of rounds.

"Mariam, I love you."

"I love you too, Nick."

Nick fired the last three rounds towards his pursuer. He saw the pistol's slide lock back which meant it was out of rounds.

Abu Fahad heard the pistol when it ran out of ammunition. He waited for him to reload. He fired a few more bursts into the desk. The American did not fire back at him. He knew that the infidel was out of bullets. He went into the room and fired directly into the desk.

Nick pushed Mariam behind him so he would take the first shots himself. Abu Fahad called out to them to stand up. Nick didn't move. Abu Fahad fired several into the desk as he eased closer. He looked around the desk and saw them.

Sami decided to take a chance. He hadn't heard Nick's pistol for a few minutes so he knew that he was out of ammunition. He decided to make a run for the other side of the hangar to help Nick. Sami had spent hours at the shooting range and knew that he was a good shot. He would stand up and run sideways toward the back hallway. He knew where the shooter was firing from. He would move and aim for the very spot his assailant had been firing from. It would be risky because while the shooter would have to make a target of himself to shoot him, Sami would be in the open and susceptible to gunfire. He concentrated and got up to move.

Abu Fahad had them in his sights. "Stand up or she dies right here." Nick stood up and pushed Mariam behind him. "Move over here. Tell the women to stay behind the desk. If she moves, she dies." Nick did as he was told. "You killed my brother today." Abu Fahad pulled his Afghan dagger out of its sheath. "My custom demands, blood for blood." He threw the assault rifle out of the office and down the hallway. He charged at Nick with the knife.

Sami leapt from behind the tool dolly and started firing at the doorway. He moved rapidly, but not too fast because he wanted to be able to get a good aim on the terrorist when he showed himself.

Walid made his way slowly to the main hangar. He walked through the parking lot and he recognized the American Embassy Suburban because of the diplomatic license plates. He thought that Sami must be inside, and he ran the rest of the way.

Abdallah saw the man leap up and begin firing. He couldn't get a clear shot without moving from out of the doorway. He eased out of the doorway and began firing at the man again.

Sami saw him. He looked through the sight and got ready to pull the trigger. Abdallah kept firing the weapon on fully automatic at the moving man. Sami was hit in his side but maintained his aim. He fired and saw the rounds tear through the man. Abdallah was hit, but he walked further out the room and shot at his target. Sami took two rounds in the chest and fell to one knee. He inhaled, dropped his rifle, drew his pistol from his left side and shot Abdallah twice in the head. Sami exhaled and crumpled to the floor. Walid was running into the hanger when he saw Sami get shot. He ran to his side.

Nick parried the first strike by his opponent. He could tell by the way he held the knife and moved that he was a professional. Nick threw a lamp at Abu Fahad, who easily batted it away. As he pushed it away, Nick struck with a high hook kick to his head. Nick wanted to stay away from the knife since the man appeared to know what he was doing. Abu Fahad saw the kick approach his face, but could not avoid it completely, he leaned back and it grazed off his head. As Nick brought the kick back, Abu Fahad lunged in with the knife and slashed a deep gash through his stomach.

Nick felt the surge of pain go through his body as the knife ripped into his stomach. Nick thought this guy was well-trained and that he had to be at his best if he wanted to live. Abu Fahad pressed his advantage and moved in with a back slash of the knife to Nick's face. Nick stepped into Abu Fahad's body to slip to the inside position, ready to counter. As Abu Fahad brought his right hand down to slash Nick's face, Nick shot his forearm up to block the slash while shooting in an uppercut to his chin. Nick immediately grabbed his neck, spun him to the left and sent a knee into his solar plexus. Abu Fahad was stunned, but had enough wherewithal to slash down with the knife against Nick's arm. Nick's body reacted instantly to the wound; he felt the blade cut to the bone of his forearm. Nick yelled in pain. Abu Fahad moved in again and slashed Nick's leg.

Nick decided that for him to live, he had to be willing to die as his instructor had told him. He couldn't be afraid to be hurt even if he was hurt. If he wanted to live, he had to be willing to sacrifice his body.

He decided to bait Abu Fahad. He feigned a high roundhouse kick with his left leg; Abu Fahad cut his leg as he brought it up. He immediately did a foot switch and sent a low oblique kick with his right foot into Abu Fahad's left knee. Abu Fahad felt the ligaments tear in his knee as he fell to the ground. He tried to slash at Nick as he went down. Nick slid out of his range before moving back to strike again.

Abu Fahad could not believe the skill of this American. His knew his knee had just been destroyed when the American kicked it. Nick did a spinning back kick into Abu Fahad's head. His head jerked back so violently, Nick thought maybe he had broken his neck. Abu Fahad head snapped back. He was dizzy and dazed but he was a Mujahid (holy warrior). He needed to exact revenge for his brother's death. He tried to stand and fell back to the one knee because of the pain.

Nick knew he had to press on. This man had attacked the embassy and killed three of his staff. He sent in a finger jab into his right eye and stuck with an open hand strike on his collarbone; the bone broke on contact. Nick slid around Abu Fahad, shot his right arm around his neck and grabbed his right wrist with his left hand. Nick stood him up and leaned back while he tightened his grip around his neck. He heard his neck snap in three seconds. Nick pushed Abu Fahad's limp body off his, and they both fell to the ground. Mariam rushed to Nick as he collapsed.

Walid sat with Sami. "Nick needs your help. Promise me you will help him."

"I will, cousin. I will call an ambulance for you." Walid got up to call for help when he noticed that Sami was dead.

Nick and Mariam walked out of the hallway and saw a man sitting with Sami. Nick recognized him as Sami's cousin. Nick ran over to Sami and stared at his body. Mariam looked at him and tears came in her eyes. She looked over to his left and saw Fatima's small body lying in a puddle of blood. She fell to her knees and cried uncontrollably.

"He wanted me to help you," said Walid.

"What else did he say?"

"That was it."

Nick could not believe that his friend was dead. He forgot about his wounds and just stared at his body. There were no words to express the loss that he felt.

Police and medical personnel had started arriving. Walid got up and went to greet them.

-Fifty-Seven-

The tar of my country is better than the honey of others
— Arab proverb

"Weep not for a friend that is distant nor for an abode, but turn thyself about with fortune as it turns about."
— Samarkand proverb

Walid had explained to the police what had happened and that Nick, as an American diplomat, needed to get to Tunis tonight. The police agreed and arranged for him to take one of the private planes in the airport late that night. The medical staff was worried about his stomach. He had a deep gash that cut to the outer lining of the stomach. His forearm caused them the next greatest concern because of how deep the arm was cut. The blade had scraped the bone. They explained to Nick that he would need physical therapy to get full use of his hand back. The cuts on his leg were not as bad. They bandaged him up the best they could and told him to see a doctor as soon as possible. They also treated Mariam for her earlier assault.

Nick saw them carry off the bodies of the terrorists, the guards, Fatima and Sami as they took them to the morgue. Nick was sad but was worried about Mariam. While she was in there with the medical personnel, Nick went to see Walid.

"Walid, I want to offer my condolences for your cousin. He was a fine man who lived his life with honor and courage. He was my closest friend here in Algiers. I will never forget him. I know he doesn't have any immediate family still alive, but if I can do anything for his extended family, let me know. These are my numbers in Tunis and in Washington. Thank you for your help." Nick held out his hand and shook hands with Walid.

"The plane will leave in 30 minutes," Walid said. "You can wait in the main terminal. I know my cousin thought highly of you. Sami had never brought a foreigner to our family home before. He said you were a man that he respected and cared about. His last thoughts were of you. He was closer to no one else in the world. You were like his brother, as he thought of you that way. This makes you Kabyle; you are a part of us. You will always have family here in Algeria." He hugged Nick and kissed him on both cheeks. Nick walked away, very distraught.

259

He saw Mariam and walked over to her. "How are you?"

"I am feeling better. They bandaged my wounds and gave me some pain killers."

"I am so sorry about Tima. I know it doesn't seem fair." Nick walked with her, his arms around her.

"I just can't believe that they would kill a little girl like that." Mariam started to cry again. He squeezed her closer to him.

Many of the emergency personnel were still there. They walked into the terminal and sat in the small cafe.

Mariam had stopped crying and looked at Nick. "I am sorry about Sami. I know what he meant to you. He was a special man and I know you will miss him."

Nick didn't say anything for a few moments, then, "The plane leaves in 30 minutes. They will come and get us when we can board."

"I can't go with you, Nick."

He turned around and looked at her. "What?"

"I'm sorry but I can't go with you, Nick, to Tunis or America."

Nick was stunned. He could not say anything.

"Nick, so much has happened in the last four days. The life that we were going to have seems so long ago. I love you, Nick, with all my heart, but I can't leave my country now. One of the reasons that I was going to leave was because of Fatima, and she's gone now. Nick, I want to help my country. I don't want to abandon it. Sulaiman was right about continuing my father's dream. So much has happened; my parents and brother were killed, I was assaulted, Tima was killed and Sami, too. I will live out my father's legacy and serve as a leader of this country. I will fight the FIS and the GIA with everything I have. Algeria is my country. I will fight like my father fought the French to keep it democratic and free. If the extremists take over the country, the core identity of Algeria will be destroyed. I will meet with the FLN leaders on Sunday to discuss our strategy to fight the Islamists.

"Nick, you remember what Sami said. He said that he would not give the country away to the fanatics, neither will I. They killed my family, all of my family. As we drove through the countryside, did you see all the burned out cars and buildings? That is not the Algeria I remember. This country was beautiful once and I want to make it beautiful again. You must understand. I can't go. It's about family honor and not letting their dream die and having their sacrifice go wasted."

"But it will be dangerous for you, Mariam."

"Nick, they have tried three times to kill me and they haven't. I should be dead already. There is a saying here in Algeria, 'the drowning man is not troubled by the rain.' I have no family left and nothing else to lose.

"My father had his life threatened hundreds of times over the last few years, yet he persevered and continued his work. I would be a failure to myself if I left. I know you would have me leave only for a few months, but at that time it could be too late; the FIS could be in power. I love you, Nick, like no other, and a few days ago, I would have gone anywhere with you. But a lot has happened in four days. I will not run away. I have a responsibility to my country and my family. I will not only help stabilize the government but I will bring those who killed my family and the others to justice. They will pay for their crimes. I am so sorry, Nick. I know you have given up so much to be with me. If the situation improves, you will be back." Nick knew if she stayed, he wouldn't see her again.

"I want what's best for you. I love you and I would do it again if I had the choice all over again. I want to be with you, but I can't stay."

"I know, Nick. I will always love you."

Nick and Mariam kissed passionately. Mariam cried. Nick saw that a man had come to tell him that the plane was ready to go.

"How will you get back?" he asked her.

"Walid will take me back to his house for the night. I will contact my relatives tomorrow. I will be all right. I truly do love you, Nick."

"I know, Mariam, and I love you." Nick was so drained from the day's events, he could not argue with her. He knew she had made up her mind. Nick wished her luck, kissed her again and walked off toward the runway. The man escorted him to the plane. Nick was still very sore from the wounds; he could barely open and close his left hand.

"Mr. Phillips, we will be leaving in a few minutes. The trip will take about 30 minutes to Tunis. Please button up your safety belt," said the flight attendant. As it was a private plane, she was the only hostess aboard. The plane took off and Nick sat back as it gained altitude.

Nick looked out of his window and stared at the countryside. Tears started coming down his face, not only because Mariam had broken his heart. He also cried for his friend, Sami, who he didn't have a chance to say goodbye to. "I will miss you, my brother."

-Epilogue-

Four weeks later

Nick was sitting in the George Washington Hospital's physical therapy department waiting to be called. He picked up the newspaper and read the headline in the world news section: "New Islamic Government formed in Algeria." He thought about Mariam and wondered whether she was still alive.

He had not heard anything about her since he had left. He had tried to call Walid and Mariam's house but could not get though. CNN had reported that the extremists had disrupted all the communications coming in and out of the country.

The State Department put Nick on medical leave because of his injuries. Nick had been taken to Tunis but was immediately medically evacuated to the U.S. because of the severity of the wounds to his arm and stomach. He had spent two weeks at the GW hospital because they had to reconstruct part of the outer lining of his stomach and reattach some of the tendons in his forearm. Nick had a meeting with the senior review panel in three days to go over his conduct during the crisis. He had watched from his hospital bed as CNN reported that the American Embassy had been evacuated from Algiers; they had described his actions as heroic. He had wondered how they knew what happened until Sarah had visited him and explained that she and Gunny had told the news channel what happened, anonymously of course. Nick did not know what the reaction of the Department would be to the CNN story or his actions in Algiers. He was wondering whether he should update his resume when the nurse called his name.

* * *